The Loner:
CROSSFIRE

The Loner:
CROSSFIRE

J. A. Johnstone

PINNACLE BOOKS
Kensington Publishing Corp.
www.kensingtonbooks.com

PINNACLE BOOKS are published by

Kensington Publishing Corp.
119 West 40th Street
New York, NY 10018

All Kensington titles, imprints, and distributed lines are available at special quantity discounts for bulk purchases for sales promotions, premiums, fund-raising, educational, or institutional use. Special book excerpts or customized printings can also be created to fit specific needs. For details, write or phone the office of the Kensington special sales manager: Kensington Publishing Corp., 119 West 40th Street, New York, NY 10018, attn: Special Sales Department; phone: 1-800-221-2647.

ISBN-13: 978-0-7860-2619-7
ISBN-10: 0-7860-2619-7

First printing: October 2011

10 9 8 7 6 5 4 3 2 1

Printed in the United States of America

Chapter 1

All roads lead home. Conrad Browning had heard someone say that once. He didn't understand it, and he definitely didn't agree with it. Maybe it was true for some people, but not for him.

In order for it to be true, he would have to *have* a home. And he didn't, not anymore. Looking at Carson City, Nevada, he felt nothing. Although he had lived here, it was just the place where his wife had been kidnapped, a crime that had culminated in her brutal murder.

He had been raised in Boston, but that wasn't home, either, as he had discovered on his most recent visit. It was the place where he had met Pamela Tarleton and become engaged to her, the single worst mistake of his life. The mistake that ultimately had brought him nothing but tragedy and grief.

Standing on the steps of the hospital in Carson City, Conrad gave a little shake of his head to break himself out of that grim reverie. He went inside, a tall, sandy-haired, ruggedly handsome man in his middle twenties wearing a black suit, black boots, and a black Stetson.

And a black leather gunbelt and holster that held a new Colt Frontier revolver with checkered, hard rubber grips embossed with an oval containing the Colt symbol.

It was a heavy, double-action weapon chambered for .44-40 cartridges, the same ammunition used by the Winchester Model 1892 rifle he owned. He had bought the Colt soon after he arrived in Carson City, and in the two weeks since, had practiced with it as much as possible, until he was able to handle the gun like it was another part of his body.

That was important, considering how often someone tried to kill him. There hadn't been any attempts on his life since he'd arrived, but he knew that was bound to change.

He took off his hat and went to the desk in the hospital lobby where a white-uniformed nurse greeted him with a smile. Conrad knew a lot of the nurses were smitten with him, but that didn't mean much to him.

"Good morning, Mr. Browning. You're here to see your friend?"

Conrad nodded. "That's right. How's he doing?"

"Mr. Vincenzo is doing very well," the nurse reported. "Dr. Taggart says he's getting stronger all the time. You can go on up to his room if you'd like."

"Thanks." Conrad returned her smile. He'd been raised to be polite.

Arturo's room was on the second floor. Conrad went up the wide, curving staircase, still holding his hat. Nurses and doctors passed him in the corridor, most of them smiling and nodding to him, occasionally speaking. He was a familiar sight. He had spent practically every visiting hour available at the hospital since he'd brought in his friend.

Conrad pushed open the door of the private room. It was a bright, cheery place, at least for a hospital. Morning sunlight spilled brilliantly through a window with the curtains pushed back. It was the finest room available, as Conrad had ordered. He could afford the best.

Arturo Vincenzo was sitting up in bed with pillows propped behind him, reading a novel by William Dean Howells. When he was healthy, he was a tall, slender, vaguely bird-like man with thinning brown hair. In the hospital, he was paler than usual, not having seen the sun for a while, and the ordeal he had gone through had etched some additional lines in his face and given him a certain gaunt aspect.

Arturo had suffered a bullet wound in the chest—a bullet intended for Conrad—and had come very close to dying. The local medico in Cavendish, Nevada, the small settlement where the shooting had taken place, wasn't much good as a doctor, but somehow he had kept Arturo from bleeding to death and had stabilized his condition enough so Conrad was able to get him on the train and take him to Carson City.

Once the train arrived, an ambulance wagon had carried Arturo from the depot to the hospital, and the doctor who had taken over the case had operated almost immediately to repair the damage caused to Arturo's right lung where the bullet nicked it. The slug had broken a rib, too.

Now it was just a matter of rest and recuperation, and Conrad thought Arturo looked a little better, a little stronger, every day. For a man who had never appeared to be much of a physical specimen, Arturo had proven to be surprisingly hardy and resilient.

He marked his place in the book and set it aside. "Good morning, sir."

Conrad smiled. "I think you can stop calling me sir," he said, although he knew it probably wouldn't do much good.

"I *am* still in your employ, am I not?"

"Of course you are. You've got a job for as long as you want it, either with me or Claudius Turnbuckle. Claudius made that clear in his wire."

Turnbuckle was a partner in the San Francisco law firm of Turnbuckle & Stafford. He and John J. Stafford were also good friends to Conrad and had been handling many of his business affairs for years, ever since Conrad had inherited half of the lucrative Browning financial holdings from his late mother Vivian.

The other half of Vivian's estate had gone to

Conrad's father, the notorious gunfighter Frank Morgan, better known as The Drifter. Like Conrad, Frank didn't take any active interest in the business. He had never paid much attention to it. Frank was content to wander, as he had been doing for decades before he inherited a fortune, and most of the time Conrad had no idea where his father was.

As soon as Arturo was out of immediate danger and recovering from surgery, Conrad had gotten in touch with Turnbuckle and made arrangements to have all the medical expenses taken care of. He had also advised Turnbuckle that he would be arriving in San Francisco sometime in the relatively near future. Turnbuckle knew the details of the quest that had taken Conrad across the country from Boston, and Conrad knew he could count on the lawyer for help.

When Conrad broke his engagement to Pamela Tarleton in order to marry beautiful, blond Rebel Callahan, Pamela had been pregnant, something Conrad hadn't known at the time. She had returned to Boston and given birth to twins, a boy and a girl, naming them Frank and Vivian after Conrad's parents.

Then she had hidden them away before embarking on a campaign of vengeance against Conrad, whom she blamed not only for breaking their engagement but also for the death of her railroad baron father, a criminal who had actually been murdered by his own partner in corruption.

Pamela didn't see it that way, and her lust for revenge had resulted in Rebel's death and in numerous attempts on Conrad's life, even after Pamela herself had been killed accidentally while trying to carry out one of her schemes.

One of her cruelest blows had come from beyond the grave, in a letter she'd written that was delivered to Conrad by one of her relatives. In that missive calculated to tear his heart out, she had informed him that he was a father and practically dared him to find his hidden children.

Since then, with the help of Arturo, a valet and all-around assistant who had come to be a good friend, Conrad had been on a cross-country search for the twins.

He knew Pamela had taken the children and set out from Boston for San Francisco. Fearing she might have stashed them somewhere, he had taken his time and asked questions about them at every settlement along the railroad. Because of that, he knew the twins had still been with Pamela when she had reached Nevada.

It wasn't far to San Francisco, and every instinct in his body told him she had taken them with her all the way to the coast. He had decided to bypass the rest of the smaller settlements and head directly for the city by the bay. Although it was a gamble, his instincts told him it might pay off.

Arturo broke into his thoughts. "You're brooding about Miss Tarleton and the children again, aren't you, sir?"

Conrad sighed. "Sorry. I should be more worried about you right now."

"Nonsense," Arturo responded without hesitation. "I'm feeling much better, and Dr. Taggart says my condition is improving on a daily basis. In fact, he told me there's no reason for you to remain here for the duration of my recuperative period. You can proceed to San Francisco any time you wish."

Conrad smiled. "Are you sure Dr. Taggart said that, or is that you talking?"

"It's true that I don't wish to delay you"— Arturo rolled his eyes—"and Lord knows the evidence indicates you have a difficult time taking care of yourself without me around."

"That's true," Conrad said, thinking of all the times Arturo had helped save his life.

"But you can ask the doctor for yourself if you'd like," Arturo went on. "He and the nurses are perfectly capable of looking after me, and since all the financial arrangements have already been made with Mr. Turnbuckle"—Arturo shrugged— "there's really no reason for you to stay, is there?"

"I suppose there's not," Conrad agreed. "Other than the fact that I'll miss you."

"I'll be well enough to travel in another week or ten days, according to the doctor. At that time, I'll come straightaway to San Francisco and contact Mr. Turnbuckle. You'll keep him apprised of your current activities and whereabouts?"

"I'm sure I will."

"Well, there you go. Good-bye. Have a good trip to 'Frisco'."

"I've heard the people who live there don't like that name," Conrad said with a smile.

"Perhaps not, but we don't live there, do we?"

Grinning, Conrad shook his head. "Nope." He put his hat on. "All right, I won't argue with you. I'll head for the train station right now and see when the next westbound is due." He put out his hand. "Thanks for everything, Arturo. I'm sorry you may miss out on the end of this."

"As long as your quest is successful, sir, that's all I care about." Arturo shook Conrad's hand.

"I'm going to find the doctor and talk to him before I go, just to make sure he thinks it's all right."

"I would expect nothing less from you, sir."

Dr. Liam Taggart, a middle-aged man with the sad face of a hound, nodded and agreed with Arturo's suggestion when Conrad talked to him a few minutes later. "Mr. Vincenzo's recovery is coming along splendidly. We'll take good care of him. You can go on about your business without worrying, Mr. Browning."

"I'm glad to hear that. If you need anything, Doctor, don't hesitate to wire my attorneys in San Francisco. They'll handle everything."

Taggart nodded. "Of course."

Conrad left the hospital. It was a beautiful day. The air was crystal-clear, and the mountains near Carson City seemed close enough to reach out and touch. As he gazed at the splendor around him, he avoided a certain area. He didn't want to look at, or think about, Black Rock Canyon, the place where Rebel had died. Unfortunately, once those dark thoughts entered his head, it was almost impossible to banish them.

The sudden roar of a shot and the sound of a bullet whipping past his ear did the job.

Chapter 2

Instinct took over, as it always did when danger threatened. Conrad's hand stabbed toward the Colt on his hip as he whirled.

His keen eyes instantly spotted two men with guns about twenty feet from him. They stood next to a parked wagon, evidently intending to use it for cover if they needed to. Smoke curled from the revolver held by one man, and the other would-be assassin was lining up his shot.

Conrad crouched and fired as the second man squeezed off a round. The two reports blended together into one blast. The gunman's aim was a little high and Conrad heard the slug whine over his head.

Conrad's bullet slammed into the gunman's left shoulder. The impact was enough to make him cry out in pain and spin to the pavement as he dropped his gun and clutched at his bullet-shattered shoulder.

The first man fired again, but he was on the move. His shot went wild and missed Conrad by several feet. Someone screamed behind him and he knew the stray bullet must have found an unintended target.

As the gunman darted around the horses hitched to the wagon, Conrad held his fire. He didn't want to hit any of the animals.

The man he had wounded was groping for the gun he'd dropped a few seconds earlier. Conrad kicked the revolver as he dashed toward the wagon and sent the gun spinning along the street, well out of reach. The wounded man groaned and slumped on the pavement again as he appeared to pass out from the shock of his injury.

Conrad knew the man he had shot ought to survive. It was unlikely he would bleed to death since he was practically on the front steps of the hospital. Wanting at least one of the bushwhackers alive to question, Conrad ran after the one who had disappeared into the mouth of the alley across the street, between a saloon and a hardware store.

All along the street, people were yelling and scattering, getting out of the line of fire. He pressed his back to the front wall of the saloon next to the alley and listened.

He didn't hear running footsteps, but was pretty sure he heard harsh breathing coming from deeper in the alley. The man was waiting for him. As soon as he showed himself, he'd be silhouett in the mouth of the alley and the gunman would open fire.

Instead of waltzing right into that trap, Conrad slapped aside the batwings and hurried into the saloon. People gawked at him and got out of his way as he headed toward the stairs at the back of the room. A bartender with a bungstarter gripped firmly in his hand moved to block Conrad's path. "Hey, mister, what do you think you're—"

He stopped short and stepped back from the cold-eyed glance Conrad gave him.

Taking the stairs three at a time, Conrad got to the second floor landing in a hurry. Turning to the right, beside the alley where the bushwhacker was hidden, he jerked open the closest door and found the shabby bedroom inside empty. He went to the open window and peered out cautiously.

He saw what he wanted to see. About a dozen feet from the street, the gunman crouched behind a rain barrel, watching the mouth of the alley. His gun was leveled over the top of the barrel, and all his attention was focused in that direction as he waited for Conrad to appear.

It would have been easy for Conrad to gun him down from the window. But when you shot somebody, there was always a risk you would kill them. He didn't want that. He wanted the man to talk and reveal who had hired him to murder Conrad Browning.

As if the answer would come as any surprise . . .

The window in the next room was almost directly above the place where the gunman was hidden. Conrad hurried there and opened the door. He wasn't lucky enough to find the room unoccupied. A redheaded woman clutched the sheet on the bed to her naked bosom, which was ample enough that it wasn't easily covered. Beside the bed, a fat, pale, hairy gent was struggling frantically to get back into his clothes.

Conrad saw the anger on her face and knew she was about to yell at him. He held the index finger of his left hand to his mouth in a shushing gesture and showed her the gun in his right hand. Her eyes, as well as her mouth, opened wide, but the only sound that came from her was a frightened little squeak.

Half dressed, the redhead's customer rushed past Conrad and out the door, obviously determined to get as far away as fast as he could.

Conrad moved silently toward the open window and looked out. The bushwhacker was still below in the alley, crouched behind the barrel.

Judging the distance from the window to the ground, Conrad decided the drop wouldn't be too bad. He slid his Colt back in its holster and lifted a leg over the windowsill. He had just gotten his second leg out the window and was perched on the sill when heavy footsteps pounded into the room behind him and a deep voice bellowed, "Hold it right there, mister! You can't just—"

Conrad glanced over his shoulder and saw a big man with a lawman's badge pinned to his coat entering the room with a shotgun in his hands. Somebody had called the law on the loco hombre who had run into the saloon brandishing a six-shooter.

The man in the alley heard the shout, and jerked his head up toward the window. His eyes widened in surprise and he lifted his gun up, but Conrad had already let go and leaped toward him.

Conrad crashed on top of the man and drove him against the rain barrel, which turned over and sent water flooding into the alley. They rolled over the barrel and were spilled into the dirty lake that had formed. Conrad clamped his left hand on the man's right wrist and shoved the gun aside as a shot blasted from it. The slug thudded into the wall of the hardware store next door.

Smashing his right fist into the man's face he drove the back of the man's head into the mud. The man heaved and bucked but Conrad twisted his wrist so hard that bones ground together. The man howled in pain and dropped the gun.

Conrad grabbed the man's coat, rolling over in the muck as they struggled. He twisted his body aside just in time to take the vicious blow aimed at his groin on his thigh instead. His leg went numb for a moment, but at least it didn't incapacitate him as it would have had it found its intended target.

As they fought the gunman managed to lock his hands around Conrad's throat. Conrad looked up past the man's furious face and saw the lawman leaning out the window on the second floor. The star packer was yelling, but Conrad couldn't make out the words over the roaring of his blood in his head as the bushwhacker tried to choke the life out of him.

Cupping his hands, he slapped them over the man's ears as hard as he could, assaulting the eardrums. The man yelped in pain and loosened his grip. Conrad broke it and flung him off. The man rolled across the muddy alley and came to a stop against the wall of the hardware store.

Conrad scrambled after him. The man jerked a leg up and tried to kick Conrad in the stomach, but Conrad grabbed his foot and twisted it. The man yelled and was forced to roll over onto his belly to keep Conrad from breaking his leg.

Conrad let go of the leg and dropped on top of the man, landing hard with both knees in the small of his back. He grabbed the man's hair and slammed his face into the ground twice. That was finally enough to knock the fight out of the man. He stopped struggling and lay there gasping.

"By God, stop attackin' that fella or I'll shoot!"

Conrad looked up at the lawman, who had his shotgun pointed at the two men in the alley. Conrad was a little out of breath. "Be careful . . . with that Greener, Marshal. If it goes off . . . you'll kill both of us down here."

"Stand up and move away from that man, you damn loco weed!" the badge-toter ordered. "You're under arrest for attempted murder, assault and battery, unlawfully dischargin' a firearm, trespassin', and anything else I can think of!"

Conrad gestured toward the semiconscious man at his feet. "Blast it, he's the one who tried to kill me! Him and his partner I wounded out on the street."

"So you're the one who shot that hombre! I might a' knowed it. Take your gun out and drop it."

Conrad snorted in disgust. "Not hardly. It's nearly brand-new. I'm not going to drop it in the mud."

The lawman sputtered angrily for a moment, then said, "Stay right there! Don't you move, you hear me?"

"I'm not going anywhere," Conrad said.

Not until he found out for sure who had tried to have him killed.

Chapter 3

By the time the burly lawman got down the stairs in the saloon and reached the alley, three more men wearing badges and carrying shotguns had run up. They were standing next to Conrad. The first lawman waved his Greener and ordered, "Disarm that man and take him into custody!"

"Settle down, Hargity," the other deputy said. "This is Conrad Browning. We're not going to arrest him."

Hargity scowled. "Who?"

"He used to live here. In fact, he was one of Carson City's leading citizens. Owns railroads, mines, banks, ships, you name it. Friend of the governor."

"That don't matter," Hargity snapped. "He shot a man on the street, raised hell in that saloon, and assaulted this fella. I say he's under arrest!"

"If you'd bothered to question any witnesses," said the lawman who had introduced himself to

Conrad as Deputy Wallace, "you'd know this man and the one Mr. Browning shot tried to kill him right in front of the hospital. That's the first thing Stevens and I determined when we got here. Mr. Browning fired his gun in self-defense, and he was trying to apprehend the second gunman." Wallace nudged the bushwhacker, who lay on the muddy floor of the alley. "Looks like he succeeded."

"But . . . but . . ." Hargity sputtered.

"No offense, but I'm chief deputy," Wallace said. "You and Stevens take this man and lock him up."

"I'm going to want to ask him some questions later," Conrad said.

Wallace nodded. "That's fine, as long as Marshal Owens goes along with it. Right now I want to go see how that man you wounded is doing. Are you coming along?"

"Yes, I am," Conrad said. "He may be able to tell me what I want to know."

"Who paid the two of them to ambush you?"

Conrad nodded. "That's right. I've got a pretty good idea, but I'd like for it to be confirmed."

The slender, solemn-faced Wallace motioned for Conrad to follow him and left the alley, heading across the street to the hospital. The lobby was in an uproar, not surprising since there had been a gun battle right outside. Dr. Liam Taggart was talking to several men, some in white coats, the rest in business suits.

Taggart spotted Conrad approaching with

Deputy Wallace and came across the lobby to greet them. "Are you all right, Mr. Browning? The rumor is that you were the target of an assassination attempt."

"That's true, but I'm fine," Conrad said. He looked down at his mud-splattered clothes. "Nothing hurt but my dignity and my wardrobe."

"I'll have a nurse tell Mr. Vincenzo right away that you're all right. He was quite worried when he heard the shots. He seemed to think it was a foregone conclusion you were involved in the trouble, whatever it was."

Conrad smiled. "Arturo knows me pretty well."

Taggart crooked a finger at a nurse and gave her the message to deliver to Arturo, then Conrad asked the doctor, "What about the wounded man? I assume he was brought in here."

Taggart nodded. "Yes, he's in surgery at the moment to repair his shoulder. You shot him?"

"Seemed like the thing to do at the time," Conrad said.

"Your bullet did an extensive amount of damage. I doubt he'll ever be able to use his left arm properly again."

"Then maybe he won't try to bushwhack anybody else," Wallace said. "We're going to want to talk to him."

"You'll have to wait a good long time. It'll take a while for the ether to wear off."

Wallace shrugged. "We have another prisoner we can question, I suppose. In the meantime, I'm going to assign a deputy to guard this one. There'll be somebody outside the man's room all the time until he's healthy enough for us to take him to jail."

"That's fine, Deputy, as long as it doesn't interfere with anything of a medical nature we have to do."

"There's something else, Doctor," Conrad said. "During the shooting, I heard someone cry out when one of the shots missed me. Was somebody hit by a stray bullet?"

"As a matter of fact, that's right," Taggart said. "A young woman was struck."

Conrad frowned worriedly. "Was she badly hurt?"

"Scared out of her wits more than anything else. The bullet barely nicked her hip before smashing into a lamppost. She'll be sore and limp for a week or so, but she'll be fine. We have her in a ward right now, mostly because she's bordering on hysteria. She's so upset about being shot."

"Send all her bills to Claudius Turnbuckle. He'll see to it they're taken care of."

"That's pretty generous of you, considering the young lady's injury was an accident."

"The only accident was that she got hit instead of me," Conrad said. "I'm getting mighty tired of things like that happening."

The prisoner was a lantern-jawed man with a drooping black mustache. His gray tweed suit was covered with drying mud stains. Conrad hadn't noticed those details during the brief shoot-out and the fight that followed. He had been too busy trying to stay alive.

"His name's Ed Gillespie," Chief Deputy Wallace told Conrad as they stood outside the cell. "We didn't have any trouble identifying him. He's a cheap holdup artist and gunman. Been in and out of jail for years, but we've never been able to convict him of murder and send him to the gallows, even though we're pretty sure he's killed several people. The man you shot is probably Walt Farley. He and Gillespie have been mixed up in plenty of shady deals together."

Gillespie sat on the bunk inside the cell not saying anything. He kept his eyes turned toward the floor and didn't acknowledge that Conrad and Wallace were there. His jaw was swollen and sported several bruises from Conrad's fist.

Wallace grasped one of the bars in the cell door. "Gillespie, you can make it easier on yourself if you'll answer a few questions."

Gillespie didn't look up. It was like he hadn't heard Wallace and didn't know the deputy was there.

"Come on," Wallace said. "You're going to prison no matter what you do, but you know we can make it a lot rougher on you if we want to. You and Farley didn't go after Mr. Browning and try to kill him in broad daylight on some whim.

You'd only do a thing like that if you were being paid to. I want to know who you're working for."

Gillespie continued staring at the floor.

Wallace looked at the prisoner for a moment, then sighed and shook his head. "Sorry," he muttered as he turned to Conrad. "We can work him over until he talks, but it may take a while."

Conrad looked along the section of cell block in the city jail. The other cells were empty. "Or you can step outside for a few minutes and let me talk to him." He rested his hand on the butt of the Colt at his hip.

"Now wait a minute." Wallace held up his hands. "You can't just—"

"Why not?" Conrad broke in. "You said yourself he's a killer who's gotten away with murdering people in the past. Anything that happened to him now would be a fitting punishment, don't you think?"

For the first time Gillespie's eyes flicked up, then back down. He had heard what Conrad said and knew what he meant.

"Marshal Owens would never forgive me if he found out I let you get at a prisoner," Wallace said. "It'd mean my job, Mr. Browning. I'm sorry."

"What do you make in a year, Deputy?"

Wallace frowned and named a figure.

"I can pay you twice that and never even know the money is gone. You can probably find another job in two year's time, don't you think?"

Wallace rubbed his jaw and appeared to be pondering the idea. "I'm sure I could," he muttered. "If things got too loud back here, though, I might have to spread around a little more cash to keep it quiet."

"Whatever it costs." Conrad's voice was as cold as the snow that capped the mountain peaks outside Carson City. "The money doesn't matter."

Gillespie swallowed hard. "Wait a minute. Deputy, you can't let this—this—"

"You hear something, Mr. Browning?" Wallace asked. "It's funny, I was talking a minute ago and nobody seemed to hear me. Now I'm not sure I can hear anything."

Gillespie came up off the bunk and grasped the bars. "Wait, damn it! I'll tell you what you want to know. Just don't let this loco varmint anywhere near me!"

Wallace leaned his head to the side, indicating Conrad should back away from the bars. Conrad cooperated as Wallace glared through the bars and asked, "Who paid you to kill Mr. Browning here?"

A cunning look appeared on Gillespie's battered face. "First you gotta tell me . . . is Walt all right?"

"You're concerned about your friend." Wallace sneered. "How touching. Yeah, he's in the hospital. They fixed his busted shoulder. He'll be laid up for a while . . . and then he'll be in prison.

Maybe the judge'll put the two of you in the same cell. That sound good to you?"

"Shut your nasty mouth," Gillespie snapped. "Walt's a good hombre. Always been square with me. That's all. As for who paid us to go after this fella, you go talk to Carl Monroe. That's all I got to say."

Wallace jerked his head in a nod. "I reckon that'll do, for now."

"You . . . you wouldn't have really turned that lunatic loose on me, would you, Deputy?"

Wallace's answering smile was wolfish. "I wouldn't count on it."

Once they were outside the cell block, Conrad asked, "Who's Carl Monroe?"

Wallace grunted. "Lawyer. Crooked lawyer. I wasn't surprised to hear Gillespie mention his name. Gillespie and Farley have been tied in with Monroe before. Don't you remember Monroe from when you lived here before? His name turned up in the paper quite a bit, any time there was some big swindle or scandal."

"I was busy with other things," Conrad said.

Like running a business and being married to a beautiful, wonderful woman, he thought. He hadn't spared any attention for petty crooks.

"We'll haul Monroe in and talk to him, but I don't know how much we can get out of him," Wallace said. "He's got a reputation for being pretty tight-lipped. I'm not sure a little act like the one you put on for Gillespie would work on a hardboiled character like Monroe."

"Act?" Conrad repeated with a faint smile.

He left Wallace standing outside the cell block as the deputy watched with a worried frown on his face.

Chapter 4

Conrad went straight to his hotel, where the desk clerk handed him a city directory. It took only a moment to look up the address of Carl Monroe's office. Wallace had said the authorities would question Monroe, but Conrad wanted to get to him first.

The clerk gave him directions to the address. The building was only about four blocks away. Monroe's office was on the second floor, above a bank. The building had one of those newfangled elevators, but Conrad took the stairs.

Gilt letters on the pebbled glass upper half of a door in the hallway read CARL MONROE, ATTORNEY AT LAW. Conrad didn't knock. He grasped the knob with his left hand while his right hovered near the butt of his Colt. He didn't expect to walk into another ambush in the lawyer's office, but it didn't pay to take too many chances. He turned the knob and shoved the door open.

An attractive woman with blond hair swept into an elaborate pile of curls on top of her head looked up from a typewriter on her desk. "Yes? May I help you?"

He glanced around the room. It was a typical outer office, with the desk, a coat rack and hat tree, and a couple filing cabinets. A portrait of President McKinley hung on the wall, looking down in solemn dignity. For all that, the rug on the floor was a little threadbare, and the walls could have used a fresh coat of paint.

"I need to see Mr. Monroe," Conrad said.

"I'm not aware of any appointments he has at this time," the blonde said. "Is this concerning a legal matter?" She looked at him a little dubiously, probably because he hadn't taken the time to change his clothes and still wore the mud-stained suit.

Conrad nodded. "You could say that. It involves a couple associates of his named Gillespie and Farley."

The blonde frowned and shook her head. "I'm not familiar with those names." Even as she spoke, Conrad saw her shift slightly in her chair, and his keen ears picked up the faint sound of a buzzer from behind the door leading to Monroe's private office. He knew the woman had used her foot to press an alarm button. Monroe probably had another way out of his office.

Conrad didn't wait. He moved past the blonde's desk in a hurry. She leaped up from her chair and tried to grab his coat. "You can't—", but she was too late. He was already ramming his shoulder against the door of Monroe's office. It slammed open, and he saw movement from the corner of his eye. A bulky figure was halfway through another door, on his way out.

Conrad drew his Colt and eared back the hammer, even though that wasn't necessary since the revolver was a double-action model. He figured the sound of the gun being cocked might be enough to stop the fleeing figure in his tracks.

It worked. The man froze in the doorway. "Don't shoot!"

"Turn around," Conrad told him. "Slowly."

The man did as he was ordered. He was short, heavyset, had a florid face, and hair that looked like it had been slicked down with black shoe polish. His suit, like his offices, appeared to be of good quality at first glance, but another look revealed its worn, shabby nature.

"I don't know who you are, friend, but you don't have to bust in here with a gun," Monroe said. "I'm always glad to talk to anyone, especially a potential client."

"I'm not a client. I'm Conrad Browning."

The look of alarm that flashed in Monroe's eyes told Conrad the lawyer recognized his name. Monroe controlled the reaction quickly, and said,

"If you'll put that gun away, Mr. Browning, I'll be happy to discuss whatever it is that's bothering you."

"What's bothering me is that you paid Ed Gillespie and Walt Farley to kill me."

"My God!" Monroe exclaimed. "I never did such a thing! I don't even know who you're talking about."

Conrad went on as if Monroe hadn't said anything. "What I want to know now is who paid you to hire them. Tell me that and our business is done."

"It's impossible. I can't tell you something I don't know anything about!"

"Mr. Monroe?" the blond secretary said from behind Conrad. "Do you want me to summon the authorities?"

Monroe's eyes flicked toward her over Conrad's shoulder. "No, no, I'm sure that's not necessary—"

Something in Monroe's expression warned Conrad. He turned around in time to see the blonde had picked up the freestanding hat tree and was swinging it at his head. He twisted quickly, and the base crashed against his shoulder instead of his skull.

The impact was enough to make him stagger and drop his gun. The blonde drew the hat tree back and tried to ram it into his belly. Conrad caught hold of it and wrenched it out of her hands as he heard the rapid slap of shoe leather behind him. A glance over his shoulder told him Monroe was running again.

Conrad turned to go after him, but the blonde leaped on his back. The unexpected weight sent him to his knees. She wrapped one arm around his neck and clawed at his face with the fingernails of her other hand. He jerked his head away from her and reached back to grab the pile of blond curls. Leaning forward he pulled, and the woman cried out as she slid over his back and went crashing to the floor. The chivalrous part of him hated to treat a female that way, but he ignored it for the moment as he sprang to his feet and leaped over her.

The struggle had delayed him long enough that Monroe had gotten away. The door into the corridor stood open. Conrad snatched up his Colt, then raced through the door and looked along the hall. The door of the elevator cage was just sliding shut. As it did, Conrad caught a glimpse of Monroe's frightened face through the narrow opening.

Conrad made a dash for the same stairs that had taken him to the second floor. He bounded down them two and three steps at a time and got to the lobby just as the door of the elevator cage opened a few yards away.

The look of fright on the face of the elderly black elevator operator warned him. The man flinched aside as Carl Monroe thrust a small pistol at Conrad and pulled the trigger.

As the little gun cracked spitefully, Conrad threw himself forward and down. The bullet went over his head and ricocheted off the marble floor of the bank occupying the ground level of the building. While he was scrambling back to his feet, Monroe bolted from the elevator and made a run for the front doors with surprising speed for a short, fat lawyer.

He clutched the pistol in his hand, and with pandemonium breaking out in the bank because of the shot, it was an unlucky break for Monroe that he was armed. The guard at the doors drew his own weapon, a .38 caliber Smith & Wesson double-action revolver, and yelled at Monroe, "Hold it right there!"

The lawyer didn't slow down. It was impossible to tell whether he brandished his gun at the guard on purpose or if the muzzle just swung in that direction because Monroe was pumping his arms as he ran. Either way, as the barrel of Monroe's gun rose toward the guard, he fired.

And not just one shot. Thinking a bank robbery was taking place, the guard kept squeezing the trigger and emptied all five rounds in the Smith & Wesson's cylinder into the lawyer's chest. Monroe's momentum kept him going forward even though his body jerked violently under the impact of each slug. His feet went out from under him as his nerves and muscles stopped working, and he pitched forward to land on his face with a soggy thud and slide across the slick marble floor until he came to a stop almost at the stunned guard's feet.

The guard slowly lowered his gun and stared at the dead lawyer with horrified eyes. "Holy cats!" he yelped. "That's no bank robber! That's Mr. Monroe!"

As Conrad came to his feet, he felt sorry for the guard. The man had heard the shot, seen somebody rushing toward him with a gun, and hadn't paid any attention to who it was. Thinking he was about to be gunned down by a fleeing robber, the guard had opened fire. Nobody could blame him.

But they might blame Conrad for starting the ruckus. He long legged it back to the nearby stairs and went up them in a hurry, heading toward the still-open rear door of Monroe's office. He could plainly hear the commotion downstairs and knew it wouldn't be long before the law showed up.

He went into the office warily, just in case that homicidal blonde was still there and might try to brain him again. He didn't see any sign of her in either office. Clearly, she had realized a lot of trouble was about to come crashing down and had taken off for the tall and uncut while she had the chance.

Conrad went straight to Monroe's desk and started pawing through the papers on top. He was looking for a name he might recognize or any sort of communication with a San Francisco address on it. All across the country as he searched for his missing children, Conrad had run into traps set

for him by Pamela years earlier. She had hired
men to try to kill him, and he was convinced the
latest attempt on his life was one more instance of
that. Maybe Pamela had made the arrangements
with Monroe directly when she passed through
Carson City with the twins, but she might have
used an intermediary in San Francisco to set it up.
That was the name Conrad was looking for.

Not finding anything among the papers on the
desk, he jerked open the drawers and pawed
through them. That proved just as fruitless, leaving only the filing cabinets in the outer office.

He hurried in there and yanked open a drawer.
He pulled out a handful of papers and started
skimming through them, discarding them when
he didn't find any helpful information. The
sheets of correspondence, bills, and legal docu-
ments drifted down and soon covered the floor
around his feet.

He was working on the third drawer when he
found a stack of memorandums dated almost
three years earlier. One of them bore the scrib-
bled notation *D.L. Golden Gate $5000 C.B.* Below
that, written in a slightly different colored ink,
probably at a different time, were the initials *E.G.*
and *W.F.*, followed by *$300*.

Ed Gillespie and Walt Farley, Conrad thought.
Someone had paid Monroe $5000 to set up the
ambush, and he had turned around and paid
Gillespie and Farley the princely sum of $300 to
carry out the killing. You get what you pay for,

Conrad told himself, and Monroe hadn't gotten much out of Gillespie and Farley except spectacular failure.

And a final payment of five .38 caliber bullets in the chest from the guard downstairs in the bank.

Conrad had no doubt the *C.B.* on the note meant him. And *Golden Gate* could certainly refer to San Francisco. The Golden Gate was the opening between the Pacific Ocean and San Francisco Bay, and it was also a popular name for businesses in the city.

But who or what was *D.L.*? Conrad had no idea. Claudius Turnbuckle might be able to find out. Conrad would wire him with the information immediately, so Turnbuckle could start working on the problem while Conrad was on his way to San Francisco.

He stuffed the memorandum in his pocket and turned away from the filing cabinets, the papers on the floor crackling and crinkling under his boots as he did so. When he came around to face the door, he stopped short and didn't move except to raise his hands slightly.

He was staring down the barrel of a gun.

Chapter 5

"Mr. Browning, you're making it mighty difficult for me to extend the courtesy to you that I want to," Deputy Wallace said in tightlipped anger from behind that gun. "There's only so far your reputation as one of our former leading citizens will get you."

"Take it easy, Deputy." Conrad didn't know if Wallace had seen him slip the piece of paper in his pocket, but he didn't intend to give it up unless he absolutely had to. "I haven't done anything wrong."

"Carl Monroe's lying on the floor of that bank downstairs, dead as a mackeral!"

"I didn't shoot him." Conrad shrugged. "You can check my gun. It hasn't been fired since that ruckus in front of the hospital earlier."

Wallace came farther into the office. "I know who shot Monroe. There are plenty of witnesses to what happened. I'm not going to lose any sleep over him getting ventilated. He was always too slick to get any blood on his own fingers, but he was part of plenty of dirty dealings that wound up with people getting killed. That doesn't mean you're in the clear here. Monroe got shot because he was shooting at you."

"That sounds to me like I didn't do anything wrong, like I was the victim," Conrad pointed out.

"Blast it, I knew you were gonna come here! That's why I didn't tell you where Monroe's office was and I tried to get the marshal's permission to pull Monroe in for questioning as quick as I could. But you beat me here anyway, and now he's dead!"

"There's nothing illegal about paying a visit to a lawyer in his office. Monroe panicked when I showed up and told him who I was. Seems to me that's just as good as a confession that he was mixed up in that attempt on my life."

Conrad left out any mention of him pointing his gun at Monroe. The only other person who knew about that was the blond secretary, and he had a hunch she was going to make herself scarce for a while. She probably knew about some of Monroe's crooked business, and didn't want to get mixed up in any investigation.

"What happened then?" Wallace asked.

"Can I put my hands down?"

Wallace thought about it for a second, then shrugged and motioned with the barrel of his gun for Conrad to lower his hands. "You said Monroe panicked? What do you mean?"

"He ran out of here before I could stop him. I went after him. He took the elevator, so I went down the stairs. We got to the lobby of the bank at the same time. He took a shot at me and tried to rush out. The bank guard thought Monroe was a robber and was trying to get away with the bank's money. He opened fire. That's all I know, Deputy."

"Yeah?" Wallace motioned with his gun at the litter of papers on the floor. "What about all this?"

"It was like this when I came back up here," Conrad lied. "Somebody must've come in here after Monroe and I ran out and started going through his papers."

"Somebody, eh? Who would do a thing like that?"

"Maybe somebody who worked for Monroe, or some other business associate?" Conrad suggested. "You said yourself he was mixed up in plenty of crooked work. Someone could have been trying to find blackmail material, or something like that."

"I don't know who was the slickest one here, you or Monroe," Wallace said disgustedly as he holstered his pistol in a cross-draw rig on his left hip. "I've got a strong hunch you're not telling me the whole truth, Mr. Browning . . . but I don't reckon I can prove it. Since there are more than a dozen witnesses downstairs who can confirm that you didn't shoot Monroe . . . just get out of here. You're free to go."

"I suppose you want me to stay in Carson City."

Conrad was prepared to ignore that order if he had to. Now that he had a lead in San Francisco, even a small one, he wasn't going to allow anything else to delay him.

Wallace surprised him by saying, "No, I'd rather you get out of town. The marshal may not agree with that, but considering the hell that's broken loose today, I think it would be in the interest of public safety for you to light a shuck out of here."

Conrad smiled. "That can be arranged."

"I warn you, though," Wallace went on, "Monroe had a secretary, a woman named Lorraine Eastman. I'm going to find her and talk to her. If she tells a different story than you do, I may be issuing a warrant for your arrest."

Wallace could issue all the warrants he wanted, Conrad thought. By the time the lawman got around to doing that, he would be in San Francisco and that warrant wouldn't mean a thing. If necessary, Conrad wouldn't come back to Carson City.

After all, it was no longer his home.

It was just one more in a long line of places where people kept trying to kill him.

With everything that had been going on, Conrad hadn't had a chance to get to the train station and check to see when the next westbound train would be coming through. To his chagrin he learned he had missed the train by an hour.

"But there'll be another westbound at nine

o'clock tomorrow morning, Mr. Browning," the clerk told him. "Would you like a ticket on it?"

Conrad nodded. "Yes, thanks. All the way through to San Francisco."

The delay chafed at him, but the quickest way to reach the coast was to wait for the train the next morning. He went back to the hotel to wash up, change clothes, and eat a late lunch.

He had almost accomplished the first two of those goals—he was buttoning up a clean shirt— when a knock sounded on the door of his suite, which were the best accommodations in the hotel. Considering what had already happened, Conrad figured it would be a good idea to be careful. His gun belt was draped over the back of a chair in the sitting room. He slid the Colt from its holster as he went to the door. "Yes?"

As soon as he spoke, he stepped quickly to one side, in case somebody in the hall decided to let loose with a shotgun blast through the door.

Instead, a voice he recognized as belonging to one of the bellboys replied, "I have a telegram for you, Mr. Browning."

Conrad started to ask who the wire was from, then realized the message was probably sealed up and the boy wouldn't know. He tucked the gun behind his belt where it would be handy and opened the door.

The bellboy's eyes widened a little at the sight of the black gun butt sticking up at Conrad's waist, but he didn't say anything except, "Here you go, sir," as he held out the Western Union envelope. Conrad took it, nodded his thanks, and handed the boy a silver dollar. He shut the door and tore open the envelope to slide out the yellow telegraph flimsy.

A frown creased his forehead as he read the words printed on it in a telegrapher's block letters:

WILL KNOCK ON YOUR DOOR IN FIVE
MINUTES STOP PLEASE TALK TO ME STOP

There was no signature.

Conrad studied the telegram for a long moment, then abruptly crumpled it and tossed it in a waste basket. He hurried back to his bedroom, finished buttoning his shirt along the way, and picked up his clean suit coat to shrug into it. He had brushed his hat as clean as he could, so he settled it on his head, then picked up the gunbelt on his way back through the sitting room. He pouched the iron and buckled the belt around his hips.

His hand was on the butt of the Colt as he opened the door and stepped into the corridor, which was deserted at the moment. The hotel had elevators, several of them, in fact, but there was also a stairwell down the hall to the left, and the door to it was set back in a small alcove. Conrad went to it and stepped into that alcove, then stopped and edged his head slightly past the corner so he could look back down the corridor. He had a good view of the door to his suite. He wanted to see who was going to knock on that door in a couple minutes.

He still had a lot of acquaintances in Carson City. None of them had anything to do with him now, though. It wasn't like he had tried to keep in touch over the years. In fact, some of his former friends were probably still angry with him for making it look like he had died when his house burned down, then letting everyone believe that for months.

The only other people he knew were Deputy Wallace and Dr. Liam Taggart, and neither of them would have sent him a telegram. If they'd wanted to talk to him, they simply would have shown up at the hotel and knocked on his door. There was something fishy about that telegram, and he wanted to know what it was. Staking out his suite door seemed like the best way to find out.

He stiffened as a man emerged from the elevators and came along the corridor, looking at the numbers on the doors. He wore a gray suit and a black derby and sported a close-cropped beard. Conrad had never seen him before, at least not that he recalled. He put his hand on his gun butt again as the man paused in front of his door, then took a piece of paper out of his pocket and looked at it for a second. He put the paper back, shrugged to himself, and raised his hand to knock.

At that moment, Conrad heard the faint click

of the stairwell door behind him, then a rustle of fabric. The cold ring of a gun barrel pressed itself to the back of his neck.

"I knew you'd take the bait," a woman's voice said, as down the hall the bearded man's knuckles pounded on the door of Conrad's suite.

Conrad moved with blinding speed, twisting away from the gun and whirling around. His left arm came up, hit the woman's arm, and knocked it to the side so the gun was no longer pointing at him. He drove his body against hers, forcing her back against the wall of the alcove, and closed his hand around the cylinder of the little revolver so it couldn't fire even if she pulled the trigger. He wrenched the gun out of her fingers. His other hand came up and caught hold of her chin, making her gasp. He knew he was probably hurting her and he regretted that, but he wanted answers.

"I'm not the only one who took the bait, Miss Eastman," he told the blonde he had last seen in the offices of the late and unlamented Carl Monroe.

Chapter 6

Conrad kept the pressure on Lorraine Eastman's chin, preventing her from screaming or making even the smallest outcry. Her blue eyes were wide with fear as he pinned her to the wall. He was aware of the warm, full curves of her body under her dress, but at the moment they didn't mean much to him.

Down the hall, the bearded man continued to knock on the door of Conrad's suite for a minute or so. Then the knocking stopped and he heard receding footsteps as the man walked away. A moment later the elevator door rattled as it closed and the cage started to descend.

"We're going to my suite," Conrad told the blonde. "Don't make a racket, and you won't get hurt."

She hissed something unintelligible at him. He figured she was trying to curse him. Quickly, he shifted his grip on her, getting his left arm around her waist from behind and clapping his right hand completely over her mouth. She struggled in his grasp, but he was too strong for her. He pulled her out of the alcove and forced her down the hall toward his suite.

He hoped no other hotel guests or employees came along before he was able to get her through the door. If they did, trying to force a young woman into his suite would certainly look bad for him. Luck was with him, however. The corridor stayed deserted long enough for him to open the door, which he had left unlocked. A hard shove sent Lorraine Eastman stumbling into the sitting room.

She turned toward him and opened her mouth to scream. He grabbed her again and clamped his hand around her throat, stifling any outcry.

"I know I'm not being much of a gentleman," he told her, "and I'm truly sorry about that. But you've attacked me a couple times now, and I want to know why. If I take my hand away from your throat, do you promise not to scream?"

She glared at him for a couple seconds, then a look of resignation came into her eyes and she nodded.

Conrad didn't believe her. "I can knock you unconscious before you manage to get a peep out, and I will if you don't cooperate. I'll try to pull my punch, but I can't promise you won't be injured. I have the rest of the day and all night if you want to be stubborn about this."

The fear in her gaze struck him as genuine.

When he asked again if she promised not to scream, she nodded and he believed her. He moved his hand away from her throat but held it ready to strike if he needed to.

"I'm not going to yell," she said in a surly voice. "If you'll swear to let me go, I promise to tell you whatever it is you want to know."

"You answer my questions first, and then we'll talk about what's going to happen to you," Conrad suggested in return. "That's the best deal you're going to get."

She sighed wearily. "All right. I agree. Now, will you stop pawing me and let me sit down?"

"Keeping you from trying to kill me isn't exactly the same as pawing you," Conrad pointed out. He released her and pointed to one of the well-upholstered armchairs. "Sit down."

The blonde sat. She wore the same dark blue dress she had worn at Monroe's office earlier. A matching hat perched on her head. She had tucked her hair back up as best she could after Conrad wrecked the arrangement of curls. She looked down at the floor. "What is it you want to know?"

"Your name is Lorraine Eastman, isn't it?"

"That's right. How did you know that?" Before he could answer, she went on, "Never mind. I suppose the law told you. They've been trying to get something on Mr. Monroe for as long as I've worked for him."

"How long is that?" Conrad wanted to know if

Lorraine had been Monroe's secretary when Pamela came through Carson City with the twins.

"I've been his secretary for the past year and a half."

If she was telling the truth, that meant she had probably never seen Pamela or the children.

"What happened to the secretary he had before that?"

"He fired her when she . . . well, when she turned up in a delicate condition."

"Pregnant?"

Lorraine made a face. "If you want to be crude about it."

"And I suppose Monroe was responsible for that?"

"Again, if you want to be crude about it . . . yes. I didn't really know what happened until later, when the woman came back to the office to beg Mr. Monroe for money. He . . . he laughed at her and sent her away."

"Nice fellow," Conrad said in a disgusted tone. "I suppose you were so quick to defend him earlier because the two of you—"

He stopped short at the look of utter revulsion on Lorraine's face. "God, no!" she exclaimed. "He was the most contemptible little weasel I ever met. But he paid well, and I didn't want anything to happen to him." She rolled her eyes. "That didn't work out too well, did it?"

"Is that the only reason you cared? Because of the money he paid you?"

She hesitated, then said, "I didn't want any trouble with the law. When you said he tried to have you killed, I was afraid you were going to bring in the authorities and they'd finally have something on him they could use to convict him. I knew if that happened, they would arrest me, too, and claim that as his secretary I had to be aware of all his crooked dealings."

"Well, weren't you?" Conrad demanded.

"Of course I was," she snapped. "I'm not a fool. I saw the sort of men who came and went in that office, and I typed up his correspondence and notes. I hadn't worked for him long before I knew what he was up to."

"Why come after me?" Conrad asked. "If you hated Monroe like you say, it couldn't have been to avenge him."

"I don't care that he's dead," Lorraine said bluntly. "But now the law is after me, and I need money to get out of town. I did some asking around about you, Mr. Browning. You're a rich man, even if you did come into the office with mud all over your clothes. I figured you could pay me enough to get me out of Carson City so I can start over somewhere else."

"You mean you intended to rob me at gunpoint. That's why you sent that telegram and paid some fellow you probably found in a saloon to come and knock on my door. You figured I'd be suspicious and try to spy on my visitor, and that alcove was the best place to do so. It was a cunning little trap."

"But you figured out what was going on and turned the tables on me." Lorraine's voice held some grudging respect along with the anger. "I underestimated you, Mr. Browning."

"So what do we do now? Do I turn you over to Deputy Wallace? I know he'd like to talk to you. He probably has a lot of questions about what went on in Monroe's office."

"They'll lock me up," Lorraine said with a slight quaver in the words. "I couldn't stand that. I . . . I'll do anything you want, Mr. Browning, as long as you don't turn me over to the law."

The invitation was plain in her eyes and her voice. Conrad shook his head. "That's not going to work."

"Are you sure?"

"Positive. But I might be more inclined to let you go if you can tell me what this means." He reached inside his coat and brought out the piece of paper he had taken from the filing cabinet in Monroe's office. He held it out to Lorraine, who took it tentatively and studied the words printed on it.

"Who or what is D.L.?"

Lorraine shook her head. "I have no idea. You can see from the date that Mr. Monroe wrote this note before I came to work for him."

"That's Monroe's writing? You're sure about that?"

She nodded. "Yes, I've seen it often enough." She pointed to the memorandum. "This other part, with the initials and the three hundred dollars . . . I can tell you that was written fairly recently. It's in a shade of ink that we never used until I bought some a couple months ago."

That was an interesting bit of information, Conrad thought. It indicated something or some-one had triggered the deal Monroe had made three years earlier. Conrad figured that trigger had been him setting out from Boston to search for his missing children. He had suspected all along that Pamela had hired spies to keep an eye on him. The conspiracy against him stretched across the country like a giant spider.

"Is there anything else you can tell me?"

"Well . . . the initials have to refer to Ed Gilles-pie and Walt Farley, but you know that already."

"What about Golden Gate?"

Lorraine shook her head. "That's something to do with San Francisco, isn't it?"

"But you don't recall Monroe ever saying any-thing about it?"

"No, I'm afraid not." She sat forward a little in the chair. "I've told you everything I know, Mr. Browning. I'm sorry about, well, about what hap-pened outside."

Conrad smiled. "About trying to rob me, you mean."

"I was desperate. I still am. Since you were responsible for Mr. Monroe getting killed, I thought it was fitting that you help me get away."

"Monroe was responsible for his own death. If he'd been honest, it wouldn't have happened."

"Honesty might postpone death sometimes. It doesn't prevent it."

She had a point there, Conrad thought. He opened the cylinder of the little pistol he had taken from her and shook out the bullets, then snapped the gun closed and tossed it in her lap.

"You can get more bullets. I don't want you being tempted to point that thing at me again. I don't like it."

"You're not going to turn me in?"

He slid his wallet out of his coat pocket and removed a few bills. Lorraine's eyes widened at the sight of them.

"Take the money and get out." Conrad extended the bills to her. "I don't want to lay eyes on you again. A while back I ran into another pretty young blonde who kept trying to murder me. She wound up dead."

That was true enough, although Conrad wasn't the one who killed her. He was going to let Lorraine Eastman draw her own conclusions, however.

"If I see you again, I'm liable to get suspicious," he went on as Lorraine took the money. "I won't ask questions, and I won't wait to do something about it. I'll take action right then and there."

"You don't have to worry, Mr. Browning." The bills disappeared somewhere inside her dress. "I promise you, you're about the last person I want to see again. There's an eastbound train this evening. I intend to be on it."

"I'd be careful if I was you. Deputy Wallace will probably have men watching the depot."

She laughed coldly as she got to her feet. "Those lawmen will never see me unless I want them to."

Conrad kept his hand on the butt of his gun as Lorraine went to the door. She paused and looked back at him.

"What is it that's so important about you? Why would someone in San Francisco pay five thousand dollars to have you killed?"

"It's a long story."

Lorraine shrugged. "I don't really care. I was just curious for a second. You'd better be careful. There are probably more people out there who want you dead."

"I think you can count on that."

Chapter 7

Considering the hour, Conrad ate an early supper instead of a late lunch. The rest of the evening and the night that followed passed quietly. He couldn't help wondering if Lorraine Eastman had managed to get on that eastbound train and leave Carson City, but he didn't care enough to find out.

He and Arturo had been traveling light on their cross-country journey, but once he was in Carson City Conrad had bought more clothes, as well as the new Colt. Even so, he had only a couple small bags to take with him to the train station the next morning, and he carried them himself rather than have the hotel send them over. At one time in his life he had been accustomed to having servants take care of his every need, but now he was more self-sufficient.

He wasn't surprised when Deputy Wallace strolled

up to him while he was standing on the platform, waiting for the westbound train.

"Good morning, Mr. Browning." Wallace touched a finger to the brim of his soft felt hat. "You didn't have any more trouble after the last time I saw you yesterday, I trust?"

"Not a bit." Conrad wasn't going to mention the encounter with Lorraine Eastman at the hotel.

"No one tried to kill you? No shots were fired?"

Conrad shook his head. "It appears Monroe and his hired guns were the only ones after me."

"The only ones here in Carson City, anyway."

Conrad shrugged. "It's hard to predict what a person will run into elsewhere, isn't it?"

"Not always," Wallace said. "For example, I predict that when you arrive in San Francisco, you'll find yourself in more trouble. I did some checking, and that seems to happen all the time with you."

"It's not my idea," Conrad snapped. "I just want to be left alone to go about my business."

"From what I could tell, you have teams of lawyers in Boston, Denver, and San Francisco who take care of your business for you. Or were you referring to something else, Mr. Browning?" The deputy was digging, trying to find a reason for the violence that had occurred in his city.

Conrad wasn't going to satisfy Wallace's curiosity by spilling the story. "I'm leaving town, Deputy," he said without answering Wallace's question. "Isn't that what you wanted?"

"Fine," Wallace said. "I won't be sorry to see you go."

With some apparently idle curiosity of his own, Conrad asked, "Say, did you ever find that woman who worked in Monroe's office?"

Wallace made a sour face. "No, but we will. She's still around somewhere. She couldn't have gotten out of town without us knowing about it."

Conrad would have been willing to bet the deputy was wrong about that . . . but he kept that thought to himself.

The westbound train rolled into the station a few minutes later with clouds of smoke and steam puffing from the diamond-shaped stack of the big Baldwin locomotive. Conrad lifted a hand in farewell as he climbed aboard.

Wallace wasn't sorry to see him go . . . and Conrad wasn't sorry to be putting Carson City behind him.

Conrad arrived in San Francisco that evening. The train had passed over the Sierra Nevadas and through some spectacularly beautiful scenery since he boarded it that morning, but he hadn't paid attention to any of it. He'd spent the time thinking about what he would find when he reached the city by the bay. Would he step off the train and right into the gunsights of some other hired assassin who wanted to kill him?

At first glance, the only person waiting for him on the platform was the tall, burly Claudius Turnbuckle. The ruggedly-built lawyer with muttonchop side whiskers was a distinctive figure, immediately recognizable. Turnbuckle moved forward as Conrad came down the portable steps from the railroad car. He extended a hand, which Conrad gripped firmly. "Welcome back to San Francisco. Any problems during the last leg of the journey?"

Conrad shook his head. "No, nothing happened on the train except that I got pretty bored."

"Yes, I can understand why you'd feel that way, what with no one shooting at you or anything." Turnbuckle chuckled, then grew solemn. "Seriously, I'm glad you're here, Conrad. You're too much in the habit of going it alone."

"I wasn't actually alone," Conrad pointed out. "Arturo's been with me."

"And Arturo's a fine man, but you know what I mean. We have resources, Conrad. There's no point in not taking advantage of them."

"Tell me what you've found out." Conrad had wired Turnbuckle from Carson City the previous evening, asking the lawyer to check up on the information from the note he had found in Monroe's office.

Turnbuckle took Conrad's arm and steered him toward the depot lobby. "I have a carriage waiting out front, and I'll have someone bring your bags to the hotel. We can talk while we're riding."

As they moved through the station, Conrad noticed several well-dressed but nondescript men moving along with them. A second glance showed him how tough and capable they looked, and he realized they were bodyguards hired by Turnbuckle to make sure no ambush took place at the station. Conrad appreciated that, but at the same time worried about how effective he would be in carrying out his investigation if he had guardians tagging along with him everywhere he went.

"I booked a suite for you at the Palace Hotel," Turnbuckle went on as he opened the door of a well-appointed carriage with gleaming brass trim and a team of fine black horses. Conrad climbed into the vehicle and took the rear seat. Turnbuckle followed and faced him, riding backward.

"What about D.L. and the Golden Gate?" Conrad asked as the carriage got underway.

"Do you have any idea how many Golden Gate this-that-and-the-others there are in this town? It's a popular name. But I have men combing through the city directory and pounding the pavement, trying to find some connection between a Golden Gate and something with the initials D.L. It's going to take a few days to cover all the possibilities."

"D.L. is probably a person."

"Probably, but not necessarily. Again, there are

too many people in San Francisco to put our finger on the correct one right away."

"I'm not complaining, Claudius. You don't have to defend your efforts."

Turnbuckle frowned. "I just want to do the best we can for you. You've been through so much."

"Everyone has misfortune in their lives." Conrad shrugged.

"Yes, but you've had more than your share."

Conrad thought about some of the people he had met in his travels and wasn't so sure about that. It seemed to him that tragedy, in one form or another, came to everyone sooner or later. The trick was being able to deal with it without letting it destroy you. Rebel's death had driven him perilously close to such destruction. At times he still felt like he was teetering on the edge of a cliff, poised over a bottomless abyss that would swallow him completely. All it would take to send him over the brink was the slightest push . . .

"So you don't really have anything to report?"

"Not yet," Turnbuckle said. "But we're just getting started."

Conrad nodded. "I appreciate that, I really do."

"What you should do is take a few days to rest. You have the finest, most comfortable suite in the hotel. You should relax and enjoy it. Regain some strength. You've run into trouble everywhere you've gone ever since you started searching for the children. You need to get away from all that for a while and let us worry about carrying on the search."

"I suppose you're right." Conrad leaned back against the sumptuous cushions. In truth, he had no intention of sitting back and doing nothing. Once, maybe, he could have done that, but no longer.

The carriage wheels rattled over the cobblestone pavement. Conrad felt the vehicle tilt as it started up one of San Francisco's many steep hills. Suddenly the driver cried out in surprise and the carriage lurched to the side, then came to an abrupt stop.

"What in blazes are you doing?" the driver called to someone. "Move that thing!"

Turnbuckle leaned out the window. "What's wrong, Harry?"

"Oh, some dunderhead driving a beer wagon pulled out right in front of us," the driver explained. "Nearly ran into him, I did. And now he's blocking the street."

Alarm bells began to ring inside Conrad's head. Wagons and carriages nearly ran together in the streets all the time, he supposed. That was one of the hazards of living in a big city. But his instincts told him there was something wrong.

"Are those bodyguards you hired following us?" he asked sharply.

For a second Turnbuckle looked like he was going to deny hiring any bodyguards, but then the lawyer said, "Yes, they're supposed to be back there."

The driver yelled, "Hey, what are you doing with that ax?" At the same time, a swift rush of hoofbeats sounded somewhere behind the carriage, and guns began to go off.

"Claudius, I think we'd better get out!" Conrad reached for the door.

"We'll be safer in here!" Turnbuckle protested.

"I don't think—" Conrad began, but the rest of what he was going to say was drowned out by the driver's frightened yell and a sudden rumble like thunder.

Conrad rammed a shoulder against the door and popped it open. He half fell, half jumped to the street in time to see a huge mountain of beer barrels begin to roll off the big wagon that had blocked the carriage's path, creating the thunderous sound. The first one flew off the wagon and slammed into the horses hitched to the carriage. The poor animals screamed in pain and went down under the impact.

A few weeks earlier, Conrad had witnessed an avalanche in the mountains on the border between Utah and Nevada. Right before him a small-scale avalanche was taking place on the San Francisco street, with beer barrels instead of boulders. The barrels continued to roll off the wagon. Some of them burst when they landed, spraying beer over the street, but most bounced and kept rolling. Conrad leaped aside from one that would have crushed him like a bug. From the corner of his eye he saw another barrel bounce high and then slam down on the carriage's seat, cutting short the driver's terrified scream.

"Claudius, come on!"

Turnbuckle scrambled out of the carriage as another barrel landed on the vehicle's roof, splintering it. The lawyer slipped in the flood of beer washing down the street and would have fallen if Conrad hadn't grabbed his arm and jerked him upright. They had to get out of the path of the barrels if they were going to survive.

The men who had sprung the trap had chosen a good spot for it. Buildings on both sides of the street were dark and shuttered for the night, and there were no alleys between them. There was nowhere for Conrad and Turnbuckle to go, and as more barrels rolled off the wagon and came bounding toward them, all they could do was turn and run.

Chapter 8

Things went from bad to worse a second later when Conrad saw stabs of orange muzzle flame ahead of them. He knew the hoofbeats he had heard before the shooting started came from mounted gunmen sweeping in on the bodyguards Turnbuckle had hired. Those gunmen would soon target him and Turnbuckle.

Something made him jerk his head around and glance over his shoulder. One of the barrels had bounded high in the air and was coming right at them. Conrad grabbed Turnbuckle's arm again and yelled, "Down!"

He sent them diving forward. The barrel went over them, coming so close he felt it moving through the air. They scrambled to their feet on the beer-slick pavement and started running again.

A yell of alarm sounded in front of them. Conrad spotted two men trying to get out of the way of the barrel, but they were too late. The barrel smashed into them and rolled over them, probably breaking numerous bones in their bodies. Conrad saw the guns lying on the cobblestones next to the men and knew the trap had backfired on those two, at least. They were some of the hired killers trying to wipe him out.

That gave him an idea. "Slow down!" he called to Turnbuckle. "We can't outrun those barrels. We need to dodge them!"

"You're crazy!" Turnbuckle panted. "We can't—"

"It's our only chance!"

Conrad knew he was right. He turned to face the barrels and leaped high in the air to let one of them roll under him. Muttering, Turnbuckle wheeled around and threw himself to the side to let another barrel fly past him. There were only seven or eight of the barrels left, but it would only take one to crush him or Turnbuckle.

"To your right, Claudius!" Conrad called out. "Go to your right!"

Turnbuckle flung himself in that direction while Conrad leaped the other way. One of the barrels bounced off the cobblestones and flew between them.

"Now toward me!"

It was a deadly game, like children playing tag, but the stakes were much higher. Conrad and Turnbuckle darted here and there, ducked, leaped high, threw themselves aside. The frantic action lasted only moments, but it seemed much longer before the last of the barrels had caromed past them.

The barrels weren't the only threat. The gunmen were distracted by the avalanche of beer barrels, and some of them fell victim to the bouncing, rolling, suds-filled dreadnaughts, but several killers avoided the onslaught and charged toward Conrad and Turnbuckle. Conrad heard shots booming and slugs whining off pavement, and he twisted around to meet the new threat as he reached for his gun.

The Colt hadn't fallen out of its holster during all his frenzied jumping around, and he brought the revolver up, triggering a pair of swift shots that sent two of the attackers spinning off their feet. The sharp smell of powdersmoke mingled with the earthy, overpowering aroma of spilled beer. Shifting his aim, he fired again.

Another gunman stumbled and dropped his weapon to clutch at his arm. In a voice wracked with pain, he shouted, "Let's get out of here!"

The remaining bushwhackers broke off the attack and fled into the night.

Conrad sent another shot after them to hurry them on their way, then went over to help a sprawled Claudius Turnbuckle to his feet. "Are you all right, Claudius?"

Turnbuckle was breathing hard. "Yes," he managed to say after a moment. "I'm . . . not hurt. Just soaked in . . . beer . . . and shaken up a bit."

"Come on. I want to check on the driver."

It was too late to help the man. He was lying in the wreckage of the carriage, dead. The avalanche of beer barrels had killed all the horses as well.

Conrad heard shrill whistles approaching and knew the San Francisco police were on their way, drawn by all the commotion. Explaining this mess wasn't going to be easy. It could have been passed off as an accident, if not for the bodies of the slain gunmen. Luckily, he had Turnbuckle with him, Conrad thought, and it was the lawyer's job to explain things away.

Before the police arrived, Conrad went to the abandoned wagon that had carried the beer barrels and blocked the street. There was nothing special about it. There were probably dozens just like it in San Francisco, maybe more.

Something lying on the street next to the wagon caught his eye. It was round and shiny, and although he had no way of knowing for sure that it had fallen from the driver's pocket when he jumped down from the wagon's high seat, that was certainly possible. Conrad slipped the object into his pocket before the police could arrive. He would take a better look at it later.

Uniformed men wearing peaked caps and carrying shotguns and pistols swarmed around him, their feet slipping a little on the beer-wet pavement. Conrad let the police take his gun, then lifted his empty hands to show he wasn't a threat. Not far away, Claudius Turnbuckle was already blustering in his best lawyerly bluster.

Conrad had a feeling it was going to be a good long while before he made it to the hotel for that rest and relaxation Turnbuckle had urged him to take.

Conrad and Turnbuckle finally reached the hotel long after midnight. They had spent a couple hours at police headquarters, being questioned separately and together by several different detectives on the San Francisco force. The detectives were suspicious, and Conrad knew they didn't fully believe Turnbuckle's story about how the attack must have been an attempted robbery.

On the other hand, the carriage had been an expensive one before it was wrecked, Turnbuckle was a well-to-do attorney, and Conrad was a highly successful businessman. It was *possible* they had been tempting targets for a gang of thieves.

Conrad knew it wasn't actually what had happened, of course, but he didn't admit that to the police. He had sensed all along that bringing the authorities in on his search for his missing children would be a mistake. To Pamela's warped mind, the whole thing had been a game, and instinct told him if he didn't play by her rules, he would regret it.

The police were taking the incident seriously.

Nine men were dead: the six bodyguards Turn-buckle had hired, and two strangers, who must have been members of the gang, and the driver. If the detectives knew the names of those men and who they associated with, they weren't sharing that information with Conrad and Turnbuckle.

When the two of them were told they were free to go at last, Turnbuckle accompanied Conrad to the hotel. Conrad's bags, which had been brought separately to the hotel, had arrived safely.

When they reached Conrad's suite, they found a bottle of brandy waiting for them, ordered earlier by Turnbuckle. Conrad poured drinks, then told the lawyer, "I want you to see to it that the families of the bodyguards who were killed tonight are taken care of. I'll pay for all the funeral expenses, and the families shouldn't be hurting for money for a while, either."

Turnbuckle nodded. "I'll make sure of it. I would have, anyway, even if you hadn't said anything. They were working for me, on your behalf."

"Exactly." Conrad sipped the brandy. "Do you have any sources of information inside the police department?"

"Perhaps," Turnbuckle replied with a lawyer's habitual non-committal caution.

"Maybe you can find out the identities of those gunmen who were killed. Knowing who they were and where they spent their time, might lead us to whoever hired them."

"The same thought crossed my mind. I'll have our investigators look into that, as well as continuing the search for the Golden Gate and D.L."

"All right," Conrad said. "If I think of anything else, I'll be in touch."

"And if we find out anything, I'll let you know immediately."

"Claudius . . . I'm sorry my troubles have put you in danger again." Several months earlier, Turnbuckle had been wounded by a gunman hired by one of Conrad's enemies, as part of the ongoing plot against him.

Turnbuckle waved a hand. "Think nothing of it. Since we've started representing the interests of you and your father, there's been more excitement in my life than ever before."

"Not necessarily the sort of excitement you might want, though," Conrad pointed out.

"Speaking of your father," Turnbuckle said, "have you thought about getting in touch with him to see if he could help you with your search?"

Conrad frowned. "You know where Frank is?"

"Well, not exactly. I could probably locate him, though, if I set out to do so. The last I heard, he was in Alaska."

"Alaska?" Conrad repeated with a smile. "That sounds like Frank. Always wandering."

"They don't call him The Drifter for nothing." Turnbuckle paused. "What about it? Do you want me to try to find him?"

Conrad shook his head. "No, this is my problem, not Frank's."

"He's always been glad to help before. And those children are his grandson and granddaughter, after all."

Conrad tossed back the rest of his drink and set the empty snifter on an expensive, hand-carved sideboard. "No."

"Very well. It's up to you, certainly." Turnbuckle finished his drink. "I should be going and let you get some rest. I'm glad we both survived the night."

Conrad nodded. Surviving was generally a good thing . . . although there had been a time when he wished more than anything in the world that he had died along with Rebel, so he wouldn't have to live without her.

Once Turnbuckle was gone, Conrad stripped off the clothes that stunk of stale beer and tossed them on the floor. The hotel staff could clean them or burn them or whatever they wanted to do. He washed up, then fell onto the soft, luxurious four-poster bed in the elaborately decorated bedroom.

Despite his weariness, sleep didn't come easily to him. He thought about everything that had happened, and something occurred to him. He got up and padded over to the clothes he had discarded. From a pocket in the trousers he took the little object he had picked up from the street next to the beer wagon.

It was round, about the size and shape of a silver dollar, but it was lighter because it wasn't made from metal but rather carved from what appeared to be ivory. The thing reminded Conrad of a poker chip, but it was bigger than most poker chips he'd seen, and it had a picture carved in relief on it. It might be an identification token, he decided as he turned it to get a better look in the light from the gas lamp he had turned on. Something a man might flash to gain entrance to a place, or to identify himself to others who might not know him otherwise.

He realized almost instantly the scene depicted on the item was a familiar one. Two points of land extended toward each other, with a wide stretch of water between them. Conrad had been to that place on numerous occasions, and he had ridden a ferry from one side of that strait to the other. His heart began to beat faster as he took in the implication of what he held in his hand.

He was looking at a representation of the Golden Gate.

Chapter 9

Turnbuckle arrived at the hotel the next morning while Conrad was having breakfast, which a waiter had delivered and served in the sitting room of his suite. The lawyer looked tired, which was not surprising considering his age and the fact that he had gotten only a few hours sleep.

He had news to report. He took the cup of coffee Conrad offered him and said, "I've been in touch with one of those sources inside the police department you mentioned. One of those would-be assassins killed last night was named Floyd Hambrick. He was a known criminal suspected of a number of killings along the Barbary Coast. His grandfather was a Sydney Duck."

Conrad raised his eyebrows to indicate he didn't understand the reference.

"That was a gang of Australian criminals who dominated the San Francisco underworld back in the fifties, in the days after the Gold Rush," Turnbuckle explained. "A lot of them were hanged by the Committee of Vigilance, but some survived, and even married and had children and grandchildren. In Hambrick's case, evidently the proverbial apple didn't fall far from the proverbial tree."

"Have the police been able to tie this fella Hambrick in with anybody else?" Conrad asked.

Turnbuckle shook his head. "Not so far. I suspect it may not be a very productive lead. Hambrick, and no doubt the other two men, were simply hired assassins, the sort who would kill anyone if the price was right."

Conrad sipped his coffee and nodded. It wouldn't be the first time such men had come after him since he'd started his search for the twins. Someone was always masterminding those efforts, though, someone who had been paid off directly by Pamela while she was still alive. He was confident that would turn out to be the case.

That mastermind might finally be able to tell him where his children were.

He picked up the ivory token from the table next to the fine china holding the remains of his breakfast and tossed it to Turnbuckle. "Have you ever seen anything like that before?"

The lawyer studied the token, turning it over in his fingers and running a fingertip over its carved surface. "That looks like the Golden Gate."

"I'm convinced it is."

Turnbuckle handed the token back to him.

"But, no, I've never seen one like it before, at least not that I recall. Where did you get it?"

"It was lying in the street next to the wagon carrying all those beer barrels," Conrad explained. "I can't prove the man who drove the wagon and cut the barrels loose dropped it . . . but he might have."

"I'd say it's even likely," Turnbuckle replied. "Should I take it and show it to some of our investigators?"

Conrad shook his head. "No, I'm going to hang on to it. But you can describe it to them and see if they remember ever seeing anything like it."

"Fine. I'll do that. In the meantime, what are your plans?"

"You told me to rest and relax, remember?" Conrad smiled. "That's what I intend to do."

Turnbuckle looked a little like he had a hard time believing that, but didn't say anything. He finished his coffee and left.

A short time later, dressed in a brown tweed suit, Conrad opened the door of the suite and looked out into the hall. A large man wearing a derby and sporting a red handlebar mustache sat a few feet away in an armchair he had pulled up from somewhere. The man was reading a newspaper, but he looked over and gave Conrad a polite nod.

"I suppose Claudius stationed you there," Conrad said.

"The boss says you ain't to be disturbed, Mr. Browning. It's my job to see to it things stay that way."

"What's your name?"

"Dugan, sir."

"Well, Mr. Dugan, you're supposed to prevent anyone from getting into this suite. Are you also supposed to prevent me from leaving?"

Dugan set his paper down in his lap, took off his hat, and scratched a bald, somewhat bullet-shaped head. "He didn't say nothin' about that."

"I'm surprised," Conrad said.

"Just that if you go anywheres, I'm to go with you and make sure nothin' happens to you."

"Oh. Do you have a family, Mr. Dugan?"

A grin split the big man's face. "Aye, sir. A fine wife and four redheaded little ones."

"Did Mr. Turnbuckle inform you that the last men he hired to watch over me all wound up dead?"

Dugan's grin went away. "He told me. That don't matter. I'm bein' paid to do a job, and I figure on doin' it."

"That's an admirable attitude. And I assure you, if anything happens to you, I'll see to it that your family is taken care of financially. Or if I can't, Mr. Turnbuckle will."

"And that's a reassurance indeed, sir," Dugan said. "But I don't plan on windin' up dead."

"Let's hope for the sake of those four redheaded little ones that you're right."

Conrad went back inside and closed the door. It was going to make things a little more difficult, because he was determined no one else was going to lose their life because of him.

A little more difficult, yes . . . but not impossible.

* * *

Conrad stayed close to his hotel room all day, leaving it only to eat lunch in the Palace's sumptuous American Dining Room. Dugan trailed him and took a table in an unobtrusive corner where he could keep an eye on Conrad. It was likely Dugan could not afford to eat there and Conrad assumed Turnbuckle had instructed the hotel to put the bodyguard's meal on his tab.

Conrad chose to have supper in the suite, as he had breakfast. Dugan had gone off-duty and been replaced by a short, thick individual who introduced himself as Morelli. The new bodyguard followed the waiter into the suite.

"Could be one o' them assassins in disguise," Morelli explained. The waiter, who by his accent was Russian, took offense at that, and Conrad shooed them both out and told them to take their squabble outside.

He ate supper and waited for full darkness to settle over the city by the bay. When it had, he took off his tweed suit, his cravat, and his white shirt. In their place he pulled on a homespun shirt and a rough brown coat and trousers of the sort working men wore. While he was downstairs for lunch he had stopped at the concierge's desk and made arrangements to have the clothes bought and delivered to his suite that afternoon, along with a stevedore's cap. He tugged the cap down over his fair hair and tucked the Colt behind his belt at the small of his back, where the coat would conceal it.

The Palace was as modern and up-to-date as it could be, but it didn't yet have fire escapes outside the windows the way some hotels back east did. However, it did have decorative ledges along the exterior walls. Conrad slid open the window in his bedroom and stepped out onto the ledge. It was only about six inches wide.

Facing the brick wall, he slid his feet along the ledge toward the corner of the building. His fingers went into the cracks between the bricks and gripped tightly to take some of the strain off his toes. His suite was on the fifth floor, so there was a lot of empty air underneath him, with hard, unforgiving pavement waiting at the end of any unlucky fall. There was also a drain spout at the corner, connected to the rain gutters around the roof of the building. That was his destination.

After a few nerve-wracking minutes, he reached it. Keeping his feet on the ledge and one hand holding the wall, he pulled on the spout to test its strength. Satisfied it would hold him, he moved both hands onto it and got a good grip. Supporting himself with the drain spout, he began walking down the side of the building.

He knew it was a crazy thing to do, but he couldn't carry out the sort of investigation he wanted to if he had one or more of Turnbuckle's hired bodyguards watching him all the time. The trail led into the seamy district known as the Barbary Coast, and no one there was going to talk to the police. Those bodyguards looked like policemen, and some of them probably had been on the force, before going to work for Turnbuckle.

Conrad had to do it alone. It was his best chance to find out what he wanted to know, so he had run the risk of climbing out of a hotel window and down a drain spout.

He heaved a sigh of relief when the soles of his boots touched the floor of the alley next to the hotel.

Having spent time in San Francisco he knew how to get to the Barbary Coast. Because someone who knew him might see him and recognize him, he didn't follow the alley to the front of the hotel. He went to the rear, crossed the street quickly with his cap pulled down over his face, and found another alley that took him in the right direction. He smiled faintly, confident he had gotten out of the Palace without Morelli or anyone else knowing he was gone.

Sliding a hand in his pocket, he touched the ivory token he had brought with him. With any luck, before the night was over he would know what it meant.

And he would be one step closer to finding his children.

* * *

Because he was preoccupied, as well as because he didn't have eyes in the back of his head, Conrad didn't see the hulking, shadowy figure that appeared at the mouth of the alley beside the hotel. He didn't realize he was being watched, didn't feel the dark, almond-shaped eyes tracking his every move as he crossed the street and entered the other alley. The figure was clad all in black and was next to invisible in the shadows.

After a moment, the follower emerged from the alley and crossed the street as well, moving so swiftly and silently despite its size anyone watching might have taken it for a trick of the eyes, not something real and substantial.

The figure entered the other alley and the darkness swallowed it completely again, as if it had never been there.

Chapter 10

The area known as the Barbary Coast had grown up during the turbulent days following the discovery of gold at Sutter's Mill, when Argonauts by the hundreds of thousands poured into San Francisco and used it as a jumping-off point in their quest for riches. Some of them decided to stay instead of heading for the goldfields, some came back when they abandoned their dreams of finding a fortune, and many of those who were lucky enough to strike it rich returned to San Francisco intent on spending some of their newfound wealth.

Naturally, there were plenty of tinhorns, whores, and bartenders willing to take that money from them.

Gambling dens sprang up around the old Spanish plaza known as Portsmouth Square. Houses of prostitution spread along the waterfront. A man could get a drink in any of them, or in scores of other saloons, taverns, and dives.

The atmosphere in those places ranged from high-toned and luxurious to downright squalid, and sometimes you could find examples of both in the same block along Clay, Kearny, Pacific, and Grant Streets. The boundaries of the rather nebulous area people called the Barbary Coast drifted here and there with time and according to the vigilance of the local law enforcement agencies, but the core of its existence remained the same, the twin titans of Lust and Greed. They made up the foundation upon which the Barbary Coast was built.

That was where Conrad was headed. A damp chill hung in the air along the bay, and tendrils of fog crept up from the water and curled through the streets.

The only time Conrad had visited the Barbary Coast was when he was a much younger man, still in college. He and some of his wealthy classmates from back east were in San Francisco on a lark, and naturally they wanted to see the lurid denizens of the notorious area and sow some wild oats.

In those days, Conrad had been as arrogant and obnoxious as his companions, so he had gone along willingly on the expedition. They had caroused and whored all night, and they had been extremely lucky they hadn't wound up shanghaied, bleeding and robbed in some alley, or wasting away from some pustulent disease. He had heard it said that God looks after drunkards and fools, and he and his friends had fit into both categories.

Now, of course, things were totally different.

Time and tragedy had humbled him, stripped away most of the arrogance and pretense. But he remembered how to get to the Barbary Coast, and a short time after slipping out of the Palace Hotel, he entered a saloon called the Bella Grande, which didn't live up to its name at all. Conrad kept his eyes down and moved in a somewhat furtive manner, but in reality he was keenly studying everything around him.

He made his way across the crowded, smoky room to the bar and slid a dime onto the hardwood. "A schooner of beer," he told the man in the dirty apron who came to take his order.

The bartender tapped the bar next to the dime. "I'll need another of those, and a nickel besides."

"Two bits for a schooner of beer?" Conrad protested. "What is this place, the damn Palace?"

"It's the goin' rate, friend," the bartender said. "You must've been at sea a long time if you didn't know that."

Conrad shrugged, picked up the dime, and pawed around in a handful of coins he pulled from his pocket. The ivory Golden Gate token was among them. The bartender couldn't help but see it, but he didn't react in any way as far as Conrad could tell. The man scooped up the twenty-five-cent coin Conrad dropped on the bar and drew the beer from a big keg. He used a paddle to cut off the head and slid the big glass in front of Conrad.

"Seen Floyd around tonight?" Conrad asked.

"Floyd who?"

"Hambrick. Floyd Hambrick."

The bartender frowned and shook his head. "Don't believe I know the gent."

"Sure you do. He said he always drinks here."

"Maybe he does, but I don't know him by name, mister. What's he look like?"

Conrad didn't have Hambrick's description. Turnbuckle's source inside the police department hadn't been able to come up with anything except the name. Conrad just shook his head disgustedly. "Ah, never mind. I'll just have a look around."

"You do that."

Conrad picked up his beer and moved off into the crowd. He circulated for a few minutes, then set the schooner on an empty table and slipped out a side door. He wanted to keep a clear head, so he couldn't be guzzling down suds every place he went. One of the saloon's customers would snatch up the schooner and polish off the beer, probably by the time Conrad reached the street.

Over the next hour, the scene in the Bella Grande was repeated with minor variations in half a dozen other saloons. If anybody knew Floyd Hambrick, they weren't admitting it. Nor did anyone react when Conrad flashed the ivory token.

He was in a place called Spanish Charley's when he got his first break. The bartender, who wasn't Spanish at all but rather a fat blond Dutchman, had professed never to have heard of Floyd Hambrick, and he didn't blink at the ivory token.

Conrad still had it lying in the palm of his hand, along with some coins, when one of the women who worked in the place sidled up beside him. "Ooh, you've been to the Golden Gate."

Conrad looked over at her and revised his original opinion. Despite the painted face and the low-cut dress that revealed her breasts to the upper curve of her brown nipples, she wasn't a woman but rather a girl, no more than fifteen or sixteen years old.

He swallowed his disgust that a girl so young would be working in a place like that and put a leer on his face. It was probably what the girl was used to. He hadn't missed what she'd said. "The Golden Gate, eh?" he repeated.

"*Sí.*" The girl, at least, was Spanish, or Mexican, more likely. Maybe a descendant of one of the proud Californio families that had settled the area long before any gold-seeking Americans arrived. "The nicest place down here. Or so I have heard. I have never been there." Her blush was visible even with her dusky skin. "It is not a place for one such as I."

"Don't say something like that, darlin'. You're worthy of going anywhere you want to go."

The bartender rested a hand with fingers like sausages on the hardwood. "Where she'd really like to go is upstairs with you, *mynheer.* Ain't that right, Carmen?"

The girl batted her dark eyelashes at Conrad. "*Sí.* I mean yes." With a noticeable lack of enthusiasm, she pushed her breasts against Conrad's arm and cocked a hip so it pressed against his, though without any real urgency.

"She will cost you only a dollar, *mynheer*," the Dutchman went on.

Conrad pretended to think about it. The girl—Carmen, the bartender had called her, but more than likely that wasn't her real name—was the first person he'd encountered who admitted to knowing anything about the carved ivory token. He wanted to talk more with her, and some privacy would probably make the conversation more productive.

With pretended reluctance, he slid a silver dollar across the bar. The coin disappeared into the Dutchman's fat fingers. "She better be worth it," Conrad said.

"Oh, she will, she will," the bartender promised. "Won't you, Carmen?"

"You will never forget me, señor." The girl linked her arm with his. "Come with me."

She led him toward a staircase on the other side of the room. Conrad looked up at the second floor and saw a large number of rooms arranged along a balcony.

They were rooms only in the strictest sense of the word. Thin wooden partitions a foot short of reaching the ceiling separated them, and curtains closed off the front. The room where Carmen was taking him wouldn't provide much privacy, but it would be better than nothing.

She kept bumping her hip against him, seemingly out of habit, as they went upstairs. When they reached the balcony, she led him to the nearest room where the curtain was pushed back, but he steered her toward one farther along that had an empty room on each side.

"You're going to be yelling in pleasure," Conrad told her with the leer still on his face. "We don't want to disturb anybody else."

"Oh, señor, I am sure I will be," she said listlessly. She didn't argue as Conrad took her into the room and jerked the curtain closed.

As he turned toward her, she had already reached down and grasped the hem of her dress to pull it over her head. "Wait a minute," Conrad said. "Just hold on."

Carmen frowned at him in confusion. "You do not want me to take off my dress?"

"Not just yet. Why don't you sit down?"

She shrugged and sank onto the narrow bed. It was little more than a cot, and it was the only piece of furniture in the room other than a small, rickety-looking table. The light came from gas fixtures hung over the balcony. Their glow spilled over the short partitions, making the room a little dim, but Conrad had no trouble seeing the puzzled expression on Carmen's painted face as she looked up at him.

"What is it you wish me to do?" she asked.

"I thought we'd talk for a few minutes first. I like to get to know a girl before I—"

"Then you are an unusual man," Carmen said. "Most men don't want to know anything about me."

"I'm not like most men. You should know that because I have that token from the Golden Gate, right?"

She nodded. "Oh, yes, only the best people go there. Well, the best people for this part of town, anyway. I have heard there are crystal chandeliers. Is this true?"

"I never paid that much attention to the lights." Conrad dodged the question.

"And a long bar made of the finest mahogany. I would love to see it."

"I'm sure you will, one of these days. Maybe I'll take you. How'd you like to go sporting in there on my arm?"

"Oh, señor, that would be wonderful." She sounded more like she meant it. She started to push her dress off her shoulders, obviously figuring she would disrobe in the other direction, since he'd stopped her from pulling the garment over her head.

"Hold on, hold on. It's been a long time since I've been there. The Golden Gate's on Kearny Street, right?"

Carmen shook her head. "No, no, on Grant, near where the Chinese live."

"Oh, yeah, that's right. On Grant Street. I told you it's been a long time."

Carmen reached for her dress again. "Please,

señor, if we do not do what we came up here for, I will get in trouble."

"I never said we weren't going to."

"But I am only allowed so much time with each customer—"

Conrad took the token from his pocket and held it up. "You have to show one of these before they'll let you into the place, right?"

"Into the private rooms on the second floor, yes, or so I have heard." Carmen frowned again. "But you would know that, if you have been there."

"I just wasn't sure what the procedure was now, since I've been gone for a while."

His explanation didn't lessen the suspicion in her eyes. She stood up suddenly. "Did you bring me up here because you like me, señor, or because you are some sort of spy?"

"Spy?" Conrad repeated. "That's crazy. I just—"

Without warning, she darted past him and jerked aside the curtain that closed off the room. As she rushed out, Conrad reached for her but missed. "Dutchy!" she cried as she ran onto the balcony. "Dutchy!"

Conrad hurried after her. She was at the landing at the top of the stairs. The fat bartender had come out from behind the bar and was waiting at the bottom of the stairs with an angry expression on his florid face. "What in blazes is goin' on up there?" he demanded as the men drinking at the bar and the scattered tables looked on with interest.

Carmen ran down the stairs. "He asks too many

questions, Dutchy! I think he is a spy for one of your competitors . . . or a policeman!"

"I'm not either of those things," Conrad insisted as he reached the top of the staircase. "I was just talking to the girl—"

"Men who come here aren't interested in talking," Dutchy said with a glare. "I don't know what you're up to, mister, but I don't like it."

Conrad knew he had found out everything he was going to. Actually, it had been a pretty productive visit. But it was time to go. He wasn't worried about the bartender being able to stop him.

But then Dutchy shouted, "Hans! Ulrich!" and two men emerged from the shadows, one at each end of the balcony. The huge, blond bruisers stalked toward Conrad, each with scarred fists and broken noses of men who had dealt out and received plenty of violence in their lives.

"Take him!" Dutchy ordered. "I show you what we do with spies, *mynheer*!"

Chapter 11

Hans and Ulrich were big, but they were slow. Conrad avoided their lumbering rush by bounding down the stairs toward Dutchy and Carmen. The girl shrieked and ran, but Dutchy stood his ground, bellowing, "Help! Stop him! Help!"

Several burly customers sprang to his aid. As Conrad reached the bottom of the staircase, a man pushed Dutchy aside and swung a mallet-like fist at Conrad's head. Conrad ducked the punch and hooked a hard right into the man's midsection. The man grunted in pain, doubled over, and staggered backward.

Unfortunately, that delay was long enough for one of Dutchy's bouncers to leap down the stairs and slam into Conrad from behind. He wrapped his arms around him and lifted him off his feet. They crashed onto a table that splintered under their weight. Conrad landed amidst the debris with his attacker on top of him, knocking the breath from his lungs, stunning him.

"Hold him, Ulrich!" Dutchy shouted.

Ulrich's arms tightened around Conrad, preventing him from drawing in any air to replace what he had lost. Almost instantly, Conrad's head began to spin and a red haze drifted over his eyes. On the verge of losing consciousness, he drove an elbow into Ulrich's belly, hoping to loosen the man's grip, but it was like hitting a wall made of thick, sturdy planks and didn't seem to have any effect.

The roaring in his head rose to a thunderous level. Conrad knew he was about to pass out. Then he heard a shout that was muffled by the pounding of his pulse, and the vise-like grip around his chest and the great weight on his back was released. He rolled over and lay with his chest heaving as he dragged in great lungfuls of air.

His blurry eyesight cleared after a moment and he saw a large, black-clad shape flashing back and forth. He pushed himself to a sitting position and got a better look at what was going on. His rescuer was a tall, broad-shouldered man who kept Dutchy, the bouncers, and the patrons of Spanish Charley's at bay by slashing back and forth with a large, heavy-bladed hatchet.

Conrad wasn't surprised when he saw the man's yellow-hued skin, dark almond-shaped eyes, and black hair braided into a pigtail that hung down his back between his shoulders. The man also had a peculiar scar shaped like a half-moon on his right cheek. The hatchet men of Chinatown were famous—or notorious was probably a better word to describe them—but Conrad didn't know any reason why one of them would be helping him.

He wasn't going to turn down the aid. As he struggled to his feet, he spotted a man with an old cap-and-ball revolver on the balcony drawing a bead on the big Chinese.

Conrad's hand flashed to his Colt still behind his belt at the small of his back. Sweeping his coat-tails aside, he brought up the revolver and fired a split second before the man on the balcony did. Conrad's bullet smashed into the man's elbow, shattering bone and throwing off his aim. The old revolver boomed, but the heavy slug smacked harmlessly into a wall. The man screamed, dropped the gun, and clutched at his wounded arm. He fell forward against the railing along the edge of the balcony, smashed through it, and plummeted into the angry crowd, knocking a couple men to the floor as they broke his fall.

Conrad put his back against that of his unex-pected ally and swept the gun around. The mob drew back.

"I'm not a spy and I'm not a policeman," Conrad said raggedly as he continued to catch his breath. "But I'm leaving here, and nobody better try to stop me."

"You lie!" Dutchy accused. "You're up to no good!"

"Back off and I'll never set foot in this place again. I promise you that!"

Gradually, the crowd parted. Conrad kept a close eye on them as he edged toward the door with the Chinese man beside him.

Evidently anyone who had the impulse to pull a gun thought better of it, having seen what had happened to the man on the balcony. Conrad and his companion reached the door. They couldn't go through it together. The Chinese man jerked his head toward the door, indicating Conrad should go first. He didn't argue and ducked outside.

No sooner had his boots hit the street than a shot rang out from his right. He heard a bullet whip past his head and twisted in that direction. Some of Dutchy's friends must have come out a side entrance and up the alley to the street. More shots blasted as orange muzzle flame stabbed from the darkness of the alley mouth.

Conrad crouched and returned the fire, triggering two swift shots as he aimed at the flashes. Beside him, the Chinese man emerged from the saloon and took a hand in the fight, too. His arm flashed back, then forward, and the hatchet he held spun through the air. Conrad heard a distinctive *chunk!* and a man screamed.

The shooting stopped as a figure reeled forward into the dim light spilling through the grimy windows of Spanish Charley's place. The man pawed with both hands at the hatchet blade buried in his upper chest. His strength deserted him, and he pitched forward.

Conrad grabbed the sleeve of the black jacket the man wore and tugged on it. "Let's get out of here!"

As furious shouts rose behind them, they ran along the street. A few wild shots followed them, but none of the men from Spanish Charley's gave chase. Conrad and his companion had proven to be too deadly.

After putting several blocks behind them, the two men slowed. Conrad heard shrill whistles in the distance and knew the police were converging on the saloon in response to reports of the gunfire. They would be too late, as usual. The ruckus was over.

Conrad looked at his companion. He didn't know if the man spoke English, but he said, "Thank you. I wouldn't have lasted much longer back there without your help."

The man grunted.

"What's your name?" Conrad asked. "Did you just happen to come along and see what was going on?" He didn't believe that for a second, but wasn't aware of any other explanation.

The Chinese man didn't say anything. He looked at Conrad with narrowed eyes for a second, then turned and loped away into the night.

"Hey, wait!" Conrad called after him, but it didn't do any good. In a matter of moments, the man disappeared into the shadows, just like he had shown up suddenly and mysteriously.

Conrad shook his head. He had no explanation for what had just happened, but he knew he'd been lucky to get out of Spanish Charley's alive. Now that he'd been given another chance, he intended to make good use of it as he continued his search for his children.

He had what might be his best clue so far. One of the men who had taken part in the attempt on his life had a connection to the Golden Gate, a saloon or gambling den on Grant Street. Should he turn over that information to Claudius Turnbuckle and see what the lawyer's hired detectives could find out about it?

Or should he continue his own investigation and pay a visit to the Golden Gate himself?

He knew which way he was leaning, but he had done enough for one night. He still had to find a way to sneak back into the Palace Hotel without Morelli spotting him.

That proved to be easier than Conrad expected. He used a tradesman's entrance in the rear to get into the hotel, then climbed the stairs to the fifth floor, where a stealthy look around the corner revealed that Morelli was sitting back in his chair with his hat tipped forward over his eyes, snoring heartily. Conrad crept past him silently, unlocked the door of his suite, and let himself in. The door squeaked as he opened it, and Morelli began to stir.

Conrad had lost the stevedore's cap during the fight at Spanish Charley's. Stepping into the bedroom, he grabbed a long, thick robe and wrapped it around himself as he strode back to the door and jerked it open. He surprised Morelli in the act of raising a hand to rap on the door.

"Mr. Browning!" the bodyguard said. "What . . . I thought I heard . . . Is something wrong?"

"Only you sleeping on the job," Conrad said in a chilly tone. "My God, man, I could hear you snoring while I was all the way in the bedroom."

Morelli snatched off his derby and stammered, "I-I'm sorry, Mr. Browning. It won't happen again, I swear. I won't close my eyes the rest of the night. Y-you can see your way clear not to say anything to Mr. Turnbuckle about this, can't you?"

Conrad kept a frown on his face for a moment, but when he figured he had maintained the act long enough, he shrugged. "All right. But stay alert, Morelli." He added caustically, "I don't know if you've heard or not, but somebody wants me dead."

"Yes, sir, I know, but they'll not get past me, sir, you've got my solemn oath on that!"

Conrad made a shooing motion with his hand, sending Morelli back to the armchair. He closed the door, drew in a deep breath, and let it out with a sigh. His ribs ached from that bear hug Ulrich had put on him. But the Palace, haven of luxury that it was, had hot running water available in all its suites, so Conrad drew a bath, stripped off the workingman's clothes, and sank down in a massive, claw-footed porcelain tub to soak away those aches.

He made sure his Colt was fully loaded and lying on a chair within easy reach of the bathtub, and alongside the gun he had placed the carved ivory token from the Golden Gate. After soaking for a while, he reached over to the chair, picked up the token, and studied it, idly turning it over in his fingers.

Tomorrow he would find out more about the place it came from. If someone connected with the Golden Gate had the initials D.L., he would know he was still on the right trail. And if not . . . well, he would keep looking.

Nothing was going to stop him from finding and claiming his children. This was the endgame, and Pamela wasn't going to win.

Chapter 12

The redheaded, mustachioed Dugan was on bodyguard duty again the next morning when Conrad opened the door to Claudius Turnbuckle's knock. Conrad nodded and smiled at Dugan and ushered Turnbuckle into the suite. "Coffee?"

"Don't mind if I do," Turnbuckle replied.

Conrad had been eating breakfast, which had been delivered to the suite by a waiter from the hotel dining room. He had also been reading that morning's issue of the *San Francisco Chronicle*, which had been brought up with the food and coffee. Tucked away in the paper's rear pages was a small story about a brawl at a saloon in the notorious area known as the Barbary Coast resulting in the death of two men, one from a gunshot wound and the other from injuries inflicted with a hatchet, which had been found still lodged in the victim's body. The presence of the hatchet led the author of the story to speculate that perhaps one of the tongs from nearby Chinatown had been involved in the violence.

The same possibility had occurred to Conrad once he had time to think over the events of the evening. The criminal societies known as tongs had ruled San Francisco's Chinatown for more than four decades, ever since the Chinese began to arrive in the gold rush days along with everyone else. The rulers of the tongs used assassins known as hatchet men to maintain their iron grip on the neighborhood and also to battle each other in bloody wars over who controlled what in Chinatown.

The big man in black who had come to Conrad's aid certainly fit the description of a hatchet man, but for the life of him Conrad couldn't see why such an individual would invade a "round eyes" saloon to rescue him. He had no connection with the tongs whatsoever.

Conrad poured coffee for Turnbuckle, who put his hat and overcoat on a side table and took the steaming cup gratefully. "Anything to report?" Conrad asked as he sat down at the table again.

Turnbuckle shook his head and looked weary. "No, I'm afraid not, perhaps by the end of the day. Until we know something my men will continue to investigate." He took a sip of the coffee. "Any problems here last night?"

"How could there be, with your man Morelli on duty?" Conrad asked with a bland smile. "And in the finest hotel in San Francisco, to boot."

Turnbuckle grunted. "Nothing about this affair surprises me anymore."

Conrad smiled to himself. He suspected if Turnbuckle knew everything that had happened the previous night, he would be surprised, all right.

The lawyer was a friend who had gone to great lengths to help him on more than one occasion, and Conrad felt bad for withholding information, but thought he might have more luck investigating the latest lead by himself. He could always bring Turnbuckle in when he knew more.

They talked rather aimlessly for a few more minutes, then Turnbuckle asked, "What are you going to do today?"

Conrad picked up the folded newspaper. "I thought I might go down to the *Chronicle* offices."

"Why?" Turnbuckle asked with a puzzled frown.

"Newspapermen are famous for knowing what's going on. I want to talk to a journalist I know who works there."

Turnbuckle shook his head. "No offense, Conrad, but that's a bad idea. You wanted to keep this matter quiet if possible. That's why we haven't brought the police in on it. Talking to a reporter is like asking to have your personal affairs shouted from the rooftops."

"You're probably right in most cases, but I believe the man I'm thinking of will respect my wishes if I ask him for privacy."

"Never trust a newspaperman, that's my motto," Turnbuckle said stubbornly.

Conrad smiled. "Some people say the same thing about lawyers," he pointed out.

Turnbuckle grunted. "Of course you should do whatever you think is best. I've given you my advice. That's my job."

"And you're excellent at it."

"If you go out, at least take Dugan with you."

"I don't think the estimable Mr. Dugan would have it otherwise."

Turnbuckle finished his coffee and left. Conrad dressed in his black suit and flat-crowned black Stetson. When he stepped out of the suite, Dugan stood up immediately from the armchair.

"Goin' somewhere, Mr. Browning?" the bodyguard asked.

"I am, and you're coming with me," Conrad answered. "Do you know how to get to the offices of the *San Francisco Chronicle*?"

"I sure do. You need to put an advertisement or a notice in the paper?"

"Something like that."

They left the hotel and walked several blocks to the impressive redbrick building that housed the offices of the *Chronicle*. A woman at a counter in the lobby directed Conrad and Dugan to the third floor, where they found a large open area littered with desks where men sat pecking at typewriters. Conrad spotted the slender, balding man he was looking for and walked over to that desk, trailed by Dugan.

The reporter glanced up as they approached, then looked again with eyes grown wide with surprise. "Conrad Browning!" he exclaimed as he came to his feet. "I heard rumors you were in town, but I hadn't been able to confirm them yet."

"Hello, Jessup." Conrad shook hands with the man. Despite the lack of hair on the reporter's head, he was about Conrad's age. In fact, they had been in college together for a while before Jessup Nash had decided he had no interest in running the textile mills his family owned and had disappointed them severely by going into journalism.

"Jessup, this is Patrick Dugan," Conrad went on, having asked the big bodyguard his first name earlier. "Dugan, meet Jessup Nash."

Dugan grunted as his hairy paw all but swallowed Nash's smaller hand. "I've seen the name in the paper. Never thought I'd be meetin' the fella it belongs to."

"It's a pleasure, Mr. Dugan." Nash turned back to Conrad. "What brings you to San Francisco? Business or pleasure?"

"For some people it's the same thing," Conrad pointed out.

"Yes, I remember when it was like that for you. But from everything that I've heard, ever since—" Nash stopped short and looked horrified. "Damn it, Conrad, I was so glad to see you that for a minute

I forgot . . . I'm sorry. I'm so sorry for your loss. I couldn't believe it when I heard about your wife, and then everybody said you were . . . I mean—"

"I know what you mean"—Conrad nodded—"and I appreciate the sentiments, Jessup. But sympathy's not why I'm here. I'm looking for information."

"Of course." Nash pulled a chair from an empty desk over beside his desk. "Why don't you sit down?"

"You want me to stay, Mr. Browning?" Dugan rumbled.

"I think it would be all right for you to go down to the lobby where you'll be comfortable. I'm confident no one will try to assassinate me here in the *Chronicle*'s editorial offices."

Dugan frowned. "Sounds good, but I'm supposed to keep my eye on you."

"I'm not going anywhere," Conrad promised. "I'll come get you when I'm ready to leave."

"If you're tryin' to trick me, you know I'll lose my job over this."

Conrad smiled. "I wouldn't do that to those four redheaded little ones of yours."

"I'll hold you to that," Dugan said ominously. He walked back to the stairs and disappeared down them.

As Conrad and Nash sat down, the reporter said, "Your friend Mr. Dugan has the appearance of someone who's been hired to look after you. By Claudius Turnbuckle, say?"

"Jessup, before I tell you anything, or ask you anything, I have a request."

Nash looked pained. "You don't want me to print anything that we're about to discuss."

"That's right."

"That's a very difficult thing for a journalist to promise, Conrad. Our business is finding things to print."

"I know that. And I can give you a good story— maybe a better story than you've ever had—but only when the time is right."

"You'll promise me an exclusive in return for my discretion and cooperation now?"

"Exactly."

Nash thought about it for a moment before saying, "Normally I wouldn't agree to such a thing. But since we're old friends . . . and since I have a hunch you're right about it being quite a story . . . I'll take a chance. What is it you want to know?"

"I have your word you won't write anything about this until I tell you it's all right?"

Nash nodded, although he still looked a little reluctant. "My word."

"What can you tell me about a place in the Barbary Coast called the Golden Gate?"

"The Golden Gate what? Walk around this city and you'll find everything from the Golden Gate Saloon to the Golden Gate Laundry. You mentioned the Barbary Coast, which leads me to think you're more likely talking about the saloon."

"There is such a place?"

"Oh, yes. One of the biggest drinking and gambling establishments in the area. Other things go on there as well, if you get my drift."

Conrad reached in his pocket and took out the ivory token. "Is this from there?"

Nash barely glanced at the token before he nodded. "Sure. How did you get hold of one?"

"Never mind that now. What's its purpose?"

"Twofold, actually. All the people who work at the Golden Gate carry them, and the owner also hands them out to certain customers so they can gain entrance to the second floor, where the real drinking and gambling and those other things I mentioned go on."

"The owner," Conrad repeated.

"That's right. If you have one of those tokens, you must know him. His name's Dex Lannigan."

Dex Lannigan. The name echoed in Conrad's head.

He had found D.L.

Chapter 13

Conrad tried to keep the reaction he felt from showing on his face. "Dex Lannigan, eh?"

"Are you telling me you *don't* know him?" Nash asked with a puzzled frown.

"That's right."

"Then how did you get that token?"

"That's part of the story I've promised you when the time is right. What can you tell me about Lannigan?"

Nash grunted and spoke quietly. "He owns a successful saloon on Grant Street, smack-dab between the Barbary Coast and Chinatown. That ought to tell you everything you need to know about the man. Despite a veneer of smoothness, Dex Lannigan is no more honest than he has to be. He's shrewd, ruthless, and dangerous. I suspect some of his competitors found that out to their regret. Before their bodies were dumped in the bay or out at sea, that is."

"So you think he's a killer?"

Nash leaned back in his chair. "I don't know if he's ever killed anyone personally, although it wouldn't surprise me if he had. But I'm confident he's ordered plenty of executions. So are the police, but they haven't been able to prove it."

"How long has he been around?"

Nash cocked his right ankle on his left knee and toyed with a pencil on the desk. "That's an interesting question. He bought the Golden Gate about three years ago. Old Cletus Snyder owned it before that, but Snyder was in bad health and wanted out of the game. Lannigan came out of nowhere and took over the place. Some of us looked into his background afterward and found he'd been involved with some of the gangs along the Barbary Coast, but only as a low-level hoodlum. There was nothing in his history to indicate he had the money to buy a place like the Golden Gate or the skill to run it. Obviously he had both, since he's made it more successful than it already was." Lowering his voice he went on. "Some important people in San Francisco have been known to patronize the private rooms of the Golden Gate. I suspect Lannigan has a pretty good blackmail racket going on."

Conrad nodded. He was intensely interested in everything Nash had said so far. The timing of Dex Lannigan's rise to power was very suspicious. Pamela had arrived in San Francisco about three years ago, Conrad thought. If she had somehow made contact with Lannigan, she could have bank-rolled his purchase of the Golden Gate Saloon. She wouldn't have done that without getting something in return, though, such as his promise to send killers after Pamela's former fiancé if Conrad showed up in the city by the bay looking for his missing children.

It was also possible Pamela had enlisted Lannigan's help in finding a place to hide the twins. Conrad knew he was going to have to have a face-to-face talk with Mr. Dex Lannigan, and soon.

"What else can you tell me about him?"

Nash shrugged. "There's not much else to tell. His wife's a bit of a social climber. He's managed to get them invited to some parties where a cheap sharper like him has no business being. That's another reason I think he indulges in a little blackmail. Sometimes instead of money he demands at least an illusion of respectability for himself and his wife."

That was an interesting angle. "You don't know if Lannigan's going to be attending one of those society parties any time soon, do you?"

"Not my department," Nash replied with a shake of his head. He smiled. "But I know how we can find out. Come on."

They stood, and Nash led him out of the big editorial room and into a corridor lined with smaller offices.

"Where are we going?" Conrad asked.

"To see Francis Carlyle. I'm sure you remember her."

As a matter of fact, he did. Francis Carlyle wrote a popular column for the *Chronicle* about the doings of San Francisco's high society. Not many women were involved in journalism, but Mrs. Carlyle, a widow, held an important and respected position among the city's elite. Conrad had met her on several occasions when he'd accompanied his mother to San Francisco, before Vivian Browning's vicious murder at the hands of an outlaw gang . . . a murder which had later been avenged by Frank Morgan.

Conrad didn't like to think about those days. Some of those same outlaws had kidnapped and tortured him, mutilating one of his ears before Frank was able to rescue him. He kept his hair long enough to hide that deformity.

If he had found himself in such a situation now, he would have figured out a way to kill those varmints himself, rather than relying on Frank to save him. He had changed a great deal since then.

But not enough to keep Francis Carlyle from recognizing him when Nash ushered him into her office after knocking on the door and being told to enter. Mrs. Carlyle, a still-attractive woman in her late forties with a husky voice and dark, curly hair only lightly touched with gray, stood up behind her desk. "Well, for heaven's sake. If it's not Conrad Browning himself." She came around the desk and extended a hand. "Conrad, my dear boy, how are you?"

Conrad took her hand and bent to brush his lips across the back of it in the courtly European manner. He recalled that while Mrs. Carlyle was quick to use her column to cut through what she regarded as pretense and hypocrisy, she enjoyed being played up to. He held her hand in both of his as he straightened. "I'm fine, Mrs. Carlyle. You haven't changed a bit, as beautiful as ever."

She smiled, obviously pleased, then grew solemn. "My deepest condolences on your loss."

Conrad nodded. "Thank you."

"I was very happy when I heard you were alive after all. That blasted Claudius Turnbuckle was tight-lipped about it for a long time."

"At my request," Conrad said.

"Yes, well, I'm accustomed to people talking to me. I maintain a position of absolute trustworthiness."

Mrs. Carlyle could be trusted, all right . . . trusted to gossip—which, of course, was exactly why Conrad was in her office. He understood why Jessup Nash had taken him there.

"Sit down and tell me what brings you to San Francisco," Mrs. Carlyle went on. She waved a hand at Nash. "Thank you for bringing Conrad to see me, Jessup. You can go now."

Nash looked pained, but didn't argue. "Stop by my desk on your way out," he told Conrad, who nodded in agreement.

After Nash left, Conrad settled on the opposite side of the desk. "I'm relying on your absolute discretion here, Mrs. Carlyle."

"My goodness, call me Francis. It's not like you're a callow youth anymore. You're a grown man." The blatant interest in the woman's gaze made it clear how aware of that fact she was.

Conrad smiled. "All right, Francis. I want to ask you about a man named Dex Lannigan."

A look of surprise and distaste appeared on Mrs. Carlyle's face. "Dex Lannigan?" she repeated. "Why are you interested in a cheap hoodlum like that?"

"From what I hear, he's not all that cheap. He owns a very successful business."

"A saloon. And a saloon in the Barbary Coast, at that."

"And he's become a member of San Francisco society."

Mrs. Carlyle shook her head. "More of a pretender than a member. But for reasons I can't fathom, he's been issued invitations to a number of soirees the likes of him and that crass woman he's married to never should have attended. I think she must be the one behind it. She has that desperate hunger for approval you find in women who come from a less than sterling background."

As Conrad recalled, Francis Carlyle's background wasn't all that sterling itself. Her father had been a railroad conductor. But she had married a man who was a stockholder and an important executive with the Southern Pacific, and that had been her entry into society.

Conrad didn't say anything about that. "Do you know if Lannigan is going to be attending any of those parties in the near future?"

"Why do you ask? Don't tell me you want to meet the man!"

"It might be mutually beneficial for the two of us to have a conversation."

It might be easier to do while they were on neutral ground, Conrad thought, rather than him trying to approach Lannigan at the Golden Gate. If Lannigan wanted to keep his wife's position in society secure, he wouldn't cause a scene at a party.

"You intrigue me." Mrs. Carlyle's eyes narrowed suspiciously. "Something's going on here, and I want to know what it is."

"I'm sorry. I can't tell you any more . . . right now." Conrad's words held the promise of future information, as they had with Jessup Nash.

"*Quid pro quo*," Mrs. Carlyle snapped. "I know you studied Latin. You're familiar with the concept."

"Of course. But my hands are tied at the moment. However, I can tell you this much. If my conversation with Lannigan goes as I hope, I can promise you there *will* be a story, and a good one."

"And that story will be mine?"

Conrad shrugged and inclined his head, indicating agreement without actually saying as much.

Suddenly, Mrs. Carlyle laughed. "You're trying

to trick me, young man. It won't work. I'm on to all the tricks young men use to make poor women like myself believe they've promised something when they really haven't." She picked up a copy of the newspaper lying on the desk and tossed it closer to Conrad. "I won't haggle with you, especially since what you want to know is already in print. And you'd already know it *if* you had bothered to read my column this morning," she added caustically.

Conrad picked up the paper, which was that morning's edition folded back to Mrs. Carlyle's column. He had scanned those pages that very morning while eating breakfast, but hadn't noticed what seemed so obvious to him now.

One of the notes in the column was about a party to be held in four days at the Nob Hill mansion of Mr. and Mrs. Madison Kimball. Among a long list of guests expected to attend were Mr. and Mrs. Dexter Lannigan. The name had meant nothing to Conrad when he read it in the paper that morning, but he should have noticed the D.L. initials, he told himself.

It hadn't occurred to him the man possibly responsible for trying to have him killed would be attending a high society ball.

He looked up at her. "Do you think you can arrange for me to be invited to that party?"

"I don't think it'll be any trouble at all," Mrs. Carlyle said. "If Roberta Kimball knew you were in town, you would have already gotten an invitation, even if she had to deliver it personally. I'll mention that I've seen you, and you should hear from her before the day's over. Where are you staying?"

"At the Palace."

"Of course you are. I'll tell Roberta."

"Thank you." Conrad put the newspaper back on Mrs. Carlyle's desk.

"Oh, a simple thank you isn't going to be enough. Not by a long shot."

"Then what can I do to repay you for your help?" he asked with a smile.

"Let me share the story with that little reporter Nash when the time comes. And have dinner with me."

Conrad had a hunch Francis Carlyle's plans for him included more than dinner. But he would deal with that when the time came. As for sharing the story with Jessup Nash, he was confident he could make some sort of arrangement.

"I think that's fair enough." He got to his feet. "Thank you for your help."

Mrs. Carlyle came around the desk and laid a hand on his arm. "Don't forget, we have a deal."

"I won't," Conrad promised.

"If there's anything else I can do for you while you're in town, don't hesitate to let me know."

Conrad leaned closer and kissed her on the cheek. "Of course," he murmured.

She was smiling when he left the office. As he

eased the door closed, his thoughts immediately turned back to Dex Lannigan. Waiting four days to confront the man would be difficult, but that seemed like the best course of action. He would just have to be patient, Conrad told himself.

He had waited this long to find his children. A few more days wouldn't hurt anything.

Chapter 14

"Did you find out what you wanted to know?" Nash asked as Conrad stopped at his desk.

Conrad nodded. "I hope so."

"The old witch didn't make you promise your firstborn in return for her help?"

Conrad managed not to wince. Nash didn't know anything about the reason he was in San Francisco, he reminded himself. The reporter didn't mean anything by the comment about Conrad's firstborn.

"We reached an equitable arrangement. And I'd hardly call Francis Carlyle an old witch."

Nash shrugged. "I'm probably being unfair to her. But watch yourself when you're dealing with her, Conrad. She'll steal a story right out from under you if you're not careful."

"But I'm not a reporter," Conrad pointed out.

"She can be a little predatory when it comes to young men she finds attractive. At least so I've heard," Nash added. "I don't seem to be her type, thank God."

Conrad shook hands with his old friend. "I'll be in touch."

When he reached the lobby, he spotted Patrick Dugan sitting in a chair next to a potted palm. Dugan was reading a newspaper, or at least pretending to. His gaze roved around the lobby constantly as he kept a lookout for trouble, the way a good bodyguard should.

He spotted Conrad and stood up, leaving the paper in the chair. "Get your business taken care of?" he asked as he walked over.

Conrad nodded. "Yes, we're going back to the hotel now."

He wasn't sure how he was going to fill up the time during the next four days as he waited for the ball at the Kimball mansion. Maybe he could actually force himself to rest and relax, as Claudius Turnbuckle had suggested, although if he was being honest with himself, he considered that possibility rather remote. After everything that had happened, he didn't think he was capable of going back to a life of leisure.

A thought occurred to him as he and Dugan walked back toward the Palace. "Were you ever a policeman, Patrick?"

"Because I'm a big, redheaded Irishman, you mean?"

"Because you seem to know what you're doing."

"Oh. Well, in that case, yeah, I was on the force

for ten years. Did right well for myself, too. Worked my way up to bein' a detective. But then Mr. Turnbuckle offered me more money to work for him, and well, I had hungry mouths to feed. I couldn't turn down the job."

"What do you do for Claudius besides bodyguard work?"

"Whatever needs doin'. I've handled quite a few investigations for him, workin' on one case or another."

"When you were with the police, did you ever have anything to do with the tongs?"

Dugan bristled. "What do you mean? Are you askin' if any of those heathen Chinamen ever paid me off to look the other way while they went about their mischief?"

"Good Lord, no," Conrad said without hesitation. "I just wondered if you handled any cases involving them."

"Oh. Sorry," Dugan muttered. "Reckon I jumped to a conclusion there. Yeah, some of the cases I worked on took me to Chinatown, and you can't turn around in Chinatown without bumpin' into somebody from one of the tongs."

"Are they still at war with each other?"

"There's still some trouble now and then, but it's not like it used to be. Diamond Jack took care of that."

"Diamond Jack?"

"Yeah. His real name is Wong Duck, but he calls himself Diamond Jack because he's got a little diamond mounted right here." Dugan tapped a blunt fingertip against one of his two front teeth. "He came up through the Woo Sing tong and finally took it over. That wasn't enough for him, though. He managed to talk the other tongs into callin' a truce. He said they could all make more money if they weren't fightin' each other all the time. That makes sense, of course, but I didn't figure he'd ever talk all those other Chinamen into goin' along with the idea. Somehow he did."

"So they don't have hatchet men anymore?"

Dugan laughed. "Oh, the tongs still have their hatchet men, all right. The leaders don't trust each other all *that* much, and I reckon none of 'em completely trust Diamond Jack." The bodyguard frowned. "Why are you askin' about tongs and hatchet men and such like?"

Conrad couldn't very well explain about his perilous adventure at Spanish Charley's the night before. Dugan would tell Turnbuckle about the incident, and Turnbuckle would increase the number of guards watching over Conrad until it would be impossible to get out from under their scrutiny.

"I saw a big fellow on the street the other day," he said vaguely, deciding he might be able to risk a description of the man who had come to his rescue. "He was Chinese, dressed all in black, with a half-moon shaped scar on his right cheek." Conrad traced a finger along his own cheek to indicate the path of the scar. "When I saw him, I said to myself, now that looks like a hatchet man. So the sight made me curious, that's all."

Dugan grunted. "Sounds like a hatchet man, all right. Most of them are big, ugly scoundrels. You want to stay away from them, Mr. Browning, and you should steer clear of Chinatown, too. There's nothin' down there but joss houses, opium dens, brothels, and eatin' joints where they serve things you're better off not knowin' what they are. No reason for a white man to have anything to do with that place."

Conrad was sure plenty of white customers patronized those places Dugan had mentioned, but he didn't point that out. "I'm not going there. I was curious, that's all."

"You just listen to old Pat Dugan, sir. I won't steer you wrong."

"I'm sure you won't," Conrad agreed.

At the same time, he wondered about the man who had saved his life in Spanish Charley's. Dex Lannigan's Golden Gate Saloon was on the boundary between the Barbary Coast and Chinatown. Was it possible there was a connection between the tongs and his mission to find his children?

Would Pamela have hidden the twins somewhere in the depths of the Chinese quarter? Conrad didn't want to think so, but at the same time, was anything beyond the realm of possibility when it came to Pamela Tarleton?

Despite what he had told Dugan, he might have to pay a visit to Chinatown after all.

* * *

The rest of the day passed quietly, and that evening Conrad was sitting in his suite after supper when someone knocked on the door. Morelli was on duty in the corridor again, and Conrad knew that after being caught sleeping the night before, the bodyguard was unlikely to let anybody into the suite who wasn't harmless. Conrad opened the door and found a man in a sober black suit standing there, bowler hat in hand.

"Mr. Conrad Browning?" the man asked. Morelli stood a few feet away, watching with his arms crossed and a suspicious frown on his face.

Conrad nodded. "That's right."

The man extended a square envelope with a fancy seal pressed into the wax holding it closed. "With the compliments of Mr. and Mrs. Madison Kimball, sir."

Mrs. Carlyle had kept her promise, Conrad thought as he took the envelope and broke the seal. Sure enough, a fancy, gold-printed invitation to the ball at the Kimball mansion was inside on a heavy, gilt-edged card.

Conrad knew the man in the black suit—probably the Kimballs' butler—was waiting for a response to take back to his employers. "Please tell Mr. and Mrs. Kimball I'll be honored to attend."

The man inclined his head. "Thank you, sir. I certainly shall. Good evening."

When the butler was gone, Morelli asked, "Goin' somewhere, sir?"

"Not tonight. But four nights from now I'll be attending a party at the Kimball mansion."

Morelli let out a low whistle. "I've heard of the place. Never been there." He frowned. "Mr. Turnbuckle's gonna want me to come along with you, and I ain't sure they'll let me in."

"If they think you're my driver, they'll let you wait outside with the other drivers."

Morelli shook his head. "I don't know if that'll be good enough to suit Mr. Turnbuckle."

"I'll speak to him," Conrad promised. "I'm sure we can work something out. You'll be close by, even if you aren't in the mansion itself."

"Sometimes close is still too far away."

Conrad knew the truth of that perhaps better than anyone. He had been close enough to see Rebel in Black Rock Canyon . . . just not close enough to save her from being killed.

He forced that thought out of his head and closed the door. Tossing the invitation onto a side table, he went back to the chair where he'd been sitting. A newspaper and a copy of *Harper's Weekly* were on the table next to the chair. He had already been having trouble concentrating as he tried to read, and now that he knew he was going to the Kimballs' ball, he was even more distracted. He began thinking about how he would approach Dex Lannigan. If Lannigan was behind the attempts on his life, the man probably knew what he looked like and would recognize him. It was highly unlikely Lannigan would pull a gun and start blazing away at him in the middle of the party, but Conrad couldn't rule out the possibility entirely.

He needed a smaller gun, something he could carry without anyone noticing it. Tomorrow he would look for such a weapon, he decided.

Something small, but with stopping power at short range. If there was a gunfight at the Kimballs' ball, all of San Francisco society would be scandalized, but Conrad didn't care about that.

If there was a gunfight, he intended to win.

Chapter 15

Accompanied by Patrick Dugan, Conrad visited a gunsmith's shop the next day and picked out a Smith & Wesson .38 caliber double-action revolver with a five-shot cylinder and a barrel that wasn't much more than two inches long.

"The barrel was three and a quarter inches starting out," the gunsmith explained, "but I took some off that to make it easier to carry in the inside pocket of a coat or in a shoulder holster. You can get a smaller gun, Mr. Browning, but the .38 will put a man down where a .32 won't always."

Conrad nodded as he checked the heft and balance of the weapon and liked what he felt. "With such a short barrel, you can't expect much accuracy, can you?" he commented.

"Only at close range," the gunsmith admitted. "But that's where you're most likely to need a gun such as this, isn't it?"

Conrad couldn't argue with that. He bought

the gun and a shoulder holster the gunsmith was only too happy to sell him.

Conrad had told Dugan about attending the ball at the Kimball mansion. He figured Morelli had already reported to Turnbuckle about the butler delivering the invitation the night before, so there was no point in trying to keep it a secret. As they walked back to the hotel with Conrad carrying the case containing the revolver and the holster, Dugan said, "You bought that gun to wear to the party, didn't you, sir?"

"With everything that's happened, I think it's probably a good idea to be armed at all times." Conrad was carrying his Colt at the moment, in the black holster and gunbelt strapped around his hips. While it was a little unusual to see someone who was openly armed walking around San Francisco, it wasn't unheard of. Conrad smiled and added, "Even though I have a fine bodyguard with me."

Dugan grunted. "Considerin' what I know about you, Mr. Browning, I reckon if trouble broke out it'd be more likely for you to save my life than the other way around."

"Let's just try to avoid trouble," Conrad suggested.

"But be ready for it if it comes."

Conrad nodded. "Always."

* * *

Time dragged by. Jessup Nash paid a visit to Conrad's suite at the Palace Hotel the next day, clearly hoping he could get his old friend to reveal more details about that big story he'd been promised, but Conrad remained tight-lipped. He did the same when Francis Carlyle called on him later that same day. She made it fairly obvious she would be willing to spend some time with him in his bedroom whether he told her any more about the story or not, but he eased her out of the suite discreetly and without hurting her feelings.

That evening, with twenty-four hours to go until the Kimballs' ball, Claudius Turnbuckle arrived at the suite with an excited expression on his face. "Good news," he said when Conrad led him into the sitting room. "I think my men have finally found D.L. and the Golden Gate."

Conrad didn't have the heart to tell his old friend he had known the probable identity of D.L. for several days. "Tell me about it."

"There's a saloon on Grant Street in the Barbary Coast called the Golden Gate," Turnbuckle said, "and it's owned by a man named Dex Lannigan!"

"And you think he's the one who sent those killers after us?"

"I'm certain of it. The initials match, and my investigators report that the men who work for Lannigan carry a token like the one you found in the street to identify themselves. I'm sorry it's taken so long, Conrad, but I'm convinced this is the answer we've been looking for!"

Conrad nodded. "I think you're right. Excellent work, Claudius, as always."

Turnbuckle went on. "Lannigan has a reputation as a power in the criminal underworld along the bay, but he came out of nowhere about three years ago. About the same time he could have struck a deal with Pamela, in other words."

"It all makes sense," Conrad agreed.

They continued to discuss the situation for several minutes, and if Turnbuckle noticed Conrad wasn't quite as excited as he might have been if all the information were new to him, he didn't mention it. After telling Conrad more about Lannigan's background, the lawyer said, "Here's the really interesting part. Acting probably at his wife's behest, Lannigan has bullied his way into society, and as a matter of fact, they're both supposed to be in attendance at a party given by Madison Kimball and his wife tomorrow night."

Conrad raised his eyebrows. "The ball at the Kimball mansion? I'm going to that affair, Claudius!"

"I thought you might be. I had one of my men dig up a picture of Lannigan, so you'll recognize him if you see him there." Turnbuckle held out a folded newspaper.

Conrad didn't have to feign eagerness as he took the paper. He didn't know what Dex Lannigan looked like, so as he studied the photograph printed on the front page of the newspaper, his interest was genuine.

The picture showed a man standing beside a carriage parked in front of a large building that appeared to run the length of an entire city block. The man was tall and seemed to be well built, wearing an expensive suit and a derby. The hair under the hat was fair. His face was rugged and a little angular, and although the photographer hadn't been close enough for Conrad to get a good look at Lannigan's eyes, there was something hawkish about the saloon owner. Maybe it was just his imagination, Conrad told himself, but Lannigan looked dangerous.

The building behind him had large, fancy windows, and a large sign on it read THE GOLDEN GATE—FINE WINE AND SPIRITS—GAMES OF CHANCE—ENTERTAINMENT—EVERYONE WELCOME!

"This was taken not long after the place opened," Turnbuckle explained. "One of my men dug it out of the morgue at the *Chronicle.*"

Conrad nodded. He should have thought of that idea himself. He was sure Jessup Nash would have helped him. But at least he had an idea what Lannigan looked like, although he suspected the man's appearance would be somewhat different in evening wear, at a fancy Nob Hill party.

Conrad would know Lannigan when he saw him, though. He was certain of that.

"You're going to have to be careful if you confront him there," Turnbuckle cautioned. "Lannigan has a reputation as a bad man to cross."

Conrad thought about the short-barreled S&W .38 he was already wearing in the shoulder rig so he could get used to it. "I intend to be."

"What we need now is something we can hold over Lannigan's head in order to make him talk," Turnbuckle mused. "That won't be easy. Criminals like that can be very closemouthed."

"Maybe what I should do is pretend *not* to know him. That way I can introduce myself and act like I'm not suspicious of him at all. He might let something slip."

Turnbuckle rubbed his chin and frowned in thought. "Perhaps. I think it's more likely we're going to have to have him followed and maybe send undercover agents into that saloon of his to find out anything that's really useful."

"Whatever you say," Conrad replied with a nod.

"Really?" Turnbuckle looked surprised. "That's not like you, Conrad. No offense, but you always want to be right in the middle of things."

"That hasn't worked too well so far," Conrad said, although in reality it had worked better than Turnbuckle had any idea about. "Maybe it's time to give your way a try."

Turnbuckle nodded emphatically. "I won't let you down, you have my word on that. But do try to find out whatever you can by talking to Lannigan at the Kimballs' ball. It can't hurt."

"I will."

Turnbuckle bustled out excitedly, leaving Conrad to smile, shake his head, and pour brandy into a snifter. He was sitting in one of the armchairs, sipping the drink, when a commotion suddenly broke out in the hallway. Frowning, Conrad set the brandy aside and got to his feet.

A woman screamed in the corridor.

Conrad jerked the door open to see Morelli struggling with a small, shapely female. Scratches on his face oozed blood where she had scratched him. As Conrad stood looking on in surprise, Morelli succeeded in getting his arms around the girl in a bear hug and lifted her off her feet from behind.

"I told you, girl, no little trollop like you is gonna be botherin' Mr. Browning!" Morelli panted.

"Let me go!" she cried. "I must talk to him—"

"Morelli!" Conrad said sharply. "What's going on here?" He hadn't gotten a good look at the woman. She and Morelli were turned partially away from him, and her dark hair hung in front of her face. As Morelli turned toward the door, his captive gave a defiant toss of her head, throwing her hair back. A shock went through Conrad as he recognized her as Carmen, the young prostitute from Spanish Charley's.

"Please, señor," she begged. "You must help me! No one else can, and if you don't . . . they will kill me!"

Chapter 16

"Let her go, Morelli," Conrad ordered.

The bodyguard's bushy eyebrows rose. "But, sir, a girl like this ain't for the likes of you! I'm not sure how she even got into the hotel. Usually the staff don't let such tramps get anywhere near the guests."

"I know her," Conrad said, not caring whether he shocked Morelli. "Now let her go." The flat, hard tone of his voice left no room for argument.

Morelli lowered Carmen until her feet were on the floor, then released her, stepping back with a frown of deep disapproval on his face.

"What you do in your personal life is none o' my concern, sir—" he began.

"That's right, it's not," Conrad cut in. He took hold of Carmen's arm. She looked like a terrified doe about to bolt. In a steady, calming voice, he went on. "Come with me. You'll be safe here. I give you my word on that."

Her dark eyes were big with fear. "Hans and

Ulrich may have followed me. I tried to get away from them, but I don't know if I did."

"I'm not afraid of Hans and Ulrich, and I'll wager that Morelli here isn't, either."

"No, sir," Morelli chimed in without hesitation. "I don't know who those lads are, but I ain't afraid of anybody that draws breath."

Conrad managed to steer Carmen toward the door of the suite without making it seem like he was forcing her. As they went inside, Morelli started to follow, but a hard look from Conrad made him stop. Conrad closed the door behind them, leaving the bodyguard in the hallway.

"All right, Carmen," he said gently. "Can I get you anything?"

"Maybe a drink, señor?"

Conrad hesitated, unsure whether he should be giving liquor to someone as young as she was, but considering where she worked and what she did for a living, he supposed it was a little late to be worrying about things like that. He poured a little brandy into a glass and handed it to her. She clutched it with both hands, which were trembling slightly, and drank down the brandy.

That seemed to steady her nerves. She took a deep breath. "*Gracias*, Señor Browning."

"How do you know my name? How did you know you could find me here?"

"After the big fight at Spanish Charley's . . . after Ling Yuan came in to help you get away . . . I followed you. It was Dutchy's idea."

Conrad hadn't realized anyone had followed him away from the dive that night, but he supposed a slender young girl like Carmen could have slipped through the shadows behind him without him noticing.

"Why did Dutchy want you to follow me?"

"I think he wanted to take revenge on you for starting trouble. He would have sent Hans and Ulrich to kill you later. But when I told him I followed you all the way here to the Palace . . . he seemed to change his mind about that."

Conrad wasn't surprised. Dutchy must have realized there was more to his troublesome visitor than met the eye.

"I thought you must work here, maybe as a bellboy. I-I have a cousin who works in the hotel as a maid. Dutchy told me to talk to her, to tell her what you look like, and find out if she knew you. She told me there was no one working here who looks like you, Señor Browning. Then she told me about one of the guests . . . about *you*."

"And you told Dutchy," Conrad guessed.

"I had to! He would have killed me if I tried to lie to him."

Conrad didn't know if that was true or not, but Carmen believed it was.

"When you told him, he was even more interested than he was before, right?"

Carmen's head bobbed up and down. "*Sí*."

Dutchy probably sensed a possibility for blackmail. A man wealthy enough to stay in one of the Palace

Hotel's finest suites who prowled around squalid saloons and taverns like Spanish Charley's . . . usually had secrets he would be willing to pay to keep quiet.

"I know you didn't have any choice in what you did," Conrad told Carmen as she looked down at the richly carpeted floor in shame. "I'm not upset with you."

"Truly, señor?" she murmured.

"Truly."

She moved closer and reached up to throw her arms around his neck before he could stop her. "Oh, *gracias, señor, gracias*! I thought you would be angry with me for betraying your secret. I-I will do anything to earn your forgiveness."

"There's nothing to forgive"—Conrad untangled her arms from his neck— "and even if there was, all you'd have to do to earn it is ask. But there's not, so you don't have to worry." He held her hands to keep her from grabbing him again. "Now what's all this about Hans and Ulrich threatening to kill you?"

"Dutchy said he knew someone who would pay him a great deal of money if he told them about you. But he and I were the only ones who knew, and I think he was worried I might try to reach this person, whoever it is, and sell the information first. So he decided to get rid of me, even though I work for him and killing me would cost him money." She pouted. "I am only a cheap Mex whore. Dutchy can make more by selling the truth about you than he can from me."

Conrad had a hunch he knew who Dutchy intended to sell that information to: Dex Lannigan. Lannigan must have put out the word that he was interested in anything he could learn about Conrad Browning, and Dutchy would know what a powerful, important man Lannigan was in San Francisco's underworld and would be eager to curry favor with him.

"How do you know Hans and Ulrich intended to kill you?"

Carmen made a face like she wanted to spit. "I overheard them talking in their mongrel tongue. They think I do not know what they say, but I understand a little. Enough to know Dutchy told them to kill me and dump my body in the bay. I slipped out and ran away, but I . . . I didn't know where to go. Then I thought of you."

"You already sold me out to Dutchy, remember? What makes you think I'd be willing to help you?"

"Because I remembered how kind you were to me at Spanish Charley's. You could have done what you paid for and then asked me your questions, but you did not." A shrewd look appeared on her face. "And I remembered as well how you asked about the Golden Gate. Dex Lannigan owns that place, and I think Dutchy plans on telling him about you. But maybe I *could* get to Señor Lannigan first. . . ."

"So you're not above a little blackmail of your own, eh?" Conrad asked with a faint smile.

"My life has been a hard one, señor."

Conrad didn't doubt that for a second.

"I have learned to do what I must to survive," Carmen went on.

"How much do you want?" Conrad asked.

Carmen shook her head. "Nothing. No money."

Conrad frowned. "Then what *do* you want?"

"I told you I have a cousin who works here in the hotel. Her father, my uncle, is a fisherman. If I could get to his boat and hide there, he could take me away from San Francisco, take me to some place safe. This is what I want."

"Why do you need my help to do that?"

"Because Hans and Ulrich and maybe Dutchy himself will be out searching for me. I am sure if any of them see me, they will kill me on sight. But I saw the way you fought, señor. I know you could protect me from them and make sure I got away safely. *This* is what I want from you."

Conrad studied her closely and didn't see any sign that she was lying. Her story held together and made sense.

"We'd need to go tonight."

"*Sí, señor,* as quickly as possible."

As usual, Conrad didn't take long to make up his mind. He didn't owe the girl anything, and helping her escape from the men who wanted to kill her wouldn't gain him anything . . .

Except the knowledge that he had not only saved her life but also helped free her from a hellish existence. He couldn't turn his back on her, even though that might be the smartest thing to do. She had already told Dutchy who he was; she couldn't do anything else to hurt him.

"All right. Let me get my hat." Conrad already had the shoulder rig for the Smith & Wesson in place, so he left it on and didn't strap on his regular gunbelt.

When the two of them stepped into the corridor, Morelli got up hurriedly from the chair. "I have to go out for a while, Morelli," Conrad said.

"Then I'm goin' with you, sir. Beggin' your pardon, of course, but I've got my orders."

"It may turn out to be dangerous," Conrad warned.

Morelli shook his head. "Doesn't matter. Mr. Turnbuckle said to keep my eye on you, so I'm keepin' my eye on you."

"Very well. The señorita will tell us where we're going."

"To the waterfront," Carmen said. "Where the fishing boats are docked."

"Lead the way," Conrad told her.

As they went downstairs, Conrad described for Morelli the three men they were watching out for particularly. The bodyguard was intensely curious, but didn't ask any questions. He nodded and said, "Yes, sir. If I see any of the scoundrels, I'll be ready for 'em."

They left the hotel through the rear entrance Conrad had used a few nights earlier. As far as he could tell, no one paid any attention to them. But he hadn't noticed Carmen trailing him the other night, so he warned himself not to be too confident.

After they had gone a block or so, he hailed a horse-drawn cab and helped Carmen into it. Morelli jerked a thumb at the driver's seat. "I'll ride up top."

As the cab rolled up and down San Francisco's steep streets toward the waterfront, Carmen said, "I cannot tell you how grateful I am to you for your help, Señor Browning." She sat forward. "But maybe I could *show* you."

"That's not necessary," Conrad told her as he lifted a hand to stop her from moving any closer to him. "Where are you going to go, Carmen?"

"I have some cousins who live in Morellirey. They will take me in."

Conrad held out some folded bills and pressed them into her hand. "Take this money. It'll help you make a fresh start."

"Oh, *gracias, señor, gracias.* I . . . I cannot believe anyone can be as good as you are."

"Far from it. I just want you to have a chance."

The cab dropped them off in an area where the night air was thick with the smells of salt water and rotting fish. Little slapping noises came from the docks where the waves washed against the pilings. Carmen pointed. "My uncle's boat is down here." She started along the wharf, flanked by Conrad and Morelli. When they came to one of the docks that extended into the water with boats tied up on both sides of it, Carmen said eagerly, "Along here."

The area was dimly lit by lanterns hanging here and there casting feeble yellow glows into the gathering fog. Something stirred inside Conrad, a sense that not everything was as it should be. No one was around. The docks shouldn't have been completely deserted, even at that time of night.

When he heard footsteps on the damp planks behind them, he knew his hunch was right. He stopped and started to turn, then froze as he felt the sharp point of a knife in Carmen's hand penetrate his coat and shirt, and dig into his flesh.

Chapter 17

"I am sorry, Señor Browning," Carmen said. "I really am. If I had not done what they wanted, they would have killed me."

Morelli said in alarm, "What's this?"

"A trap," Conrad said, "and the señorita was the bait."

It was true. Half a dozen big men had followed them onto the dock, blocking their escape. Conrad didn't see Dutchy, but even in the bad light he recognized two of the men as Hans and Ulrich. The others were strangers to him but equally large and dangerous-looking. Conrad had no doubt they worked for Dex Lannigan.

Morelli started to reach under his coat.

Carmen cried, "Don't! I will kill Mr. Browning."

"Sir?" the bodyguard said in a voice taut with tension and strain. "What do you want me to do?"

Conrad didn't answer for a second. The wheels of his brain were spinning rapidly. It wouldn't take much strength for Carmen to slide that blade between his ribs and pierce his heart.

Not much physical strength, that is, Conrad thought, but it would take the sort of resolve he wasn't sure the girl possessed. The odds were against him and Morelli, but Conrad had faced long odds before. Besides, he figured the chances of them surviving if they surrendered were non-existent.

To think was to act, where Conrad was concerned. He answered Morelli with action, twisting his body away from the knife in Carmen's hand, planting a hand against her shoulder, and giving her a hard shove. With a startled cry, she reeled away from him and plunged off the edge of the dock into the water.

He hoped she could swim, but if she couldn't, there were a lot of boats tied up along the dock. She could grab a mooring line to keep herself from sinking.

While the splash from Carmen falling into the water hung in the air, the six bruisers charged toward Conrad and Morelli. The bodyguard pulled a thick black leather sap from under his coat and met their attack, wading into his enemies as he struck out right and left with the shot-filled weapon.

Morelli couldn't stop all of them, though. Conrad reached for his gun, but one of the men tackled him before he could pull the .38. The impact of the collision drove him backward, his boots slipping on the damp planks. He went down, sprawling on the dock.

Seeing a big, ham-like fist coming at his face, he jerked his head aside. The punch landed on the dock, causing the attacker to howl in pain. Conrad brought his elbow up under the man's chin and forced his head back. A heave threw the man off to the side, and he barely caught himself before he rolled off the dock.

Conrad scrambled to his feet just in time to meet the charge of another man, who landed a hard, straight left catching Conrad in the chest with such force it seemed to paralyze him for a few seconds. A second looping punch landed on Conrad's jaw and knocked him down again. He lay there stunned.

A few yards away, Morelli bellowed curses at the top of his lungs as he battled against three men. His sap laid out one, but another grabbed his arm and held it while the third man sunk a brutal punch in the bodyguard's belly.

Conrad rolled aside from a kick aimed at his ribs. Reaching up, he grabbed the attacker's foot and twisted. A heave sent the man crashing to the dock.

The first man Conrad had knocked to the dock made it back to his feet, and reached down to haul Conrad upright. A punch from behind slammed into the small of his back and sent pain shooting through him.

Conrad was a good bare-knuckles brawler, but there were just too many of them. They were all around him, and no matter which way he turned trying to escape the punishment, another man was there to smash a fist into his face or body.

The same was true for Morelli. The bodyguard put up a valiant struggle, but he was outnumbered by men who were his equal when it came to fighting. He didn't have any more chance than Conrad did. Both were forced to their knees, driven down by blow after blow, and then the kicking and stomping started in earnest.

Deep inside, Conrad raged in disbelief. He had traveled so far, endured so much, come so close to finding his missing children. No hired killers were going to prevent him from completing his quest!

Newfound strength surged through him. As another kick thudded into his side, he grabbed hold of the man's leg and began pulling himself up.

"Get him off me!" the attacker yelled, swinging a fist at Conrad's head. Conrad hunched his shoulders and butted the man in the stomach. The man lost his balance and went over backward with a startled shout.

Conrad made it to his feet.

Then one of the other men stepped up behind him, holding the sap he had taken away from Morelli, who lay bleeding and motionless on the dock a few feet away. He hit Conrad in the back of the head.

It was like a gigantic explosion going off inside his skull. He saw a brilliant flash and felt like his head was coming apart. The odd thing was that the devastating explosion was silent. Completely noiseless. Instead of blackness, a great white void expanded and engulfed him. He didn't hear anything, didn't feel anything, and didn't know anything as he fell endlessly through nothingness.

He crashed face-first onto the dock, out cold.

The man who got off the train the next morning was tired from sitting up the whole way during his journey. He could have booked a sleeping compartment if he'd been willing to wait for a later train; certainly he could afford the cost of such a luxury. What he hadn't been able to afford was the time.

So he had ridden sitting up in a Union Pacific passenger car from Montana to Salt Lake City, dozing when he could, then caught the next Southern Pacific westbound for San Francisco. He would have preferred to take a couple weeks and make the trip on horseback, but there was no time for that, either.

He looked out of place as he disembarked among men in expensive suits and ladies in fancy dresses. He was medium height, but the high-crowned, cream-colored Stetson he wore made him appear taller than he really was. Broad, powerfully muscled shoulders stretched the faded fabric of a blue work shirt. He wore jeans and plain, functional boots.

The Colt revolver holstered on his right hip was

plain and functional, too, as was the Bowie knife sheathed on his left hip.

He carried a simple carpetbag containing a few spare clothes and several boxes of ammunition. He hadn't brought his saddle because he hadn't brought a horse with him, and didn't expect to need one. He felt that lack keenly. Despite everything that had happened in the past forty years, a part of him was still the young cowboy he had been. Part of him felt that a man without a horse just wasn't a man.

He shrugged off the feeling and walked through the lobby of the train station. When he stepped onto the street, San Francisco spread out before him. A sigh escaped from him before he could stop it. He didn't like big cities. Never had, never would.

But it was where he was needed.

A buggy pulled up in the street outside the depot. Claudius Turnbuckle climbed out and strode hurriedly toward the newcomer. "Frank! I meant to be here when your train arrived, but I was delayed at my office." He added grimly, "By the police."

"What's wrong?" Frank Morgan asked as he shook hands with Turnbuckle.

"It's Conrad," Turnbuckle said. "I don't know how to tell you this, but . . . he's missing."

Frank's rugged face was set in tense lines as he repeated, "Missing?"

"I'm afraid so. If you'll come back to the office with me, I'll tell you everything we know."

Frank Morgan, The Drifter, the man some called the last true gunfighter, hadn't been aware he had a son until a few years earlier. Now that he had gotten to know Conrad Browning, now that they had fought alongside each other against common enemies on several occasions, Frank would move heaven and earth to help the young man if Conrad needed his help.

The lawyer motioned Frank toward the buggy. Before they reached it, a voice called from behind them, "Mr. Turnbuckle! Mr. Turnbuckle, sir!"

They stopped and looked back to see a tall, slender man in a brown suit and hat coming toward them, also from the direction of the train station. He was moving deliberately, even gingerly, as if he were injured and didn't want to make it worse. He was determined, though. That much was evident from the set of his narrow face.

"Arturo!" Turnbuckle exclaimed. "The two of you were on the same train?"

"The two of who?" the man called Arturo asked as he came up to them.

"You and Frank here."

Arturo looked at Frank. "You're Mr. Morgan, sir?"

"That's right." Frank nodded. "I reckon you must be that Italian fella I've heard about."

"Arturo Vincenzo. I had no idea we were on the same train, or I would have sought you out and

introduced myself after I boarded in Carson City."
They shook hands. "It's an honor to meet you, sir.
Mr. Browning has spoken a great deal about you,
always in the most glowing terms."

Frank chuckled. "That wasn't always the way he
talked about me, and you can bet a hat on that."

"Bet my headgear?" Arturo said with a puzzled
frown. "Why would I want to—"

"Never mind that," Turnbuckle broke in. "Something's happened that you don't know about,
Arturo. Conrad has disappeared."

"Good Lord! Tell me about it."

"Frank and I were on our way to my office. I was
going to fill him in there. You look pretty tired,
though, and I know you're still recuperating from
that bullet wound, so perhaps we should drop you
at the hotel—"

"Nonsense," Arturo said. "No offense, sir, but
I'm coming with you and Mr. Morgan. Dr. Taggart
said I was fit to travel, and I can't possibly rest
until I know what's happened to Mr. Browning."

"That's just it," Turnbuckle muttered. "We
don't know. But come along, and I'll fill you in on
all the details."

"I hope so," Frank said, "because I haven't followed much of this so far. I don't even know what
Conrad was doing here in San Francisco."

"It's not a pretty story," Turnbuckle said with
a sigh.

"It never is," Frank said.

Chapter 18

One of Turnbuckle's assistants had brought in cups of coffee for the three men. As they sat in the lawyer's elegantly appointed private office, Turnbuckle said, "I suppose the best thing to do is just start at the beginning. You're a grandfather, Frank."

"What are you talking about, Claudius?" Frank was stunned, the cup in his hand forgotten.

"Do you remember Pamela Tarleton?"

Frank grunted. "Be hard to forget her, after what she did to Rebel."

"Yes, well, that wasn't the extent of Miss Tarleton's evil. I don't wish to be indelicate about this, but it seems that when Conrad decided to call off his engagement to her, she was, ah, already in the family way."

Frank sighed. "Conrad's grown into a fine young man, but before that he could be a damned fool sometimes."

Turnbuckle didn't comment on that. "Following

the affair in New Mexico in which Miss Tarleton's father was arrested and then murdered, she returned to Boston and gave birth to twins. A boy and a girl."

"Named Frank and Vivian," Arturo put in.

That news rocked Frank. Learning he had a pair of grandchildren had been a shock without hearing they were named after him and Conrad's mother, the great love of his life. To cover how shaken he was, he took a sip of the hot, strong coffee. Then he nodded and said, "Go on."

For the next half hour, Turnbuckle and Arturo explained how Conrad had found out about Pamela's cruel plot against him and how he had set out on a cross-country odyssey to find the missing twins.

"The boy should have told me." Frank frowned. "I would have come and given him a hand."

"I believe he was determined to do this himself," Turnbuckle said.

"He had Arturo here helping him." Frank waved his hand toward the Italian.

"It's not quite the same thing," Arturo said. "Mr. Browning and I are not related, therefore no emotional complications and implications existed that would have had he called on his father for assistance."

"That never stopped him before," Frank muttered, thinking of all the times he and his gun had come to Conrad's aid.

"He was never searching for his own children before."

Frank shrugged and turned back to the lawyer. "So the trail led here?"

"That's right. Conrad felt—and I agreed with him—that he was closing in on the children at last. We located some clues pointing toward a man named Dex Lannigan who owns a saloon in the Barbary Coast. We figure Pamela Tarleton made a deal with Lannigan. He may even know where she hid the children."

Frank leaned forward in his chair and set his cup on Turnbuckle's desk. "Then I reckon it's time we went and had a talk with this fella Lannigan."

Turnbuckle held up a hand. "It's not that simple."

It's always that simple, Frank wanted to say, but he reined in the impulse.

"Lannigan is going to be at a society party tonight that Conrad was also going to attend," Turnbuckle went on. "He hoped to find out more information that way. But this morning, when one of the bodyguards I've hired to look out for Conrad went to the Palace Hotel, where he's staying, Conrad wasn't there . . . and neither was the guard who was on duty last night."

"They might've gone somewhere and just haven't come back yet," Frank suggested.

A weary sigh came from Turnbuckle. "I might have thought the same thing . . . if not for the fact that the police showed up here with the news that Thomas Morelli's body was pulled out of San Francisco Bay this morning. Morelli was the man who was with Conrad. He had been badly beaten, and his throat was cut. His wife knew he was working for me and told the police about it when they talked to her. The poor woman sent them here."

That sounded pretty bad, all right. Frank knew there was a good chance Conrad and this fella Morelli had been together. Since Morelli was dead, then . . .

Frank gave a little shake of his head. He wasn't going to let himself think the thought that had just crossed his mind. Conrad wasn't dead. He knew it in his heart. "What did you tell the police?"

"That Morelli had been guarding Conrad. There was an attempt on his life as soon as he got to town."

"Lannigan had men watching for him, probably at the train station," Frank said.

Turnbuckle nodded. "That's what we think now. We didn't know about Lannigan at the time."

"You didn't tell the police you think Lannigan's to blame for what happened to Morelli?"

"There's no proof of that," Turnbuckle said. "And I know Conrad didn't want the police involved in the matter of the children. He thought he stood a better chance of recovering them safely himself. I knew you'd be arriving today, and I wanted to consult with you first."

"Why did you track me down and send me that telegram, if you knew Conrad didn't want me mixed up in it?"

Turnbuckle's fist thumped down on the desk. "Because you and I are friends, Frank, and those are your grandchildren we're talking about! It seems to me you have a right to be involved. Besides, Arturo wired me from Carson City and told me Conrad seemed to be getting more reckless and obsessed about the whole thing."

Arturo spoke up. "I didn't want to go against Mr. Browning's wishes, but the more I thought about it, the more I came to believe you could help him, Mr. Morgan. And he needed that help." Arturo smiled. "Did you know when we first met, Mr. Browning was calling himself Kid Morgan? For the longest time I thought he was just some Western gunslinger. I had no idea he was actually a financier and businessman, and a quite successful one, at that."

"Back then he had put all that behind him," Frank said. "I reckon he thought he was Kid Morgan, too. That's who he wanted to be."

"But we can't be someone we're not," Turnbuckle said heavily. "Our pasts won't allow that."

Frank shrugged. They were drifting off the trail here. "If Conrad's still alive, Lannigan's probably got him stashed somewhere. You said Lannigan owns a saloon in the Barbary Coast?"

"That's right. It's called the Golden Gate. What are you going to do, Frank?"

The Drifter pushed himself to his feet. "I reckon it's time to pay a visit to Dex Lannigan and his Golden Gate Saloon."

The only good thing about the pain in his head, Conrad thought, was that the dead no longer felt such agonies. That meant he was still alive . . .

Unless he had died and gone to hell for all the evil things he had done in his life.

Even though he was no expert on theology, it seemed unlikely to him that hell would smell like rotten fish. That unpleasant odor filled his nostrils, with another smell lurking under it that might be salt water.

He kept his eyes closed and didn't move, making an effort to keep his rate of breathing from changing. If anyone was watching him, which certainly seemed possible, he didn't want them to realize that he was awake.

As he lay there, he concentrated on letting details about his surroundings seep into his mind, helping him to not think about how bad his head hurt. He was lying on his stomach, with his head turned to the right and his left cheek pressed into what felt like a hard wooden surface. That surface *moved* under him, not much, just a faintly perceptible rocking motion.

When Conrad put those things together—the tang of salt water, the reek of fish, the steady movement of the boards on which he lay—he came to the inescapable conclusion that he was on a boat, lying either on deck or down in a hold. Probably in a hold, because he didn't feel any air moving.

Even through closed eyes all he could sense was darkness. That meant it was either still night, or the darkness was another indication he was belowdecks.

He decided to risk cracking one eye open. He raised his right eyelid a fraction of an inch, not really enough for him to see anything but enough to let in any nearby light.

Nothing. The blackness continued to surround him.

If he couldn't see anything, that meant nobody could see him. He opened both eyes. After a moment, he lifted his head. Fresh waves of pain rolled through his skull, so intense he had to squeeze his eyes closed again until the throbbing subsided. Eventually the pain lessened.

Conrad shifted to determine if he was tied up. His arms and legs were free, which was a bit surprising.

On the other hand, if he was locked up in the hold of a ship, where could he go?

Shanghai . . .

The word sprang into his mind and a horrified shudder went through him. He was in San Francisco, after all. The town was notorious for all the men who had been drugged, kidnapped, and taken aboard ships bound for the Orient. By the time those unfortunates regained consciousness, the vessels were well out to sea, and they had no choice but work. If they refused, it was a simple matter for their captors to knock them in the head and toss them overboard for the sharks. Because of the destination that lay across the Pacific for many of these ships, it became common to say that a man had been shanghaied when he was drugged and forced to join the crew.

Would Lannigan do such a thing to him? Conrad didn't doubt for a second the man was capable of it. He might think dooming Conrad to such a hellish existence was more punishment than simply killing him. It was even possible Pamela might have come up with the idea herself when she struck her deal with Lannigan three years earlier.

But no matter whose idea it was, Conrad knew he had to get out. He could tell by the slight motion of the ship that it was still riding at anchor, probably in San Francisco Bay. If it had already sailed, it would be moving around much more as it rode the waves. If he could get out of the hold, he could still escape before the ship was out at sea.

He pushed himself into a sitting position and waited for the pain in his head to subside. Looking around, he searched for even a tiny crack of light that would indicate the location of a hatch. He didn't see anything. Maybe there wasn't a hatch that led on deck. There had to be some way into the chamber, though. A door in a bulkhead, maybe.

Before making a move, he made sure he was alone. He hadn't heard anyone else moving around, nor had he heard any breathing, but it was possible the men who had attacked them on the dock had thrown Morelli in with him. In an urgent whisper, he said, "Morelli! Morelli, are you there?"

Silence was his only answer.

But it wasn't complete silence. Now that the pounding in his head wasn't as bad, he could hear a faint sloshing sound—water moving around in the bilge—which meant he was low down in the ship. He heard something that might have been far-off footsteps, and a low, barely heard moan, but not a human one. That was a foghorn, Conrad realized.

He reached out in the darkness and felt around him, searching for a bulkhead or possibly the ship's curving hull. When he didn't feel anything he moved onto hands and knees and crawled forward, using his left hand for balance and keeping his right extended in front of him.

He hadn't gone very far when his fingertips brushed against something. At first he thought it was a wall, but in feeling around, he discovered it was a large crate.

It gave him something to lean on as he struggled to his feet. His head spun crazily as he stood up, and for a few seconds he thought he was going to fall. Forcing himself to stand still, he took some deep breaths, and the world steadied around him.

He swallowed the feeling of sickness welling up in his throat. Steadfastly ignoring it, he sat on the low crate for a few minutes, bracing himself with his hands on his knees.

With the resilience of youth and the rugged life he had led the past couple years, some of his strength came back to him. While sitting there, he took stock of what his captors had left him.

It wasn't much. He had his boots, his trousers, and his shirt. His coat and hat were gone, and so were the shoulder holster and the .38 Smith & Wesson he had carried. His pockets were empty. No coins, no matches, nothing.

If he was still locked up when the ship sailed, he would have no way to prove he was Conrad Browning . . . not that the captain and crew would have cared, anyway. They had to know what was going on. Probably Lannigan had paid them off.

His only chance was to get off the ship before it sailed.

The footsteps he suddenly heard coming closer in the darkness might be the key to doing just that.

Chapter 19

Frank insisted on paying a visit to the Golden Gate Saloon alone. "If this fella Lannigan knows who Conrad is and has spies watching him, he's bound to know who you are, too, Claudius."

"What about me?" Arturo asked.

"You've got a bullet hole in you that's still healing," Frank pointed out. "You probably shouldn't have traveled all the way here from Carson City to start with."

"The doctor assured me it would be all right as long as I took it easy."

"That means you don't need to be getting mixed up in a ruckus," Frank said.

"Do you intend to start a ruckus in Lannigan's saloon?" Arturo asked.

Frank chuckled. "I'm not exactly planning on it, but you never know what's going to happen. Sometimes I think trouble's in the habit of following me around."

"Yes, I know the feeling quite well. The same thing is true of your son."

"I don't doubt it. He comes by it honestly." Frank paused. "Anyway, no offense, Mr. Vincenzo, but you don't exactly look like the sort of hombre who'd patronize a Barbary Coast saloon."

"I suppose that's true," Arturo admitted. "But please, call me Arturo."

"That's Italian for Arthur, isn't it?"

"That's right."

"I used to know an old mountain man whose real name was Arthur, even though nobody ever called him that. He barely remembered it himself. Haven't seen him in years. He must be dead by now. He'd be almost a hundred if he's not." Frank pushed those thoughts aside and got back to the matter at hand. "The chances of Lannigan or anybody who works for him knowing who I am are pretty slim. Anyway, even if somebody recognized me as Frank Morgan, not all that many people know Conrad and I are related."

"Pamela Tarleton did," Turnbuckle reminded him. "There's no way of knowing what she might have told Lannigan."

"That's true," Frank admitted, "but I'm willing to run the risk. If I can get Lannigan alone, he'll tell us what we need to know."

"My God, Frank," Turnbuckle said. "You can't be thinking about torturing the man."

In a hard, flinty voice, Frank said, "This is my son we're talking about here . . . and my grandchildren. And a man who'd make a deal with a she-devil like Pamela Tarleton who brought nothing but suffering to everybody around her. I'll do whatever I have to, Claudius. I don't reckon it'll come to torture, though."

"If it does, I don't want to know about it."

"Deal."

Turnbuckle told him how to find the Golden Gate Saloon and described Lannigan to him. Frank said his good-byes to the lawyer and Arturo, who was going to the Palace Hotel to get some rest after the train trip from Carson City.

Frank left the building where the offices of Turnbuckle & Stafford were located. The Barbary Coast was too far to walk in cowboy boots, he decided, so he swung up on one of the electric-powered cable cars that carried him in the right direction.

It wasn't the first time he had ridden one of the cars, which ran on rails and got their power from overhead cables, but it always seemed strange to him to ride in something that wasn't pulled by a locomotive or a team of horses or mules.

The day was far enough advanced that the fog had burned off, and as a result the view was spectacular as Frank rode the cable car over the steep, high streets. He could see the blue waters of the bay stretching out to the hills on the far side. Closer at hand were the heights of Nob Hill and Telegraph Hill, and the docks along the section of waterfront known as the Embarcadero, where ships from a score of different countries were tied up. Frank would never like big cities—he was too old and set in his ways for that—but he had to admit San Francisco was a pretty place.

The Garden of Eden was supposed to have been a pretty place, too, he reminded himself . . . but a serpent had lurked in it. The same was true there, only instead of one devil, San Francisco had an abundance of them.

"Mister?"

The high-pitched voice broke into Frank's thoughts. He looked around and saw a little boy about eight years old staring at him. Frank smiled at him, emboldening the boy to ask, "Mister, are you a cowboy?"

A nice-looking woman who was probably the boy's mother sat beside him on the cable car bench near the pole Frank hung on to. She put a hand on the boy's shoulder. "Jamie, don't bother that man."

"It's no bother, ma'am," Frank assured her. To the boy, he said, "No, son, I'm not really a cowboy, although I used to be when I was younger. Some things you never forget, though, so I reckon I could still make a hand if I needed to."

"Then you must be a gunfighter," Jamie said. "You're wearing a gun."

"Plenty of folks who aren't gunfighters wear guns," Frank told him.

"Yeah, but you look like somebody who'd be in a dime novel."

As a matter of fact, a number of those lurid, yellow-backed tomes had been written about Frank, or at least about somebody the authors called Frank Morgan. He had always thought the character they depicted in their yarns had little resemblance to him. But then, people didn't read those stories because they were realistic, he reminded himself. They read them to be entertained.

"Aren't you a little young to be reading dime novels?" he asked the boy.

"I try to keep them away from him," the woman said, "but his father reads them, and of course Jamie gets his hands on them, too. He's been reading ever since he was four. He's very smart for his age."

"Yes, ma'am, I can tell that from talking to him. Listen, Jamie, I like to read, too. Always have a book or two in my saddlebags when I'm out on the trail. If you haven't already read it, you should try a book called *Treasure Island*, by a fella named Robert Louis Stevenson. I'll bet you'd like it. Got pirates and such-like in it."

Wide-eyed, Jamie turned his head to look up at his mother. "Pirates! That sounds great! Can I read it?"

"I'll see if I can find a copy for you," she promised. She looked up at Frank. "Thank you."

He touched a finger to the brim of his Stetson. "Glad to be of help." The cable car was coming up on the street where he needed to get off. "Good day to you and your boy, ma'am."

Frank dropped off the car as it slowed. Grant Street led off to his left. The Golden Gate Saloon was only a few blocks away.

That meant he might be only a few blocks away from answering the questions that plagued him.

Where was his son?

And what had happened to his grandchildren?

Conrad stood up and moved toward the sound of the approaching footsteps. He barked his left shin on something and reached down to discover he had run into another crate. He made his way around it and continued moving forward with his hands outstretched in front of him.

A moment later he touched a wall. He guessed it was the bulkhead that closed off the compartment. Running his fingers along it, he found a door. On the other side of that door, the footsteps came closer.

Not only that, but dim yellow lines appeared along the edges of the door. Whoever was coming had brought along a lantern.

Conrad pressed his back against the bulkhead, not knowing if the door would open toward him or away from him. If he was behind the door when it opened, that might give him a chance to jump the visitor. He'd have to be careful not to break the lantern and start a fire—

Or maybe that would be the best thing to do, he realized. If the ship was burning, the crew probably would be too busy to pay much attention to him. As the footsteps came to a stop outside the door, Conrad set himself, his muscles tense and ready for action.

A key rattled in a lock. Conrad took a deep breath and held it. With a creak of hinges, the door came open and light spilled into the room.

He winced from the glare, his eyes narrowing instinctively. There was nothing wrong with his ears, though, so he heard the man on the other side of the door mutter in surprise, "What the hell!"

The man stepped into the room, lantern held high in one hand, a heavy old revolver in the other. In the second before Conrad struck, he saw that the man wore the tight shirt and white duck pants of a sailor. Then he clubbed his hands together and brought them smashing down on the back of the man's neck.

The sailor staggered forward, but didn't collapse or drop the lantern or gun. He swung around and slashed blindly with the revolver, forcing Conrad to leap back or get brained by the gun. Cursing, the man pointed the weapon at him, but Conrad charged anyway, diving under the revolver and tackling the sailor around the waist.

The man went over backward, and the lantern flew from his hand and came down with a crash of breaking glass. Flames shot up as the kerosene spilled from the shattered reservoir and caught fire.

Conrad hammered punches into the sailor's body. He knew the smell of smoke would bring more of his captors on the run, and he wanted that gun in his hand before they arrived. He closed his fingers around it and tried to wrench it out of the sailor's grip, but the man held on to it stubbornly.

Lowering his head, the sailor butted it into Conrad's face. Conrad turned his head in time to take the blow on his jaw and cheek rather than his nose, which would have been pulped and flattened if the head-butt had landed where it was aimed. The impact jolted him enough to set off more explosions inside his skull.

He drove a knee into the sailor's belly, finally causing the man's grip on the revolver to loosen. Conrad jerked it free and tried to climb to his feet, but he heard the pounding of swift footsteps and knew he might be too late. By the light of the fire that was spreading through the hold, he saw several more men rushing down a companionway toward the open door.

Before he was able to get the gun turned around so his finger could find the trigger, one of the newcomers charged into the room and swung a club. The thick bludgeon cracked across Conrad's forearm and sent the gun flying out of his hand. The man swung the club in a backhanded blow at Conrad's head. He ducked under it and hammered a punch to the man's solar plexus. The sailor grunted in pain but still managed to flail at Conrad's head with the club.

"Stop it!" one of the other men yelled. "That

belayin' pin'll crush his skull, and the cap'n don't want him dead!"

The knowledge that they weren't supposed to kill him gave Conrad renewed hope. His captors had to hold back, but he didn't. He grappled with the man who had the belaying pin, sinking his knee into the man's groin. The belaying pin came loose.

Picking it up, Conrad launched into the other men, swinging the club right and left. One of the men yelled, "Grab him!" and another shouted, "We gotta get that fire out!"

Conrad landed a blow with the club and sent a man reeling out of his path. More running footsteps pounded, and he knew reinforcements were arriving for the sailors. The odds against him were rising by the second.

He kept battling anyway, knocking another man down with the belaying pin and fighting his way into the companionway. Men were all around him, and he was tackled from behind, dragged down, and hammered with fists. His already battered body barely felt the impacts. Acrid smoke drifted into his nose and mouth, stinging them and making him cough.

Several men held him down. Their weight pinned him securely to the deck. He still had hold of the belaying pin, but somebody stepped on his hand and made him let go of it. As he lay there struggling for breath, he heard a man say, "The fire's out, thank God. He could have burned us right down to the waterline!"

Knowing his escape attempt had failed made a bitter, sour taste well up under Conrad's tongue. He might not get another chance.

A moment later a voice obviously accustomed to command barked, "Get him on his feet."

Strong hands gripped his arms and hauled him upright. Somebody had brought another lantern. Its smoky light washed over Conrad as he stood in the grasp of two sailors. Several more surrounded him, ready to pummel him into submission if he tried to put up a fight again.

The man who stood in front of him wore a blue jacket and had a captain's cap tilted back on his bald head. His nose had been broken at least once in the past, and his eyes had a permanent squint. He was short but powerfully built.

"Try to burn my ship, will you?" He stepped closer and without warning swung a fist, sinking it into Conrad's belly. Conrad would have doubled over in agony if not for the men holding him up. "You'll learn. You're nothin' but an animal now, and I'm your lord and master. Yeah, it's a long way to China and back. Be plenty of time to break you."

Conrad lifted his head, spat blood past his swollen lips, and rasped, "Go to hell."

He knew what would happen. He didn't care. He saw the big, knobby-knuckled fist coming toward his face and didn't try to get out of the way. There was nowhere to go.

The blow exploded on his jaw with stunning force and drove his head back. As consciousness began to slip from him, he vaguely heard the captain say, "Who's the idiot who almost let him get loose? Sweeney? You know you weren't supposed to come down here alone, blast it! Once we're out to sea, you'll have some lashes coming, mister."

Conrad heard some pleading, but figured it wouldn't do the sailor any good. Then the captain ordered, "Throw him back in the hole."

Conrad felt himself hauled around and shoved. He couldn't keep his balance. He crashed down on the deck. The place stunk of the recently extinguished fire, to go along with the sickening smell of rotten fish.

The door closed, and darkness surrounded him again. On the other side of the door, the captain laughed harshly. "We sail tonight, Browning. Once we do, you're all mine. This voyage is gonna be a living hell for you, mister."

Too late, Conrad thought. He was already in hell.

That was his last thought as he passed out.

Chapter 20

Frank had the feeling he was being followed even before he reached the Golden Gate Saloon. The instincts developed over a long, hazardous life sensed the eyes watching him.

But when he glanced around on Grant Street, he didn't see anybody particularly suspicious. The sidewalks were busy on both sides of the street, but no one seemed to be paying much attention to him. A man dressed in range clothes was something of an oddity in the big city, but not enough to make most folks stare.

Most of the people bustling back and forth on the other side of the street were Chinese, since Grant Street was the boundary line between the Barbary Coast and Chinatown, but none of those scurrying figures even glanced at Frank. Their heads were down as they went about their business.

Frank spotted the saloon up ahead. It was large and prosperous-looking, and he couldn't help but wonder how much of it had been paid for by Pamela Tarleton's money.

It was early in the day, but even so the Golden Gate was busy when Frank went in. Quite a few men were lined up drinking at the long, horseshoe-shaped bar. To the right were tables where more men sat with glasses and bottles, and to the left were the poker tables, faro layouts, roulette wheels, and other games of so-called chance. The place was elegantly furnished with lots of polished hardwood, gleaming brass fixtures, and crystal chandeliers. The air in the Golden Gate practically reeked of money, along with the usual saloon smells of sawdust and beer.

In the rear of the room a broad, carpeted staircase led up to a second floor. Frank took note of that, but went to the bar and ordered a beer from a bartender in a red silk shirt. All the bartenders wore shirts like that, as did the men running the games. The women were clad in low-cut red gowns. The colorful getups made the workers easy to identify.

"There you go, cowboy." The bartender set the mug of beer in front of Frank. He didn't let go of the handle, however. "That'll be four bits."

Frank frowned. "Sort of expensive, isn't it?"

With a sigh of weary patience, the bartender said, "If you can't afford it, there are plenty of other places in San Francisco where you can get a drink, Tex."

"Didn't say I couldn't afford it," Frank grumbled. "Just said it was sort of high, that's all."

He dug a fifty-cent piece out of his pocket and slid it across the hardwood. The bartender let go of the beer mug and made the coin disappear.

The fella would be more than a mite shocked if he knew what this customer who looked like a down-on-his-luck grub line rider really could afford, Frank mused. He didn't waste a lot of time thinking about the riches he had inherited from Vivian Browning, but his lawyers assured him he was one of the wealthiest men west of the Mississippi. Lawyers had been known to lie, of course, but Conrad kept a pretty close eye on the ones who worked for him and his father.

Or at least he had before all the business about the missing children had come up. Frank knew what it was like to find out suddenly that you're a father, and couldn't blame Conrad for being distracted after he'd found out about the twins.

Frank had never been much of a drinker. The few times in his life he had found himself crawling into a bottle had come close to being disastrous for him. A good cup of coffee or a phosphate was more to his liking. But he was able to nurse the beer convincingly as he looked around the saloon's big main room.

His gaze lingered on the games, and the bartender asked, "Thinking about trying your luck? Our games are strictly on the up-and-up, cowboy."

Like the little boy on the cable car, the bar-

tender was making the same mistaken assumption
that Frank was a cowboy. Frank didn't bother cor-
recting him. He said, "I've heard stories about the
fella who owns this place. Rumor is he's some sort
of shady character."

The bartender shrugged. "You can't believe
everything you hear."

"This was in the newspaper."

"You can't believe everything you read, either,
especially in a rag like the *Chronicle*."

"Maybe not, but before I risk my hard-earned
money, I wouldn't mind meeting the hombre. I
can size up a fella pretty fast and tell whether or
not he's square."

"You really think you're gonna just waltz in
here with God knows what on your boots and
meet a man like Mr. Lannigan?" The bartender
laughed and shook his head. "Wise up, mister. We
don't need your business. Maybe you better just
move on."

"Hold your horses. I didn't mean any offense.
It's just that where I come from, when you do
business with a man, you get a chance to shake his
hand first."

"This ain't Texas." The bartender sneered and
glanced around.

Frank had already spotted several big, rugged-
looking gents who didn't seem to have any reason
for being there unless it was to take care of any trouble that started. He didn't want the bartender setting the bouncers on him, not because he was

afraid of the men but because he hadn't found out anything yet. He hadn't even laid eyes on Dex Lannigan, as far as he knew.

One of the bouncers had caught the heads-up from the bartender, and started in Frank's direction, his craggy face hardening into a cold mask as he approached. Frank was debating whether to leave quietly or start a brawl—that might get Lannigan's attention, he thought—when the need to do one or the other suddenly vanished.

Several men burst through the saloon's front doors, brandishing hatchets, and letting out unnerving yells as they charged at Lannigan's bouncers, upsetting tables and knocking customers aside on the way.

The violent intrusion brought screams from the women and startled yells from the men. The bouncer who had been closing in on Frank forgot about him and swung around to leap into action as he and his comrades met the attack.

Frank was as surprised as anybody, but he stayed coolheaded as trouble erupted around him. The intruders wore silk hoods over their heads that completely concealed their features, along with quilted jackets and loose-fitting trousers. It was impossible to tell from their yells what nationality they were, but he had a hunch they were Chinese. The hatchets told him that much, along with the Golden Gate's proximity to Chinatown.

One of the bouncers pulled a gun from under

his coat, but as he brought it to bear, one of the attackers leaped in and swung his hatchet. The bouncer screamed as Frank saw the gun fly into the air with the man's hand still clutching it.

The razor-sharp hatchet had chopped it off cleanly at the wrist. Blood spurted from the stump where the hand used to be.

The customers scattered as they tried to get out of the way of danger. Chaos erupted all through the saloon. One of the bartenders reached under the bar and brought up a sawed-off shotgun.

Frank was ready to dive to the floor, knowing that buckshot was about to spray all over the place, but before the bartender could fire the scattergun, one of the hatchet men threw his weapon. It spun glitteringly through the air and hit the bartender in the forehead, knocking him cold. The bartender dropped the shotgun and collapsed as crimson flooded over his face.

Guns began to roar. It wasn't Frank's fight, so he knelt between a couple overturned tables to let the violence ebb and flow around him. One of the saloon girls was on her hands and knees nearby, trying to crawl through the madly charging horde. She was about to fall down and probably get trampled to death when Frank reached over, took hold of her bare arm, and hauled her to relative safety next to him.

She threw her arms around his neck and clung to him. "Oh, my Lord!" she gasped. "Mister, help me!"

"Hang on," Frank told her. "We're gonna stay right here until things settle down."

"They're crazy! They're going to kill us all!"

"Who?"

"Those Chinamen! Diamond Jack's men!"

The girl's words confirmed his guess that the attackers were Chinese. He knew the tongs, the criminal societies ruling Chinatown's underworld, often warred with each other and with the white hoodlums from the Barbary Coast.

The daring, broad daylight attack had to be part of some ongoing hostilities between Dex Lannigan and one of the tongs, Frank decided. It was the only explanation that made any sense. He hoped Lannigan didn't get killed in some tong skirmish before he could find out what had happened to Conrad.

Most of the saloon's customers had made it to safety, either fleeing up the stairs to the second floor, piling out through the doors—or in some cases the windows—or huddling behind the bar. The battle continued, however, between Lannigan's men and the hooded invaders.

The girl shrieked and clutched at Frank as the body of one of the bouncers landed on the floor close to them. The man's throat had been laid open by a swipe from one of the hatchets, and blood poured out of the gaping wound.

The shooting stopped, and Frank risked a look. He saw that all of Lannigan's men were down, and so were a couple of the tong warriors. Some of the other hatchet men picked them up and carried them toward the doors. Somewhere outside, whistles blew shrilly as policemen rushed toward the scene of the bloody battle.

One of the remaining hatchet men suddenly strode toward the overturned table where Frank and the girl had taken cover. He was a big man, and the outlandish garb made him seem even bigger. Blood dripped from the hatchet he held.

Frank pushed the trembling girl down so he could shield her better with his body and reached for his Colt. It might not be his fight, but he sure as blazes wasn't going to just sit there while some loco hombre chopped him up with a hatchet.

The man stopped him by saying in a deep, powerful voice, "Please, Mr. Morgan, you must come with us. Your son's life depends on it."

Chapter 21

Frank was so surprised by the words he heard that for a couple seconds all he could do was kneel there and stare at the hooded figure in front of him. Then he closed his hand around the butt of the Colt and asked harshly, "What do you know about Conrad?"

"There is no time to explain. You must come with us." The hatchet man reached for the girl. "And this one, too, since she heard me speak your name."

The girl screamed in terror and tried to scramble away. Frank saw the hatchet man's hand tighten on the handle of his weapon, and realized the man might kill the girl rather than leave her behind to talk.

Frank had no doubt he could draw his gun, fire, and kill the hatchet man before the hooded killer could strike. But there were more of them, and if he gunned down one, the others might chop him up, along with the girl. Besides, they knew who he was, and they knew something about Conrad. He realized he had to play along in order to find out what that was.

"Come on," Frank told the girl as he grasped her arm again. "I won't let them hurt you."

"No! No!" She tried to pull away.

With a sigh of regret, Frank closed his other hand into a loose fist and struck a short, sharp blow to the girl's jaw that stunned her. As a Westerner, every part of his being rebelled at hitting a woman, but she didn't understand that if she didn't cooperate, the hatchet man would take the easy way out and kill her.

Frank would have to rely on his ability to take care of her. As she sagged against him, he lowered his shoulder and let her weight drape over it. As he came to his feet, his powerful muscles taking the burden of the girl without straining, he told the hatchet man, "Let's go."

As they started toward the door, he heard a voice he recognized as belonging to the bartender who had served him. "Hey! Hey, that crazy cowboy's kidnapping Connie! Somebody stop him!"

Nobody got in Frank's way, though. Not with the hulking figure beside him gripping a bloody hatchet. They passed through a lane created by the other hooded men, then suddenly were outside in the sunlight.

The hatchet man led the way across Grant Street toward a throng of people on the opposite sidewalk.

That crowd opened like magic before them, and they trotted into an alley. Gloom closed in around them, as on the sidewalk the crowd came back together as if there had never been a gap.

Frank was confident none of those folks would ever admit to seeing anything unusual if the police questioned them. The grip of the tongs on Chinatown was strong.

Instinct warned him that by going with the hooded hombres he might be waltzing right into a trap, but he didn't know of any reason why those powerful Chinese gangs would have any grudge against him. He had never clashed with the tongs during any of his rare trips to San Francisco in the past.

Except for the big hatchet man at his side and another who trailed behind them, the men who had launched the improbable raid on the Golden Gate had scattered. If they took off those hoods and hid their weapons under their jackets, they wouldn't look that different from all the other men in the Chinese quarter. They could blend in and disappear in a matter of moments.

The girl on Frank's shoulder began to stir. He stopped and let her slide down onto her feet. She was unsteady and pressed both hands against his broad chest to steady herself. As her wits returned to her, she lifted her head, stared wildly around her, and opened her mouth to scream.

"That wouldn't be a good idea," Frank told her before she could make a sound. He put his hands

on her shoulders, which the low-cut dress left
bare. "You don't want to annoy these fellas."

He felt her trembling like a bird as he took his
first good look at her. She was on the small side,
only a couple inches over five feet, and slender although her body had the sort of mature curves
that made the red silk dress look good on her.
Thick, dark brown hair fell to her shoulders. Her
gray eyes were wide with fear.

"Your name's Connie, right?" Frank asked, remembering what the bartender had yelled as they
were going out.

She bobbed her head in a shaky nod.

"Well, listen to me, Connie. You're gonna be all
right. I give you my word on that." Frank gave the
big hatchet man a hard look as he said that, so the
hombre would know he meant it. "I don't know exactly what these fellas want with me, but their only
interest in you is making sure you don't tell anybody they came into the Golden Gate to get me."

He was making a guess there, but even in the
dim light of the alley he saw the big hatchet man
and his smaller companion stiffen momentarily in
surprise. Their reaction told Frank he was right.

"Once they're through with me, they'll let you
go," he continued. "And they'll keep you safe the
whole time, or else they'll have a lot of trouble on
their hands."

Again he was making an assumption, that his
cooperation was important to the men and to
whoever they worked for. The two hatchet men

didn't say or do anything to contradict what he'd said.

"Do you understand?" He squeezed Connie's shoulders. "You're going to be all right."

She didn't look quite so terrified, although she was still plenty scared. She managed to swallow hard and nod. "I . . . I won't cause any trouble. I'll do whatever you tell me."

"Good." Frank kept one hand on her shoulder as he turned to face the big hatchet man. "All right, you can go ahead and take us to your boss now."

He heard a rumbling sound from under the hood and realized after a second it was what passed for laughter in the big man. The man said some swift words in Chinese to his companion, and they started off again.

For a while Frank tried to keep up with all the twists and turns they took through the maze of alleys and narrow streets, but finally gave it up as hopeless. He had no idea where they were or how to get back to the Barbary Coast. His frontiersman's instincts were all but useless there. Even though it was midday, the spaces between the buildings were so small and clogged with laundry hanging from lines strung across them that nothing got through except a dim, dusk-like half light. Frank's nerves crawled. He was used to wide-open spaces and didn't like being closed in.

At last the big hatchet man opened a door and motioned for Frank and Connie to go up a dark, steep, narrow flight of stairs. Connie shrank back against Frank, who turned to the man and said, "How about one of you go first so we know we're not walking into an ambush?"

The man gave that rumble of laughter again. He gestured toward the smaller hatchet man, who reached through the doorway and brought out a candle from somewhere. He lit it with a match he produced from a pocket in his quilted jacket, then started up the stairs in the lead with the candle held high. Its flickering glow revealed the stairs were covered with a dirty, threadbare carpet runner. The grimy walls seemed to close in on each side.

Frank prodded Connie into going next. His guts were tight with the impulse to draw his gun as he followed her, but he left the Colt in its holster. Not only did he have the big hatchet man right behind him, but he also felt like eyes might be watching them through hidden portals. He didn't want to spook anybody.

When they reached the top of the stairs, the man with the candle led them along a dingy hallway. From the looks of it, the building was abandoned, but Frank didn't fully believe that. The corridor made several turns, then they came to another staircase, leading down.

"Where are we going?" Connie asked in a trembling voice. "Where are they taking us?"

"I don't know," Frank said, "but I hope we'll be there soon."

They reached a landing, turned, and kept going down. Frank figured they were below street level. At the bottom of the stairs was a door, and when the man with the candle opened it, the light revealed a tunnel with earthen walls and thick beams shoring up the ceiling, like in a mine.

Connie stopped short and shook her head. "No, I can't. I can't go in there. They . . . they have earthquakes here sometimes. The tunnel could collapse. I can't go in there!"

She turned with panic in her eyes and tried to run, but Frank caught her. "It won't take us long to get through it. We'll be all right."

He wished he could be as sure of that as he sounded.

The big hatchet man motioned impatiently for them to go on. The tunnel was wide enough for Frank and Connie to walk side by side. He kept an arm around her waist to steady her as they followed the man with the candle.

Even though Frank had had no way of knowing how long the tunnel was, it turned out that what he had told Connie was right. They were in it only for a hundred yards or so, then came to another door with stairs behind it leading up. Obviously glad to be out of the tunnel, Connie climbed them without any prodding.

They emerged into another hallway where the walls were covered with colorful, intricately embroidered tapestries. The hardwood floor was polished to a high sheen, and light shone from ornate brass fixtures that held gas lamps. Frank figured they were in a completely different building. The tunnel they had used probably passed underneath one of Chinatown's streets.

The hall ended in a small, square room with a fine rug on the floor, a couple of impressively ugly chairs that didn't look all that comfortable, and some small but exquisitely detailed paintings on the walls. A pair of doors on the opposite wall were closed. The big hatchet man, who had put away his blood-stained weapon, went to those doors and opened them. "Please, Mr. Morgan."

"The girl stays with me," Frank said.

The hatchet man inclined his hooded head in agreement.

Frank led Connie into the room on the other side of the doors. It was as large and opulent as he expected it to be. This was where he would meet the boss, he sensed, the man who had sent those hatchet men into the Golden Gate to fetch him. Maybe *now* he would get some answers.

There were no windows. The walls were covered with more tapestries. The room was furnished with a divan and several well-upholstered armchairs, but the large desk in its center dominated it. It was the sort of desk you'd find in the office of a successful banker or lawyer, like Claudius Turnbuckle, Frank realized.

The man who stood behind it was dressed like

an American businessman, in a sober gray suit, white shirt, and black cravat. He was young, probably around thirty, and had sleek dark hair and a mustache. At first glance you might not even take him for Chinese, although the golden skin and dark, almond-shaped eyes testified to his heritage. He regarded Frank and Connie solemnly. "Mr. Morgan? Mr. Frank Morgan?"

Frank nodded. "That's right."

The man's eyes cut toward the big hatchet man. "Ling Yuan, I did not tell you to bring any . . . entertainment . . . with you."

The man finally pulled the hood off, revealing a stolid face that bore the marks of many battles in the past. "She heard me speak Mr. Morgan's name, and I thought it best not to leave her behind to tell Lannigan of our interest in him."

"Then you should have—"

"A thousand pardons, illustrious one, but Mr. Morgan insisted we bring her along."

Anger had flared in the man's eyes at the interruption, but he suppressed it. "Very well. You adapted to the situation and performed your task admirably as always, Ling Yuan. Since we're going to be working closely with Mr. Morgan, cooperating with him in this matter should convince him of our good faith."

"I'd be more convinced," Frank said, "if you'd tell me what you know about my son."

"Of course." The man came out from behind the desk and extended his hand to Frank. "But first, introductions are in order. My name is Wong Duck." He smiled for the first time since Frank had come into the room, and the light from the gas lamps winked on the tiny jewel embedded in one of his front teeth. "But you can call me Diamond Jack."

Chapter 22

Frank took the man's hand and shook it. "You know who I am."

"Indeed I do," Diamond Jack replied. "Frank Morgan. Sometimes known as The Drifter. You are a famous fighting man who hires out his gun."

"You're wrong about that," Frank said bluntly as he let go of Diamond Jack's hand. "I've been in plenty of fights, but never for money, only for causes I believed in or to protect folks who needed my help."

"Then your reputation does not do you justice."

Frank shrugged. "I stopped worrying about things like that a long time ago."

"It takes a man with a great deal of serenity not to worry about what others think of him."

"Just never seemed like it was worth the time and trouble to me."

Diamond Jack turned to the big man he had called Ling Yuan. "Escort the young lady to one of the other rooms so Mr. Morgan and I can speak privately."

Frank held up a hand as Ling Yuan started toward Connie, who flinched away from him. "She stays with me. I promised her I'd take care of her."

"Your concern is touching but unnecessary," Diamond Jack snapped. "She works for my enemy. Things must be said that she cannot hear."

Frank needed to find out what the man knew about Conrad, so he said, "Do I have your word she won't be harmed?"

"Of course," Diamond Jack answered without hesitation. "I'll go farther than that. Ling Yuan, defend this woman to your last breath until I release you from the task."

The big hatchet man bowed to show his obedience.

Diamond Jack turned back to Frank. "Satisfied, Mr. Morgan?"

"I reckon I'll have to be."

Connie shook her head and backed away. "No, I . . . I don't trust these men!"

"They're men of honor," Frank told her, hoping he was right about that. "They'll keep their word."

Diamond Jack smiled at Connie. "I'll have tea brought to you. You'll soon see that I'm not the monster Dex Lannigan makes me out to be."

Maybe not a monster, Frank thought, but utterly ruthless when he needed to be. Frank hadn't forgotten how ready Ling Yuan had been to kill Connie in order to silence her, and Diamond Jack had hinted at the same thing.

Ling Yuan escorted a pale, trembling Connie out of the room, leaving Frank and Diamond Jack alone. The younger man held out a hand to indicate Frank should take the comfortable red leather armchair in front of the desk.

Frank took off his hat and sat down. Diamond Jack went behind the desk and settled himself in the big swivel chair. He steepled his fingers together and said, "I hope you'll forgive me for the somewhat unorthodox manner in which I arranged this meeting between us, Mr. Morgan."

Frank grunted. "I've got a hunch most things about you are a mite unorthodox, Mr. Wong."

"Please, call me Diamond Jack, or just Jack. I suppose you've noticed that while I honor my ancestors, I don't dress or speak like them."

"No way for me to know about the honoring part, but yeah, you don't exactly look like what I'd think of as a tong leader."

"You believe I lead one of the tongs here in Chinatown?"

"Don't you?"

Diamond Jack smiled, revealing that jewel again. "Actually, yes. I am the leader of the Woo Sing tong, and some of the leaders of the other tongs look to me for advice and counsel since we have banded together to deal with the threat of a common enemy."

"Dex Lannigan," Frank said. The name was a statement, not a question.

"Indeed," Diamond Jack murmured. "Lannigan has attempted on several occasions to expand his power and influence from the Barbary Coast into Chinatown. That is one more indication of how much things have changed. In previous decades, no white man, even the most arrogant and ambitious, would have dared to do such a thing. But a new century will soon be upon us. We face new challenges and must use new methods to combat them." He gestured to indicate his suit and the desk. "I intend to run the tongs as a business . . . a profitable business."

"Of course, some of the old ways are still effective," Frank commented. "Like using hatchet men to chop your enemies into little pieces."

Diamond Jack threw his head back and laughed. "Well, some things never get old. Yes, our enemies still fear the hatchet men. They shall learn to fear even more."

Frank leaned forward. "What about my son? I don't see how he figures in this war of yours against Lannigan."

"To be honest, I don't, either. But clearly, Conrad Browning is very important to Lannigan. Otherwise he wouldn't have attempted to have your son and the lawyer Turnbuckle killed as soon as Browning reached San Francisco. Lannigan knew he was coming and wanted to get rid of him."

Frank could have told Diamond Jack what Lannigan's interest in Conrad was, but first he wanted to find out what else the tong leader knew. "I reckon you keep pretty close tabs on what Lannigan does. That made you curious about Conrad."

Diamond Jack nodded. "Indeed. My thinking was that if your son is so important to Lannigan, perhaps there is some way I could use him against my enemy."

"So you started watching Conrad, too," Frank guessed.

"Yes." Diamond Jack chuckled. "San Francisco is a city of spies, Mr. Morgan. There are eyes and ears everywhere belonging to people who work for the various factions. The normal citizens go on about their business without any idea of the undercurrents actually guiding their lives. Some of my men, including Ling Yuan, whom you met earlier today, have been watching Conrad Browning for the past few days. In fact, Ling Yuan quite possibly saved his life several nights ago when Browning was involved in a fight at a tavern called Spanish Charley's. The owner of the tavern, although your son probably didn't know this at the time, is Dex Lannigan. This situation ultimately led to the perilous circumstances in which Browning currently finds himself."

Frank leaned forward and asked tensely, "What perilous circumstances?"

"Last night, Lannigan set a trap for your son. My men did not become aware of it in time to prevent it. Browning was captured, and the man with him, a bodyguard hired by Claudius Turnbuckle, was killed."

Frank nodded. He knew what had happened to Morelli. After talking to Turnbuckle, he had strongly suspected that Lannigan was involved. Diamond Jack had confirmed it. But the most important question was still waiting for an answer. "Where is Conrad now?"

"Being held prisoner on a ship called the *Nimbus*. It sails tonight, and Browning will be forced to become a member of the crew during its voyage to China and back. He's been shanghaied, as the Americans call it." The tong leader shrugged. "Either that, or the captain of the *Nimbus* has orders to kill Browning and dump his body at sea. It's impossible to know which fate Lannigan has in mind for your son."

"Why haven't you sent your men in to rescue him?"

Diamond Jack's expression hardened. "Taking over a ship is a different proposition from intervening in a tavern brawl or making an incursion into Lannigan's saloon. I knew only a few bouncers would be working in the Golden Gate at this time of day. On board the *Nimbus* there's an entire crew of extremely tough sailors. It's almost certain I would lose some of my men, and they're valuable to me. I refuse to run that risk simply to frustrate Lannigan's plans and annoy him." The tong leader leaned forward and placed his hands flat on the desk. "I want to know what's going on here, Morgan. I want to know why your son is so important to Dex Lannigan. Perhaps then I can decide if he is that important to *me.*"

"So you brought me here to answer that question."

Diamond Jack's narrow shoulders rose and fell in another eloquent shrug. "Who better to know the affairs of the son than the father?"

Frank didn't answer that. "How did you know I'm Conrad's father?"

"I have my sources of information. There are spies everywhere, remember?"

Frank sensed he wasn't going to get a straight answer out of the man. Diamond Jack wanted to protect his sources. Frank couldn't blame him for that. The Woo Sing tong was locked in a war with Lannigan, and its leader would use every weapon at his disposal.

"What happens if I tell you what's going on?"

"Then I decide whether or not to rescue your son," Diamond Jack said.

"Based on how much of a blow that'll deal to Lannigan."

"Precisely."

Frank nodded. The tong leader represented his

best chance of getting Conrad off that ship before it sailed, so he was going to have to put his cards on the table.

"Three years ago, Lannigan made a deal with a woman named Pamela Tarleton. At least that's what Claudius Turnbuckle and I believe."

"Turnbuckle has a reputation as an astute lawyer," Diamond Jack admitted. "But I have never heard of this Tarleton woman."

"Consider yourself lucky. At one time she was supposed to marry my son, but all she wound up ever giving him was grief."

For the next few minutes, Frank sketched in the details of Conrad's relationship with Pamela and how she had set out to have her vengeance on him. When he reached the part about the hidden children, Diamond Jack arched an eyebrow.

"This woman sounds . . . impressive."

"If being downright evil impresses you, I reckon she fits the bill, all right," Frank said. "Ever since Conrad found out about the twins, he's been looking for them, and the trail led him here to San Francisco. It looks like she made an arrangement with Lannigan, since he's been trying to kill Conrad. I want to get my hands on him so I can make him tell me if he knows where my grandchildren are . . . unless those spies of yours might be able to shed any light on that."

Diamond Jack shook his head. "My people cannot look for something they don't even know exists, and this is the first I have heard about any missing children. You and your son have my sympathy, Mr. Morgan. You have suffered much at the hands of this Tarleton woman."

"Conrad more than me, but I'd be holding a grudge against her, too, if she was still alive. I sure don't want her winning, even though she's dead."

"Perhaps I can be of assistance—"

"You'll help get Conrad off that boat?"

"It can be arranged," Diamond Jack murmured, "but I must have something in return."

"What do you want?" Frank asked bluntly.

"What happens to Lannigan if he knows where the children are hidden?"

"I reckon that's up to him."

Diamond Jack smiled. "I would like to see him wind up dead. My men might be able to get to him, but at a high cost. You and your son, on the other hand . . ."

"We're not members of your tong, so our lives aren't worth as much to you."

"Look at it however you will, Mr. Morgan, but it seems to me you and Browning have ample reason for wanting Dex Lannigan dead, as do I."

"I told you, I'm not a hired gun," Frank said. "But if you rescue Conrad from that ship, I think there's a good chance the two of us will be taking the fight to Lannigan. What happens after that is up to fate."

Diamond Jack laughed. "As a good Chinese,

how can I not put my trust in fate? Very well, you have a deal. Before the *Nimbus* sails tonight, my men will take your son off the ship."

"One more thing . . . I'm going along."

"Knowing your reputation, Mr. Morgan, I expected no less."

Chapter 23

At least a year had dragged by since he'd regained consciousness the second time, Conrad thought. That was what it felt like, anyway.

But the ship on which he was being held prisoner still rocked gently at anchor, and since the broken-nosed captain had said they were sailing that night, Conrad knew only hours had passed, not months.

The first time he woke up in that hellhole he had only *thought* he hurt. The second time he was in more pain. Not just his head, but his entire body ached intolerably. A lesser man would have wanted to curl up and die.

Conrad lay there regaining some of his strength and trying to figure out a way to escape.

The second part of that challenge was going to be difficult, if not impossible. The crew member who had been careless when coming down to check on him earlier faced punishment lashes for his carelessness. Nobody wanted to be whipped. The next time that door in the bulkhead opened, there would be at least three men on the other side of it, probably more. They wouldn't take chances with him again.

It was possible they wouldn't unlock the door until after the ship had sailed. Realizing that was enough to goad him on his hands and knees again. He crawled around until he found one of the crates he had encountered earlier. Pulling himself onto it, he sat for a long time and rested from the effort.

Feeling stronger, he got to his feet and began exploring his prison. There might be another way out. A porthole, maybe. If he could find something like that and force it open . . .

There weren't any portholes. He felt his way all over the four walls of the chamber and found nothing except the door. The hinges were on the inside, but he had nothing with which to work on them. If he had a tool of some sort, he might work the pins out of the hinges and free the door.

With that thought in his mind, he stumbled through the darkness back to the crates and fell to his knees beside one of them. He ran his hands over the lid, searching for even the tiniest gap he might be able to force his fingers into. If he could pry one of the boards loose, he might be able to use a nail in it to push the pins up and out of the hinges. What he really needed was a crowbar to pry up a board . . .

That thought made him collapse in grim laughter against the crate. If he had a crowbar, he could use it to force the door open and wouldn't have to attack the hinges. He wasn't thinking straight. The beatings he had endured, plus the lack of food and water, had taken quite a toll on him. A desperate thirst gripped him. The inside of his mouth felt like sandpaper, and his tongue seemed twice its normal size.

"Feeling sorry for yourself won't do you any good, Conrad," he rasped, speaking the words aloud. "Get back to work."

Finally, on the fourth crate he checked, he found a slightly warped board on the edge of the lid. Gripping it with his fingers, he heaved up with all the strength he could muster, but the board didn't budge. He rested a few moments and tried again, then again and again.

He lost track of time. He didn't know if he'd been pulling on the board for fifteen minutes or three hours. He didn't notice when the board finally shifted a little. He just reset his grip and heaved again.

The movement was unmistakable.

Conrad slumped against the crate as emotion washed over him. He was far from being free, but at least he had accomplished *something*.

After a moment, he shook his head in the utter darkness and got back to work. With a better grip on the board and the other hand on the crate to brace himself, he put his back into the effort and pushed with his legs. Nails squealed as they slipped a little in their holes. Conrad grinned savagely and heaved again.

At last the board broke with a splintering of wood, and a piece of it came free in his hand. He lost his balance and wound up sitting down hard on his rear end. He sat there laughing until he remembered why he wanted the board in the first place. Two nails were still in place, protruding about an inch and a half from the bottom side of the board.

He climbed painfully to his feet. Having spent so much time in the dark, almost airless chamber he was able to find the door much easier, guided to it by some instinct. Working by feel, he wedged the point of one of the nails firmly against the bottom of the pin in the uppermost hinge and tried to force it up.

Putting pressure on the board wasn't enough to loosen the pin, Conrad realized after a few minutes. He set the board down and took off one of his boots. When he had the nail back in place, he used the boot as a makeshift hammer and began striking blows against the board.

Hitting upward was awkward, but the jolts finally had an effect. Conrad thought the pin had moved. When he felt it to check, he found the top of the pin sticking up half an inch above the hinge. He tried to wiggle it out the rest of the way, but it wouldn't come loose. He went back to using the nail, the board, and the boot.

A couple minutes later, the pin was in his hand. He clutched it in triumph.

There were still two hinges holding the door in place, he reminded himself. After drawing in a couple deep breaths, he went to work on the second one. In the back of his mind, he was still aware of the aches and pains in his body, but he didn't pay much attention to them anymore.

His freedom beckoned, and beyond that, his children. Those goals were more than enough to make him forget about how badly he hurt.

Besides, when he got out of there he was going to deal out some pain of his own . . . and that made him feel better.

The fog rolled in before the sun went down, cloaking the city in gloom. Once night fell, visibility shrank to almost zero. From an alley between two warehouses along the Embarcadero, Frank couldn't see the ships docked at the other end of the long wharf.

The big hatchet man called Ling Yuan waited patiently next to him. Behind them were a dozen more of Diamond Jack's men.

The tong leader had remained in his stronghold. As he had explained to Frank, he was an executive. He gave orders to warriors. He didn't take up a hatchet himself.

That was all right with Frank. From what he had seen of Ling Yuan and the other hatchet men, they could handle themselves just fine in a fight. He wouldn't have to worry about them, only about rescuing Conrad.

"The ship is supposed to sail in less than an hour," Ling Yuan said quietly. "Before then, three Woo Sing soldiers will swim around to the other side and use grappling hooks and cords to get on board. While they cause a distraction, the rest of us will go up the gangplank."

"Do you have any idea where my son is being held?"

Ling Yuan shook his head. "Somewhere below-decks. Wong Duck's agents have watched the ship all day. There has been no sign of Conrad Browning. But you and I will find him. The others will keep the crew busy while we search. We must be quick, so we can get away before the police come."

"I figured your boss would have the police paid off to look the other way."

Ling Yuan grunted disdainfully. "This is possible with some of the authorities, but an annoying number of them are honest."

"You speak English really well."

"A missionary lady from England taught me, while I was still in China. Before I came to this country."

"Is she still over there teaching?"

Ling Yuan sighed. "No. A local warlord saw the missionary teachings as a challenge to his rule. He had warned the lady and the other missionaries to leave. When they didn't his soldiers raped the women and killed them, then tortured all the men to death."

"What did you do?" Frank asked.

"What could I do? I was only one man." Ling Yuan looked off into the fog. "A month later the warlord was found in his fortress, choking on his own entrails. The heads of all his guards had been cut off. He died moments later."

Frank looked at the big man and slowly nodded. "Somehow that doesn't surprise me."

"Our men will be on board soon," Ling Yuan said briskly. "Be ready."

Frank was ready, all right. He had slipped a sixth bullet into his Colt, into the chamber he usually kept empty so the hammer could rest on it.

Ling Yuan had his arms crossed over his chest. Without looking at Frank, he said, "Since I came to this country, I have learned to read English. I have read stories about you, Mr. Morgan."

"Dime novels?" Frank guessed.

"Yes. Do they exaggerate your exploits?"

"By a whole heap."

"But you *are* a gunfighter?"

Frank sighed. "I never set out to be. But a fella pushed me until I didn't have any choice but to draw on him. He thought he was fast, but I was faster. After him there was another man, and another, and almost before I knew what was happening, I had a reputation. I had to leave the place where I'd grown up"—his voice grew wistful for a second—"had to leave behind a girl. Since then

I've never settled for very long in any one place. Tried a few times, but something always happened to make me think it was better to move on."

"The life of a true warrior," Ling Yuan said. "Trouble finds him, wherever he goes."

Frank nodded. "That's about the size of—"

A sudden shout from the ship, followed a split second later by the crack of a gun, interrupted him.

Ling Yuan pulled his hatchet from under his jacket. "We go!"

Chapter 24

Using the nail and his boot, Conrad worked at the other two hinges until he had the pins out. But the door still sat squarely in its frame, and the lock on the other side held it shut.

The gap between door and jamb on the hinged side was too narrow for him to get his fingers in it and pull the door loose. He tried prying it out with the nails and made a little progress, but the door was well-fitted and stubborn.

An idea occurred to him as he stepped back into his boot. He felt his way over to the crate with the broken lid and stuck his hand through the small opening he had made.

His hand delved through a layer of excelsior, then touched canvas shrouding. He pressed against the canvas to see if he could tell what was underneath it. He felt a long, narrow shape.

It took a moment for Conrad to realize he was touching what felt like a rifle barrel.

Excitement leaped through him. He grabbed the piece of board that had broken off and pried up the remaining section still nailed to the crate. With that bigger opening created, he was able to remove another board. He pulled out handfuls of excelsior and threw it behind him until he had uncovered more of the cargo.

Using the nails in the broken board, he poked a hole in the canvas, then ripped it larger. He cut through the next layer of protection—oilcloth— then plunged his hands into the grease coating the rifles in the crate. He pulled out one of the weapons.

Of course it was empty, and he had no ammunition. But even so, the feel of a gun in his hands made his heart leap. He set it on the crate, tore off a piece of canvas, and starting wiping the grease off the rifle, as well as from his hands. He had to tear off more canvas, but eventually he had the rifle fairly clean. It felt like a Winchester repeater. He checked the action, and it worked smoothly and easily. The rifle was probably new.

Conrad wondered if all the crates in the hold contained rifles. He had a hunch they did, and he suspected there was something shady about shipping them to China.

That wasn't any of his business, though. He just wished he had a boxful of cartridges.

That could make all the difference in the world.

Maybe he could use the rifle to bluff his way

past some of the sailors once he got out, he thought. They wouldn't have any way of knowing for sure the weapon was unloaded.

He took the rifle with him and leaned it against the wall beside the door as he went back to work trying to pry it loose with the nails in the piece of board he held. The nails were small enough to go in the gap around the door, but when he used them to lever the door out of its frame, they bent. Biting back a curse, he tried to straighten them. He still needed that blasted crowbar . . .

His muscles suddenly stiffened and his head came up as somewhere above him, gunshots sounded. The reports were muffled by decks and bulkheads between him and them, but they were unmistakable.

A ruckus was going on, and he couldn't help but think it had something to do with him. Maybe Turnbuckle had figured out where he was and sent in the police.

Or maybe that big Chinese hatchet man, his guardian angel from Spanish Charley's, had shown up unexpectedly again. If that was the case, Conrad hoped the man had brought some friends with him. Not even the formidable Ling Yuan— that was what Carmen had called him, wasn't it?— would be a match for the entire crew of the ship.

Conrad wanted to be in the middle of it, not locked up, hidden belowdecks. He pried harder at the door, but still to no avail.

He heard the slap of footsteps hurrying toward

the door and backed away, holding the broken board in his right hand and using his left to pick up the Winchester.

A man called, "Bring a light! Plant yourselves in front of that door! Nobody gets to Browning!"

The sailors were going to stand guard out there. Realizing that wouldn't help him, Conrad focused on getting them to open the door. He lifted the rifle and slammed the butt of its stock against the panel. He hit the door hard, twice, and let out a yell.

"What the hell!" a sailor cried. "The Chinks already got in there somehow!"

That told Conrad who was behind his rescue attempt.

"Get your guns ready!" another man ordered. "Malley, unlock the door and get out of the way!"

Conrad backed off again, having a pretty good idea what was about to happen. A key rattled in the lock, then one of the men shoved hard on the door, thinking it would swing open.

It fell into the room, landing with a crash on the deck.

The racket hadn't even had a chance to echo in the companionway when Conrad hurdled over the fallen door, slashing right and left with the piece of board in his hand.

The protruding nails made it a vicious weapon. They tore across the face of a startled sailor, causing blood to spurt and drawing a howl of pain from him. The flat side of the board thudded into a second man's head, staggering him.

After being locked up in the dark room for so long, Conrad's eyes were almost useless to him in the lanternlight. But he could make out some dim shapes and had the advantage of knowing nobody was his friend. He tore into them, pressing his surprise.

"Look out, he's got a gun!" That was enough to make them forget the captain had ordered them to keep Conrad alive. A pistol roared deafeningly in the narrow confines of the corridor.

Conrad dropped the board and used both hands on the Winchester. He rammed the barrel into a man's belly, then slashed the stock across the sailor's face when he bent over in pain. He saw three men down, and only two still on their feet, making him realize his vision had improved.

One man held a pistol, and fired again. Conrad felt the hot breath of the slug as he leaped forward and crashed the rifle butt in the middle of the man's face. Bone gave way under the impact. The man slumped against the wall with blood pouring from his ruined nose and mouth and slid to the deck. The pistol slipped from his fingers.

Conrad snatched it up and turned toward the last sailor, only to see him fleeing for his life. The lantern he carried bobbed and weaved as he ran toward a ladder at the far end of the corridor. Conrad could have shot him in the back, but he held his fire. More interested in getting out of there, he headed for the ladder, too. The sailor scrambled up it with the dexterity of an ape and disappeared through a hatch. Enough light spilled down through the opening that Conrad was able to see where he was going.

When he reached the ladder, he dropped the empty Winchester and tucked the pistol into the waistband of his trousers. He hated to abandon the rifle, but needed both hands to climb. Looking up he saw the sailor with the lantern already climbing another ladder on the next level. His prison really had been buried in the bowels of the ship, Conrad thought.

He started up the ladder. Sooner or later he would reach the ship's deck and the open air. Even filled with the stench of rotten fish, it was going to smell good.

Rotten fish . . . and powdersmoke, because somewhere above him guns continued to roar.

Ling Yuan motioned for Frank to fall behind as they charged toward the gangplank leading to the deck of the *Nimbus*. The other hatchet men would take the lead and run interference. Frank and Ling Yuan had the important job of finding Conrad.

Shouts and curses echoed over the deck as sailors battled the men who had boarded the ship on the water side. Unfortunately, the lookout near the gangplank on the dock side of the ship didn't abandon his post to see what the commotion was. He yelled a warning and pulled a pistol from his belt as the first of the hatchet men charged up the gangplank.

The lookout didn't get off a shot. Staggering back, he dropped his gun to paw at the handle of the hatchet lodged in his chest. The Diamond Jack man who had thrown the razor-sharp weapon with deadly accuracy paused just long enough to jerk the hatchet free as he leaped past the fallen lookout.

The hatchet men scattered across the deck to meet the threat of the ship's crew. Some of the sailors were armed with revolvers, and shots began to roar. The hatchet men were blindingly quick, and avoided most of the bullets as they rushed in, chopping and slashing. Blood flew in the air.

Ling Yuan and Frank ran up the gangplank, reaching the deck. Frank's Colt snapped up as he spotted a man standing on the bridge drawing a bead on them with a rifle. The Colt blasted first, sending a slug deep into the sailor's chest, driving him backward. The rifle went off, but it was pointed at the sky by then and the bullet sailed harmlessly into the night.

"The captain!" Ling Yuan barked as he waved his hatchet toward a short, burly man wearing a blue jacket and a cap. "He can tell us where your son is!"

That sounded like a good idea to Frank. He headed for the captain with Ling Yuan at his side.

The man saw them coming and jerked a gun from under his jacket. Before he could fire, Ling

Yuan sent his hatchet spinning through the air. Slicing cleanly through jacket and shirt sleeves, it lodged in the captain's right forearm. The man screeched in pain and dropped the pistol. Falling to his knees, he cradled his injured arm against his body.

But he was tough, and still in the fight. Pulling the hatchet free with his left hand, he surged to his feet and slashed at Ling Yuan, who jerked back, barely avoiding the swipe.

Wanting the man alive so he could tell them where Conrad was being held prisoner, Frank jammed the Colt back in its holster and dived at the captain, going under the flailing hatchet. He rammed his shoulder into the man's thick but solid gut and drove him backward off his feet.

They crashed to the deck. The captain chopped at Frank with the hatchet, but Frank got his right hand on the man's wrist and kept the blow from falling. A second later, he hammered a punch with his left into the captain's face. The blow didn't faze the man. Squirming and twisting he tried to pull his left hand free to use the hatchet.

Frank hit him again, but the captain heaved his body up and toppled Frank to the side. A quick roll took Frank out of reach just as the hatchet came sweeping down at him. The blade hit the deck so hard it got stuck. The captain tugged on the handle but couldn't get the weapon free.

Frank kicked the captain in the chest, knocking him to the deck, away from the hatchet. Blood still poured from the deep gash on the man's arm. Years of a hard life at sea had toughened him to the point that he kept fighting, in spite of his weakened state.

Ling Yuan reached for the man, but the captain got a leg up and kicked the hatchet man in the stomach. Ling Yuan doubled over and took a step back, giving the captain time to scramble to his feet. He reached into a pocket with his left hand and brought out a derringer. The little weapon had two barrels, one on top of the other. At close range, it would be lethal.

From several yards away on the deck, Frank saw the range was practically point-blank. He was too far away to tackle the man before the derringer went off, but couldn't let the captain shoot Ling Yuan in the head. He palmed out his Colt again and tilted the barrel up as he squeezed the trigger. No time to be fancy, he aimed for the man's body.

Another shot sounded just as the Colt roared and bucked in Frank's hand. The captain reeled backward as two slugs ripped into him. He struggled to raise the derringer again, so Frank shot him a second time. The captain went down, landing heavily on his back. The derringer slipped out of his fingers and slid across the deck.

Frank turned his head to see who had fired the other shot and was shocked to see Conrad with a smoking pistol in his hand, halfway through a hatch leading belowdecks.

"Frank?" the younger man exclaimed in obvious

surprise. He hadn't been aware his father was anywhere within a thousand miles of San Francisco.

Frank hurried over to the hatch and extended his left hand to Conrad, who gripped it and let Frank help him out on deck. Conrad was battered and bruised and had dried blood on his face.

Frank looked him over. "Are you all right?"

"I'm fine," Conrad said, "and I'm a lot better now. How in the world—"

"No time for that," Ling Yuan interrupted. His face was a little gray from the vicious kick the captain had landed in his belly, but he was able to straighten up. "We should go."

Scattered fights between the hatchet men and the crew of the *Nimbus* were still taking place around the deck. Bodies sprawled here and there. Diamond Jack had been right. Some of his men had lost their lives in the rescue.

Frank gripped Conrad's arm and steered him toward the gangplank. Ling Yuan recovered his hatchet and flanked Conrad on the other side. The three of them clattered down to the wharf. Ling Yuan shouted something in Chinese. Probably an order to retreat, Frank thought. They didn't wait to see if the other hatchet men got away. Ling Yuan hustled them toward the safety of the dark alleys along the Embarcadero.

"I never expected to see you here, Frank," Conrad said as Ling Yuan led them through the maze and the sounds of battle fell behind them. "How did you—"

"Claudius and that friend of yours, Arturo, decided you needed a hand whether you wanted one or not," Frank said. "Not sure you did, though. You'd already gotten loose somehow."

"Yeah, but I might not have made it off that ship without your help. Thanks, Frank."

"You can thank Diamond Jack, this big fella's boss. He's the one who decided to step in and get you away from whatever Lannigan has planned for you."

"You know about Lannigan?" Conrad asked.

"I know about all of it," Frank replied grimly. "About the kids and what Pamela did and Lannigan's part in it. I hope you'll let me play out the hand with you, now that I'm here."

"Damn right I will," Conrad said. "And unless I was locked up down in that hold longer than I thought I was, I know where Lannigan is tonight. I think it's time we go and introduce ourselves to him."

Chapter 25

Ling Yuan insisted they accompany him back to Diamond Jack's stronghold in Chinatown. Since it was unlikely Conrad would have escaped without the tong leader's help, he supposed he could take the time to do that. The ball at the Kimball mansion would be going on for several hours yet.

"What will happen back on the ship?" He asked as they made their way through the streets.

"The police will arrive, yet again too late to do anything but clean up the mess left behind and blame the violence on the tongs."

"Well, you fellas did have something to do with it," Frank pointed out.

"Because we were helping your son."

"True enough," Frank admitted.

Conrad said, "If they search the ship, they'll find something interesting. There are several crates hidden down in the hold where I was locked up that

I'm pretty sure are full of brand-new Winchesters bound for China."

"As a power in the criminal underworld, Lannigan has numerous connections with smugglers. No doubt those rifles were intended for one of the warlords who controls China." Ling Yuan paused. "If I had known about the guns, I might have burned the ship."

Conrad looked over at Frank, who said, "Ling Yuan has some old grudges against the warlords. I'll tell you about it later."

Conrad nodded. "The ship won't be sailing tonight, not after everything that's happened. I'll talk to Claudius and he can make sure the authorities get tipped off about that cargo."

"We need to let Claudius and Arturo know you're safe," Frank said.

"Wong Duck can telephone Mr. Turnbuckle and inform him," Ling Yuan said. He added dryly, "We have some modern conveniences in Chinatown."

"You don't call him Diamond Jack?" Conrad asked.

"I prefer the more traditional customs."

"Like hatchets."

One of those rumbling laughs came from Ling Yuan. "Sometimes the old ways are still the best."

He took them through yet another old abandoned building and into the opulent headquarters of the Woo Sing tong.

Frank said, "This place is honeycombed with tunnels and secret passages, isn't it?"

"Our people have many enemies," Ling Yuan explained. "Deception and subterfuge are valuable weapons in our ongoing battle with those who would destroy us."

He ushered them into Diamond Jack's sanctum. The slender, well-dressed tong leader stood up to greet them.

"I was already informed you had been rescued successfully from the *Nimbus*, Mr. Browning." He smiled as he held out his hand to Conrad. "Welcome to my home."

Conrad shook hands with him. "I understand I have you to thank for what happened tonight."

Diamond Jack shrugged. "Don't think me too altruistic. If Dex Lannigan wants something, *I* want to deny it to him. Clearly he wanted your death, or at least your exile."

Conrad smiled. "He's going to be mighty surprised in a little while when I walk into that party at the Kimball mansion."

Diamond Jack arched his narrow eyebrows. "You're going to a society ball? Not looking like that, I hope."

"I guess I could clean up a little."

Diamond Jack spoke to Ling Yuan in Chinese. The big man nodded and said to Conrad, "Come with me."

Conrad frowned. "Where?"

"By now you must trust us."

Conrad didn't, not completely, and he was all too aware he was in the middle of another place where escape would be very difficult. But Ling Yuan had a point. So far no one connected with the tong had done anything except be helpful to Conrad.

"What about you, Frank?" Conrad asked.

Before Frank could answer, Diamond Jack said, "Your father will stay here with me while your needs are attended to. He can tell me more about the quest that brought you here."

"I reckon it'll be all right," Frank put in. "If Jack wanted us dead, his men could have seen to it before now."

That was true enough, Conrad supposed. He nodded to Ling Yuan and allowed the big hatchet man to lead him out of the room.

They took just a few twists and turns in the corridors, but it was all that was necessary to get Conrad lost. It was just another indication of how much he and Frank were at the mercy of their "hosts."

They hadn't taken away the revolver he had brought with him from the ship, so as long as he was armed, he was willing to play along with the Chinese criminals.

Ling Yuan took him to a room where a young woman in a red silk dress waited on a divan. At first glance Conrad thought she was Chinese, because she had dark hair and eyes, but then he took a closer look and saw that she was white. She was short and slender but well-curved. The skimpy dress she wore looked like something you'd find on a saloon girl.

Her eyes were big with fear, especially when she glanced at Ling Yuan.

"Who are you?" she demanded of Conrad. "When am I going to get out of here?"

"I can't answer the second part of that, but my name is Conrad Browning."

Her eyes widened with recognition. "You're Mr. Morgan's son! The one he was looking for."

"You know Frank?" The girl's words had taken Conrad by surprise.

"We met earlier today. It's because of him that I'm being held prisoner by these . . . these . . ." She glanced at Ling Yuan again, obviously too scared to go on.

The big hatchet man's face remained impassive. "You have not been harmed, have you?"

"Well . . . no. But I want to get out of here."

"At the moment, that is impossible. But no harm will come to you. You have Wong Duck's word on that, and mine as well. Wong Duck has suggested that while you are here, perhaps your time could be spent productively by tending to Mr. Browning's injuries."

"What? I'm no nurse. I'm a . . . Well, it's pretty obvious what I am, isn't it?"

Ling Yuan ignored that question. He gestured toward a door at the side of the room. "Through that door is a place where you can get a basin of water, as you have no doubt already discovered.

There are cloths in there as well. Please help Mr. Browning clean his injuries while I bring fresh garments for him to wear."

Conrad said, "Not, uh—"

Ling Yuan laughed. "You do not want to wear the garb of a hatchet man, my friend? Do not worry. As you have seen, Wong Duck prefers Western-style clothing to go with the Western name he has adopted. I will bring you something suitable."

With that, he inclined his head in what Conrad recognized as a gesture of farewell and left the room, closing the door firmly behind him.

Conrad was alone with the frightened girl. "You know who I am. What's your name?"

"Connie," she told him. "You're really Conrad Browning?"

"That's right."

"Well, I guess it won't hurt anything if I help out, like that big monster said."

Conrad wasn't sure he would describe Ling Yuan as a monster, but the man might look like that to her.

She went into the other room and came back with a basin of water and several clean white cloths. "Sit down on the divan. I'll see if I can get that dried blood off your face. What did they do, beat you?"

"Yes. Not Ling Yuan and his friends, though, if that's what you're thinking. They're the ones who rescued me."

She caught her bottom lip between her teeth

for a second as she sat down next to him and dipped a cloth in the water. "Our names are sort of alike, aren't they? Conrad and Connie?"

"I noticed that."

She started dabbing at the blood on his face. "My real name is Constance, but I like Connie better. Some of the girls who work at the Golden Gate don't use their real names. They make up something instead. But I never saw any point in trying to pretend I'm somebody I'm not, did you?"

He could tell she was talking mostly to keep her jagged nerves under control. Thinking about the time he had spent as Kid Morgan, he said, "I can understand why somebody would feel that way. Maybe they want to forget the lives they left behind."

"Or maybe they're just ashamed to admit they work in a saloon." She gave a defiant little toss of her head. "If anybody doesn't like who I am or what I do, they can just go—"

Conrad winced a little as she wiped the wet cloth over one of the scrapes on his forehead.

"Oh, I'm sorry," she exclaimed. "I didn't mean to hurt you."

"It's all right," he assured her. "It just stings a little."

"I wish we had some whiskey. I'd use it to clean all these scrapes and scratches." She giggled. "Of course, that would sting even more."

He was glad to see she was relaxing a little. "So you work at the Golden Gate."

"That's right. I was there earlier today when your father came in, then a bunch of those Chinamen busted in and all hell broke loose. I got knocked down in the rush to get away from the trouble, and I probably would have been trampled if it hadn't been for Mr. Morgan. He grabbed me and got me to safety." She paused and made a face. "Of course, then the Chinamen grabbed *him* and took him out of there, and they brought me along, too. But it could have been worse." Her voice dropped to a whisper, as if she was afraid someone was listening in on their conversation. "I think that big one they call Ling Yuan wanted to kill me, right then and there."

"Probably not." Although in all honesty Conrad had to admit he didn't really know what Ling Yuan was capable of. The men were criminals, after all. He figured they could be pretty ruthless.

When she had finished cleaning the blood off his face, Connie said, "You've got blood on that shirt, too, and Ling Yuan said he was bringing you some clean clothes. Why don't you go ahead and take it off? You may have some other wounds that need attention."

"I'm sure I'll be fine."

She smiled. "There's no reason for you to be shy, Mr. Browning. It's not like I'd see anything I haven't seen before. In fact, you could take *all* your clothes off and I wouldn't see anything I haven't—"

He held up a hand to stop her. "It's not that. I just don't think it's necessary."

"Maybe not . . . but we don't have to have a good reason for *everything* we do in this life, do we?"

For a long time after Rebel's death, Conrad had had no interest in women, not like that, anyway. He was in mourning, and even after a suitable period of time had passed, he still felt like he would be disloyal to her if he took up with another woman.

He had let his guard down with the redheaded bounty hunter, Lace McCall, and almost without realizing what was happening, he had developed genuine feelings for her. Then she had been wounded because of another scheme tracing back to Pamela Tarleton, and shortly afterward Conrad had found out about his missing children. He had been busy since then, but Claudius Turnbuckle was keeping tabs on Lace while she recuperated from her injuries. Conrad intended to get back in touch with her . . . someday.

In the meantime, he had too much on his mind to consider dallying with the saloon girl, no matter how attractive she was.

The door opened and Ling Yuan came back in carrying an expensive black suit. "Appropriate to wear to a party such as the one you will attend this evening, according to Wong Duck." He held out the clothes to Conrad, who took them and agreed with the assessment.

Ling Yuan turned to Connie. "You will come with me."

Instantly, her fear was back. "What are you going to do with me?"

"You will be taken to Wong Duck's home and will continue to be his guest there."

"I thought this was his house," Conrad said.

Ling Yuan shook his head. "This is his place of business."

"I . . . I don't want to go," Connie said. "I want to stay with Mr. Browning."

"You can't do that," Conrad told her. "I have places to go."

She pouted. "And I won't fit in there, will I?"

"It's not that. It might be dangerous for you. Lannigan will be there, and if he sees you with Frank and me, he'd likely think you'd betrayed him. You wouldn't want that, would you?"

The way she paled at the thought gave Conrad his answer.

"All right," she said reluctantly. "If you think it'll be safe for me to go with this Wrong Duck."

"That's Wong Duck," Ling Yuan said in a stiff voice.

Conrad smiled. "I think the lady knows that." He took Connie's hand. "Thank you for helping me. Maybe I'll see you again later on."

"I hope so." She sounded like she meant it.

Ling Yuan ushered her out of the room. Conrad stripped off his filthy clothes and put on the clean white shirt, the black trousers, the vest, and the black coat. He tied the silk cravat he found in the breast pocket of the jacket and fastened it down with an ivory-headed stick pin.

Ling Yuan came back and handed him a small revolver that Conrad recognized as the Smith & Wesson .38 he had bought a couple days earlier.

"I found it on the docks last night where Lannigan's men captured you," the big hatchet man explained. "You must have lost it during the struggle."

Conrad checked the loads in the gun, then slipped it into his waistband where the suit coat would conceal it. "Much obliged. I'd lost track of it. All I knew was that I didn't have it anymore."

He ignored the dull headache he still had as Ling Yuan took him back to Diamond Jack's office. Stopping just inside the door, Conrad gave a surprised grunt when he saw his father wearing a suit every bit as elegant and expensive as the one he wore. "Never thought I'd see you decked out like that, Frank."

"Never thought anybody would ever catch me in one of these monkey suits, either. But Jack pointed out we might not get into that mansion where the party's going on if we showed up looking like we did. It's bad enough that face of yours looks like you've gone fifteen rounds with Gentleman Jim Corbett."

"Did you ever see Corbett fight?" Diamond Jack asked with interest from behind the desk.

Frank smiled and nodded. "Shoot, I was even the referee at one bout . . . but that's a long story and we don't have time for it right now."

"That's right," Conrad said. "We need to get to Madison Kimball's house. There's no way of knowing for sure how long Lannigan will be there."

"I have a carriage waiting for you," Diamond Jack said. "Don't worry, the driver is white, so he won't look out of place. I have a few of your people working for me, for situations such as this. Money, I've found, has no color other than green."

Conrad nodded. "We appreciate all your help."

"Remember . . . should Dex Lannigan not survive this night, I would feel the spirits of my ancestors smiling upon me."

"I can't guarantee that," Conrad said, "but if Lannigan doesn't tell me what I want to know, there's a good chance those ancestors of yours will be grinning before the night is over."

Chapter 26

The big house on Nob Hill, one of many in the exclusive neighborhood, was lit up brilliantly. Dozens of carriages and buggies gleaming with expensive brasswork sat parked in the curving driveway running in front of the porticoed entranceway. Conrad had been to many places like that. He had been a fixture at the lush, lavish parties given by his mother and also at the parties thrown by her millionaire friends.

Looking at the Kimball mansion as he and Frank swung down from the carriage Diamond Jack had provided, Conrad was struck by the thought that normally he would have preferred to be in the high country somewhere, watching an eagle wheel through the blue sky, or out in the lonely vastness of the desert where a man could truly find peace. That realization brought home to him exactly how much he had changed over the past few years.

But the man who might be able to tell him where

to find his missing children was inside the mansion, so at that precise moment in time, there was nowhere else he would rather be.

Frank tugged at his cravat and sighed. "I don't see how some fellas wear these dadgum things all the time. Feels like somebody's about to slip a black hood over my head and drop me through a trapdoor in a gallows floor."

"It's not *that* bad," Conrad said. "And stop pulling at it. We're supposed to look like we belong here, remember?"

Frank stopped fidgeting with his cravat and patted the slight bulge under the jacket at his waist. That prompted Conrad to touch the .38 tucked away in his waistband, even though he could feel the weight of the gun. He took a deep breath and blew it out. "Let's go."

They walked to the door, where a man in butler's livery stopped them. "I need to see your invitation, sir," he told Conrad.

The invitation was still in his suite at the Palace Hotel, Conrad realized. He hadn't thought to retrieve it. "I'm afraid I don't have it with me," he said easily, "but if you have a list of invited guests, I'll be on it. Conrad Browning."

"And how might I be certain you are indeed who you say you are, sir?" the butler asked with a trace of a sneer on his face.

Conrad reined in the annoyance he felt at the man's attitude. Considering his battered, beard-stubbled appearance, he supposed he couldn't blame the butler for being suspicious of him.

"Why don't you check with Mr. or Mrs. Kimball?" he suggested. "Both of them are personally acquainted with me."

"I'm sorry, sir, but I couldn't think of disturbing them while they're occupied with their guests."

Conrad was torn between the urge to punch the stuffed shirt in the face and the impulse to pull out his gun and force his way in. Thankfully, he didn't have to do either of those things. At that moment, a familiar husky voice called, "Conrad! There you are. I was beginning to think you weren't going to make it."

He looked past the butler and saw Francis Carlyle coming toward him. The newspaper columnist was quite attractive in a dark green gown that set off her eyes. Conrad wasn't surprised to see her there. Despite having a job, Mrs. Carlyle was still a member of the society circles about which she wrote for the *Chronicle*. Of course the Kimballs had invited her so they could get a favorable write-up in the paper.

Conrad smiled. "Hello, Francis."

The butler turned to her. "Do you know this man, Mrs. Carlyle?"

"Of course I do. He's Conrad Browning." Mrs. Carlyle slapped the butler on the arm. "Now get out of the way and let him and his friend in."

The servant rolled his eyes, but he moved aside.

Conrad and Frank walked into a foyer with a beautiful parquet floor.

Mrs. Carlyle looked Frank up and down with obvious interest. "Who's this?"

Frank glanced at Conrad, who thought he saw a hint of desperation in his father's eyes. Even given the seriousness of the situation, Conrad had to suppress a chuckle. "This is Frank Morgan. An old friend of mine."

"Not that old." Mrs. Carlyle took Frank's hand. "Morgan, Morgan . . . There's something familiar about that name. You're not related to J.P. Morgan, are you?"

"Not that I know of," Frank said.

"Well, it'll come to me." She moved between Conrad and Frank and linked arms with both. "Come with me. I'll show you around. You've been here before, of course, Conrad, but it's been a while."

"Yes, it has." He lowered his voice as they moved into a huge, fancy ballroom filled with men in sober suits and women in glittering gowns. "You remember that I'm here to see Dex Lannigan."

"Of course," Mrs. Carlyle replied. Still smiling, she nodded to partygoers they passed. "I'm taking you to him. By the way, what happened to your face? You look like you got caught in a threshing machine." The reference was a reminder of her humble beginnings.

Conrad said, "It's a long story, and I'll make sure you and Jessup Nash get all the details later."

"If you decide to leave Nash out of it, I won't argue with you." Before Conrad could respond to that, Mrs. Carlyle stopped and nodded her head. "Over there, under that big painting of Madison and Roberta . . . that's Lannigan and his wife Winifred."

Conrad tried not to be too obvious about staring at him. The man was tall and rather rawboned, with an angular face and white hair that was somewhat premature for his age, which Conrad put around forty. The woman standing next to him, smiling radiantly in a light blue gown, was about ten years younger, with a pile of lustrous black curls on her head and a richly curved body that filled out her gown nicely. She was pretty rather than beautiful and had a sweet look about her face. She didn't strike Conrad as the sort who would be married to a powerful criminal . . . but he supposed there was no particular type for doing such a thing.

Lannigan was talking to several well-dressed men while his wife stood by smiling pleasantly. Conrad kept drawing his eyes back to her for some reason. Leaning closer to Francis Carlyle he asked, "Lannigan's wife's name is Winifred, you said?"

"That's right."

"Was he already married to her when he bought the Golden Gate and started working his way into San Francisco society?"

"Why, I don't really know. I might be able to find out for you."

Conrad nodded. "If you could do that, I'd appreciate it." He wasn't sure why he was so curious about Winifred Lannigan, but he had learned to follow his hunches.

"Why don't you and Mr. Morgan wait over there for a few minutes?" Mrs. Carlyle suggested, pointing to a small alcove. "I'm assuming you don't want to talk to Lannigan just yet?"

"That's right."

On the way from the crowded ballroom, Conrad snagged a couple glasses of champagne from a passing waiter who carried a tray full of them. Frank took the delicately stemmed glass Conrad handed him and frowned. "I never cared much for this fizzy water."

"Just sip it. We'll look more out of place if we're not drinking, and we already look odd enough, what with my battered face and your obvious hatred of that suit and cravat."

Already Conrad had spotted quite a few people who looked familiar to him, even though he didn't remember their names. Some might remember him, though, so he avoided conversation by stepping into the alcove.

He didn't want word spreading that Conrad Browning was in attendance. That news might make its way to Lannigan's ear, and Conrad didn't want to ruin the surprise fate held in store for the saloon owner.

While Frank sipped his champagne, Conrad used the glass to help shield the bruises and scrapes on his face from view. He looked around for Francis Carlyle, but the woman had disappeared into the crowd.

"Conrad? Conrad Browning, is that you?" another woman's voice asked.

Conrad had no choice but to look over and smile at Roberta Kimball, the hostess of the night's affair. She was an elegantly beautiful middle-aged woman with honey-colored hair only lightly touched with gray. She gasped quietly as she got a better look at Conrad's face. "Dear Lord, what happened to you?"

"Just some unpleasant business that has no bearing on this party," Conrad lied. He leaned closer and kissed Mrs. Kimball on the cheek. "It's wonderful to see you again."

"And you, too, of course. When Francis Carlyle told me you were in town, I knew I had to have you here so all your old friends could see you again. Oh, Conrad, I'm so sorry—"

He held up a hand to stop her. "I know. I appreciate that, Roberta."

"After the tragedy, you should have come back here. We would have taken care of you."

Conrad nodded. "I thought it best to keep busy."

In his case, keeping busy had meant tracking down the men who had kidnapped and murdered Rebel and finding out the truth from them, the truth that ultimately had led him to Pamela Tarleton. He had kept busy, all right . . . busy killing.

"I don't believe I'm acquainted with this gentleman," Roberta said as she turned to Frank.

"Allow me to introduce an old friend of mine, Frank Morgan. I hope it's all right I brought him along this evening. Frank, this is Mrs. Kimball, our hostess."

"I'm mighty pleased to meet you, ma'am," Frank said with a polite nod.

"Of course it's all right, Conrad. Mr. Morgan, please make yourself at home."

"Yes, ma'am. Much obliged."

She frowned slightly, as if his manner puzzled her, but before she could say anything else, Francis Carlyle reappeared. "Roberta, you simply must go set Madison straight. He insists it was two years ago you made that voyage to Hawaii, instead of three."

Mrs. Kimball shook her head. "I swear, poor Madison is getting so forgetful. Excuse me, Conrad, Mr. Morgan. Please, enjoy the party."

"We will," Conrad told her.

Once Mrs. Kimball had moved away into the crowd, Francis Carlyle said quietly, "I found out what you wanted to know, Conrad. Lannigan and his wife were married shortly after he bought the Golden Gate. She's a widow from somewhere back east."

"She doesn't hardly look old enough to be a widow," Conrad said.

"Widowhood can happen any time. In her case, she didn't just get a husband, she got a new father for her children."

"Children?" Conrad repeated. A hollow feeling suddenly spread through his stomach.

"That's right. She has two. They were babies at the time, actually, so it must not have been very long since her husband passed away."

"Two . . . children." Conrad's voice sounded strange in his ears, muffled by the sudden pounding of his pulse inside his head.

"That's right. A boy and a girl." Francis Carlyle paused. "Someone told me they're twins."

Chapter 27

Frank's hand closed around Conrad's arm to steady him. "Are you all right, son?"

"Son?" Mrs. Carlyle repeated.

Conrad had never been the sort who would pass out at unexpected news, but for a second the ballroom had spun crazily around him. No, not just the ballroom, he thought. The whole world had tilted off its axis and was turning the wrong way.

His children—*his children!*—had spent the past three years living with a vicious criminal. Conrad had thought all along Pamela had hidden the twins. But she hadn't. She had merely disguised them as the children of that woman Winifred, that supposed "widow" from back east. Conrad had no doubt she was actually the nurse who had accompanied Pamela and the twins from Boston. She had been paid off to marry Lannigan and pretend to be the children's mother. Everything was shockingly clear.

"My God, Conrad, you look like you've seen a ghost," Mrs. Carlyle said. "What's going on here? What's so special about the Lannigan twins?"

"They've taken his name?" Conrad grated.

"That's right. I think he legally adopted them."

Conrad dragged in a deep breath and forced himself to steady his nerves. "Thank you, Mrs. Carlyle. You've been a big help to me."

"Oh, no. You don't get off that easily. I want answers, Conrad, and I want them now."

"Sorry," he muttered. He pulled his arm loose from Frank's grip and started across the room toward Lannigan. Behind him, he heard Mrs. Carlyle ask Frank what in the world was going on, but Frank didn't answer. He maneuvered through the crowd after Conrad.

Spooked by the look on Conrad's face people stepped out of his way, opening a lane across the big room that led straight to Dex Lannigan. Conversations died away and a strained silence spread in Conrad's wake. He saw Lannigan look up and recognize him. Stunned surprise settled over the man's face.

It didn't last long. Lannigan hadn't risen to power by being easily startled. His expression hardened as he put a hand on his wife's shoulder and moved her behind him so he stood between her and Conrad. Conrad had to give the man credit for trying to protect the woman he was married to, even though she was a lying, mercenary bitch.

All eyes in the room were on them when Conrad stopped about four feet from Lannigan. "You know why I'm here."

Lannigan tried to act ignorant. "I do? I don't even know who you are, friend, let alone what you want. You look like you've been through the wringer, though. How about a drink?"

"I want my children," Conrad said.

That brought a tiny whimper from the woman behind Lannigan. The saloon owner's jaw tightened. "I don't know what you're talking about, mister."

"My children," Conrad repeated. "The twins. Frank and Vivian. Pamela Tarleton stole them from me and gave them to you."

Lannigan tried to remain calm and suave, but the man's control was developing cracks. Conrad was barely able to keep his own emotions in check.

"It's true that my wife and I are the proud parents of twins, but they're not yours," Lannigan forced out. "And they're not named Frank and Vivian. Their names are David and Rachel."

"And you're their father?" Conrad snapped.

Everyone in the room was hanging on every word.

Lannigan managed to smile. "Well, actually . . . no. My wife's first husband . . . her late husband . . .

fathered them. But I love them and feel like they're mine, so I've adopted them. They *are* mine."

It was all Conrad could do not to pull the Smith & Wesson and put a .38 slug between the man's eyes. Forcing himself to stay calm, he shook his head.

"They're not yours, and they're not hers. I'm their father, and Pamela Tarleton was their mother."

That brought some gasps of surprise from the crowd. Many of the people knew what had happened between Conrad and Pamela, even if they'd never met her. The grapevine of high-society gossip extended from coast to coast.

Conrad's words also brought an anguished cry from Winifred Lannigan. "No!" She stepped around her husband. "Stop that!" she shouted at Conrad. "Stop saying that! David and Rachel are *mine!* Don't you think I know whether or not I gave birth to my own children?"

The pain and anger on her face and in her voice was convincing, but Conrad didn't believe it. "You were paid to lie," he said coldly. "Pamela set this all up. She gave Lannigan the money to buy the Golden Gate Saloon, and she paid you to marry him and pretend the children were yours. But we all know that's not true. You stole my son and my daughter from me . . . *and I'll have them back.*"

So much for subtlety. So much for trying to get Lannigan alone and forcing him to talk. Everything had blown up, right out in the open. Conrad hadn't intended to go that way, but when he found out Lannigan and Winifred were passing the twins off as their own, the emotions running unchecked through him were too strong to resist. They had overwhelmed him, and he let himself be carried along on the wave.

Winifred's furious glare suddenly crumpled into sobs. She turned to her husband and buried her face against his chest as she shuddered and pleaded, "Make him stop saying those awful things, Dex. Make him stop!"

Lannigan patted her awkwardly on the back. "Don't worry, dear. I'll handle this." He looked at Conrad. "I'm still not sure who you are, mister, but I think you'd better leave. Otherwise I'll be forced to summon the authorities."

Conrad laughed. "Go ahead and call them. Call the police, and I'll tell them all about how you tried to have me killed, and when that didn't work, your men shanghaied me onto a ship bound for China with a shipment of rifles you're smuggling to the warlords! So go ahead, Lannigan. Summon the authorities."

A hand plucked tentatively at Conrad's sleeve. He looked into the pale face of Roberta Kimball. "Please, Conrad. I can tell how upset you are, but . . . is it really necessary to do this here?"

"I'm sorry," he told her. "I didn't set out to ruin your party. I really didn't. But when I heard how these two liars had stolen my children—"

That set off another round of bawling from

Winifred, whose sobs had subsided to sniffles until Conrad repeated his accusation.

"That's enough," Lannigan snapped. He tightened an arm around his wife's shoulders. "We're leaving—"

Conrad reached under his coat and drew the .38. "No, you're not," he warned. "Not until we've settled this."

That was just about the worst thing he could have done, he realized a second later when he heard Frank say behind him, "Conrad, look out!"

A gun roared somewhere in the ballroom.

Of course Lannigan wouldn't have come without guards, Conrad thought as panic erupted. Women screamed, men shouted curses, and everybody scattered . . .

Except the men wearing the red jackets of waiters, who charged across the ballroom with guns in their hands. Lannigan's men working the party so they would be on hand in case of trouble.

Trouble such as the real father of the children Lannigan claimed as his own showing up and pulling a .38.

Lannigan grabbed Winifred and shoved her behind him again, then lunged at Conrad and grabbed the wrist of his gun hand, twisting it so the Smith & Wesson pointed at the fancy chandeliers dangling from the ceiling. Conrad tried to wrench his arm free, but Lannigan hung on stubbornly with both hands. Conrad smashed a punch with his left hand into Lannigan's body. Lannigan grunted in pain but didn't let go.

A few feet away, Frank had whirled around to meet the threat from the saloon owner's hired guns and keep them away from Conrad. His Colt was in his hand, but there were too many innocent people in the way. He held his fire.

Suddenly a gap appeared in the crowd, and two of Lannigan's men blasted shots at Frank when they spotted him holding a gun. The slugs whistled past, one on each side of his head. His Colt thundered in return as he squeezed off three shots so fast they sounded like one long roar. One of the gunmen doubled over and spun around as he clutched at his bullet-torn gut. The other collapsed as his thighbone, shattered by one of Frank's bullets, gave out under him.

The exchange of shots made the panic in the ballroom worse as everybody headed for the doors.

Everybody except the struggling Conrad and Lannigan, the screaming Winifred, and Frank and the gunmen, who continued swapping lead as Frank overturned a table and knelt behind it for cover. Bullets chewed splinters from the heavy table but didn't penetrate it.

Conrad hooked another punch into Lannigan's body, causing him to loosen his grip. Conrad tore his gun hand free and slashed the .38 across Lannigan's face, opening a gash in the saloon owner's forehead and causing him to take a stumbling step backward.

Winifred stopped screaming, picked up a chair, and smashed it down over Conrad's head as he turned toward her. He was taken by surprise and disoriented for a second although the chair was lightweight, a spindly-legged thing that didn't have a lot of impact as it shattered. Using one of the broken chair legs she still clutched in her hand, Winifred hit him again. The blow landed solidly against Conrad's skull just above his left ear.

If he hadn't already endured so much punishment in the past twenty-four hours, he could have shrugged it off, but skyrockets exploded in his head and the room started spinning. The dizziness made him lose his balance. As he staggered to the side, Lannigan tackled him, and they crashed to the floor. Conrad lost his grip on the .38. It went sliding away across the brilliantly polished hardwood.

As Conrad struggled to regain his wits, Lannigan pummeled him viciously. The man panted in his ear, "Why . . . won't . . . you . . . just . . . *die!*"

Conrad got a hand up, and chopped at Lannigan's face. Using his other hand he grabbed Lannigan's collar and hauled him to the side. He swung another punch, burying his fist in Lannigan's midsection. Breathing heavily, both men came to their knees and slugged at each other.

The weight that suddenly landed on Conrad's back drove him forward. Winifred wrapped her arms around his neck and shouted, "I've got him! I've got him!"

Not for long. Conrad surged to his feet and slung her away from him. She cried out as she slid across the floor just like the Smith & Wesson had a few moments earlier.

That startled cry turned into a shriek of pain as she slid into the line of fire between Frank and the hired guns. She rolled onto her side and clutched at her right arm, which had been creased by one of the bullets flying back and forth.

"Winifred!" Lannigan bellowed to his gunmen, "Hold your fire! Hold your fire!"

Conrad scrambled after the .38. As he bent down to grab the gun Lannigan moved like a man possessed and lashed out with a kick that caught Conrad on the jaw. Conrad saw it coming and jerked his head aside, preventing the kick from shattering his jaw or breaking his neck. It sent him flying backward, leaving him too stunned to move after he landed.

Lannigan scooped up his wounded wife into his arms. "Cover us!" he barked at his men. "We're getting out of here!"

Still firing, the gunmen leaped up and formed a line to shield Lannigan as he dashed toward the door with Winifred in his arms. Frank crouched lower behind the bullet-pocked table and held his fire. He didn't try to bring Lannigan down. There was too great a chance of hitting the woman.

Conrad rolled over onto his stomach, pushed himself up a little, and shook his head groggily in an attempt to clear away some of the cobwebs clogging his vision. As his eyesight cleared, he saw Lannigan disappear through the front door with Winifred. The gunmen retreated as well, shooting as they went to keep Frank pinned down. The last of them darted through the door, and a silence fell over the ballroom.

Frank hurried over to Conrad and helped him to his feet. "Are you all right?"

"Yeah. Just shaken up a little. And mighty tired of getting hit on the head and kicked in the gut." Conrad clutched Frank's arm. "Lannigan got away. Now that he knows I know about the twins, he'll probably head for his house and try to fort up there."

Frank nodded. "Either that or take his wife and the kids and get out of town while he has some of his bought-and-paid-for lawdogs take care of you."

That thought shook Conrad. "If he tries to have me arrested and locked up as a dangerous lunatic, after tonight the police will probably believe him."

"I reckon after everything you've gone through, nobody could blame you for acting a mite loco—"

"Yes, they will," Conrad cut in. "This is San Francisco, not Dodge City. You can't just bust into a society party and start waving guns around. Frank, we have to get out of here."

Frank nodded. "If we can catch up to Lannigan and get our hands on those kids, maybe we can get to the bottom of this. Come on."

They started toward a rear door, figuring it would be safer to go out that way. Before they reached it, Francis Carlyle stepped out from where she had taken cover. "Conrad!"

"Mrs. Carlyle, are you all right?" He paused for a moment.

"I'm fine. That's what this was all about? Lannigan's children?"

"My children."

"Can you prove it?"

"Give me enough time and I can. Or rather, Claudius Turnbuckle can."

"I believe that. What a great story! And it's all mine, because Jessup Nash isn't here! What are you going to do now?"

"Get my kids back," Conrad said. "Settle with Lannigan."

"You'd better hurry, then, because the police will be here any minute."

Conrad nodded. "Thanks for your help."

"No need to thank me! Once I write this story, they'll forget all about Nellie Bly!"

Conrad and Frank made their way out of the mansion, twisting through hallways, pounding through a kitchen, and emerging into a garden at the back of the house. The carriage Diamond Jack had provided was still parked in front, but they would be running too great a risk of being caught by the police if they tried to reach it. They would have to find some other way to get to Lannigan's house.

With a sinking feeling, Conrad realized he didn't

even know where that was. He knew the location
of the Golden Gate Saloon in the Barbary Coast,
but that was all.

"Frank," he said miserably, "I don't know where
to—"

A large, menacing shadow loomed over them,
and they turned swiftly, bringing their guns up.

Chapter 28

"Mr. Browning, Mr. Morgan," the familiar gravelly tones of Ling Yuan said. "Please come with me."

Conrad wasn't surprised to see the big hatchet man in the fancy garden behind the Nob Hill mansion. Somehow, he had a habit of popping up wherever he was most needed.

But that didn't stop Conrad from asking, "What in blazes are you doing here?" as he lowered his gun.

"Wong Duck sent me to report on what happened here tonight," Ling Yuan replied. "I heard shots, then saw Lannigan, his wife, and a number of gunmen pretending to be waiters flee from the mansion. My feeling was that if you and Mr. Morgan survived the battle, you would take your leave this way, rather than risk running into the police."

"Your hunch was right about that," Conrad said. "I found out Lannigan's been pretending my children belong to him and his wife." He caught his breath. "Wait a minute! Your boss knew I was looking for my kids, and with the way he keeps tabs on Lannigan, he must've known that Lannigan and his wife have twins. He must have put that together, but he didn't tell me about it. Why would he keep that from me?"

"It is not my place to question Wong Duck's actions or his motives," Ling Yuan said.

"Never mind," Conrad snapped. "I can figure it out for myself. He was counting on me losing my head when I found out about the twins. He thought I'd react by starting a fight, which is exactly what happened, and he hoped Lannigan would be killed in the ruckus. But it didn't work out that way."

Ling Yuan didn't comment on that theory. "We must go. The police will be here soon."

It was true. Conrad heard clanging bells on the police wagons as they approached the mansion. "All right, but Diamond Jack and I are going to have some words about this when it's all over."

Ling Yuan didn't say anything. He just gestured with a ham-like hand at the path that ran through the garden.

"Come on, Conrad," Frank urged. "I'm betting Ling Yuan knows how to get to Lannigan's house."

"Of course," the big hatchet man said.

"Then you're right," Conrad said with a curt nod. "We have to go."

The three of them hurried along the path until

they came to a brick wall about eight feet tall. With Ling Yuan's help, Conrad and Frank clambered over it. The hatchet man was able to pull himself up and over without any assistance. They dropped onto one of the steep, narrow streets and quickly vanished into the darkness.

"You realize I'm risking my reputation for you," Claudius Turnbuckle said as he handed the gunbelt to Conrad. He had gone to the Palace Hotel to get it after a Chinese messenger had shown up on his doorstep with a note from Conrad. Ling Yuan had arranged that without much difficulty. "The police are looking for you."

"Am I wanted for anything?" Conrad asked as he buckled on the gunbelt and felt the familiar, comforting weight of the Colt revolver in the holster. He had discarded the cravat but still wore the suit. Its dark color made it easier for him to blend into the shadows outside the big estate belonging to Dex Lannigan.

"No, no charges have been brought against you yet," Turnbuckle said. "The police merely want to question you about the shooting at the Kimball mansion. But you can't expect to disrupt such an affair and have bullets whizzing around the heads of the most important people in San Francisco without getting into trouble for it."

Frank said, "The shooting wasn't our idea. Lannigan's men started that particular ball."

"That may well be true. Still, I expect complaints to be filed against Conrad, at the very least."

"But not by Lannigan."

Turnbuckle shook his head. "No, despite what you said he threatened, he won't go to the police. He can't stand to have the authorities delving too deeply into his business, even his personal affairs."

Arturo had accompanied Turnbuckle from the hotel when he found out the lawyer was engaged in an errand for Conrad. The four men stood in deep shadows under some trees along the street a block away from the Lannigan house. Ling Yuan was scouting around in an attempt to find out just what sort of situation they were facing.

Arturo said, "This fellow Lannigan probably has at least a dozen hardened killers in there to protect him and his family. You can't hope to simply break in and take the children from him."

"Ling Yuan said we could get as many men from Diamond Jack as we need," Conrad replied, "but that's too dangerous. We can't risk the children being hurt in an all-out battle like that." His mouth twisted in a grimace. "Anyway, I'm not sure I trust Diamond Jack anymore, if I ever did. He knew where the kids were, and he didn't tell me. He was using me to kill Lannigan, so his hands wouldn't be dirty."

"He's a crook, after all," Frank said. "Can't expect the hombre to be doing something out of the goodness of his heart."

"Maybe not, but I still don't like it."

Turnbuckle pulled a handkerchief from his pocket and mopped his forehead, even though it wasn't a particularly warm night. In fact, the air had a slight chill in it, made worse by the dampness of the fog rising from the bay. "If you don't intend to attack the house, what *are* you going to do?"

"I was thinking that if Frank and I can get in there and get our hands on the kids—"

"You'll be charged with kidnapping and sent to prison, more than likely," Arturo said.

Conrad shook his head. "The woman really seemed to care for them. I think we can persuade her to tell the truth. If she'll admit to the deal she made with Pamela, and to the deal Lannigan made, the police won't have anything against us. The twins are *my* children, and I have a right to them."

"What will wind up happening is the whole thing will be thrown into the courts," Turnbuckle said. "The children won't be turned over to you immediately, Conrad. This is going to take time."

"Well, at least they won't be living with a criminal like Lannigan anymore," Conrad said. "And eventually everything will come out and they'll be with me."

"I wish I had your faith," Arturo said. "In my experience, most often anything that *can* go wrong *will* go wrong."

"Not tonight," Conrad said with grim determination.

Before they could discuss the situation further, Ling Yuan came trotting out of the shadows.

"There is a carriage house in back," he reported without any preamble. "Something is going on in there. I believe a team is being hitched to a vehicle, and several horses are being saddled as well."

Conrad bit back a curse. "Lannigan's not forting up here. He's about to make a run for it."

"So it appears to me," Ling Yuan agreed.

"We have to stop him." Conrad felt a sense of desperation growing inside him. "Where's he going to go?"

"Lannigan has a hunting lodge in the mountains east of here, on the other side of the bay. He must think he and his family will be safer there."

"It's not his family," Conrad snapped. "Claudius, you and Arturo stay here. Ling Yuan, take Frank and me to this carriage house."

Arturo began, "Sir, are you sure you should—"

"I haven't come this far and gone through so much to let them slip away from me now." Conrad's voice trembled a little from the strain he felt. "Not when I'm this close."

"Then we'd best not waste any time," Frank said.

He and Conrad followed Ling Yuan toward the rear of the estate that sprawled across a hillside overlooking the bay. The view would be pretty during the day, but there was nothing much to see at night. The fog blotted out the lights of the towns on the other side of the water.

A brick wall surrounded the house and its grounds, much like the one around the Kimball mansion. Ling Yuan led Conrad and Frank to a wrought-iron gate in that wall. On the inside was a drive made of crushed stone that ran to the carriage house. Yellow light glowed through the windows.

Suddenly the big double doors in the front of the carriage house swung open. Light slanted out onto the drive. Two men on horseback trotted out, followed closely by the team pulling an enclosed carriage.

"They're coming!" Conrad said. "We have to stop them."

"Best split up," Frank said. "We'll wait on opposite sides of this gate. Once they get it open, we can jump the carriage before it goes through."

That sounded like a good idea to Conrad. He motioned for Ling Yuan to go with him. They hurried to the left side of the gate and waited with their backs to the brick wall while Frank went to the right side and did likewise.

Hoofbeats pounded along the drive, coming closer. Conrad drew his gun. Chances were, Winifred Lannigan and the children were inside the carriage, so he and his companions would have to be very careful. They couldn't just blaze away at Lannigan's men. The risk was too great that a stray bullet might hit one of the twins. Every shot was going to have to be painstakingly aimed.

The men on horseback rode well ahead of the carriage. When they reached the gate, one of the riders swung down and went over to the wrought-iron barrier. A big key rattled in the lock, and with the creaking of hinges, the two sides of the gate swung outward.

Conrad moved fast, darting through the opening and taking by surprise the man who had unlocked the gate. The gun in Conrad's hand rose and fell, thudding down on the man's head. He collapsed, out cold.

Still mounted, the second man was ready for trouble. Muzzle flame spouted from the revolver in his hand. Conrad felt the heat of the bullet pass his face.

Frank's gun roared, and the man on horseback cried out, clutching his shoulder as he swayed in the saddle. The horse bolted, dumping him.

Inside the carriage, Dex Lannigan roared, "Run them down!"

The driver did his best to follow that order. He whipped the team into a hard gallop, making the carriage lurch back and forth as it barreled along the drive. Conrad thought about shooting one of the lead horses and piling up the team, but the carriage might overturn and crash. He couldn't risk it.

Several riders had been following the carriage, and they spread out to the sides, opening fire as they galloped toward the gate. Conrad and Frank returned those shots without having to worry about hitting the children.

One of the gunmen spilled out of the saddle with a hole bored in him, a slug from Frank's .45.

Another doubled over as one of Conrad's bullets struck him. He managed to stay mounted, but his horse veered off wildly. That left two men on horseback. They pulled back behind the racing carriage.

The vehicle was almost on top of Conrad and Frank. They had failed to stop it, and they had to leap aside to avoid being trampled by the charging team. As the carriage rolled through the gate, a large, dark shape soared into the air from the top of the wall, swooping down almost like a giant bird. Ling Yuan's daring leap carried him to the roof of the carriage. He crashed down on it and caught hold of the brass railing around the edge to keep from falling off.

Conrad lunged for the carriage, too, hoping to grab hold of the back and climb onto it, but a horse of a gunman struck him a glancing blow with its shoulder and knocked him off his feet. Bullets kicked up the crushed rock of the drive as they landed only inches away from him. He rolled away from the bullets and came up in a crouch, firing his Colt at the rider who had just tried to ventilate him. The man's arms went wide and he let out a gurgling scream as Conrad's bullet tore into his throat and blew out the back of his neck.

Frank had traded shots with the remaining rider, but none of the bullets had found their mark. The man left his saddle in a diving tackle that sent him and Frank crashing to the ground. They rolled over and over, wrestling with each other.

Despite no longer being a young man, the rugged life Frank Morgan had led meant he was still strong and fit. He got hold of his opponent's shirtfront and flung him to the side, then landed on top of him. Frank drove a knee into the man's belly and hooked a hard right fist into his face. The man tried to put up a fight, but he was no match for The Drifter. Frank hammered several punches into the man's face and body, and with a defeated sigh, the man went limp.

Frank came to his feet and followed as Conrad ran out through the open gate to stare along the street. He hoped to see the carriage a block or so away where Ling Yuan had stopped it, but the vehicle was gone.

"They got away," Conrad said in an agonized voice. "They're gone!"

Frank grabbed his arm. "Somebody's coming. Is that the Chinaman?"

Ling Yuan trotted up the street toward them. He held his upper left arm with his right hand. Dark worms crawled between his fingers. Conrad knew they were trails of blood.

"How bad are you hurt?" he asked as he and Frank hurried to meet the big hatchet man.

"It is nothing," Ling Yuan replied. "A bullet straight through my arm, and it did not strike the bone. But when Lannigan shot me while I was trying to get the reins away from the driver, it was enough to make me fall off the carriage."

"So they got away." Conrad tasted sour defeat in his mouth.

"But we know where they're headed, more than likely," Frank said. "That hunting lodge in the mountains. How do they get there?"

Ling Yuan's head came up. "The ferry across the bay. That would be the fastest route."

"Then let's get to that ferry. Maybe we can still stop them."

The three men ran toward the spot where they had left Claudius Turnbuckle and Arturo. Turnbuckle had come to the rendezvous in a buggy, and Conrad and Frank would use it.

Turnbuckle and Arturo emerged from the shadows under the trees. "Good Lord, what happened up there?" Turnbuckle asked anxiously. "We heard all the shooting and didn't know if you three were dead or alive!"

"We're alive," Conrad said, "but Lannigan got away with his wife and the twins."

"Blast it! What now?"

Conrad and Frank exchanged a glance. "Frank and I are going after them. We think they're going to take the ferry over to the other side of the bay. Lannigan's bound to be headed for that lodge of his."

"How do we get to the ferry landing from here?" Frank asked.

Quickly, Turnbuckle gave them directions. Conrad remembered enough about San Francisco to be fairly certain he could follow them without any trouble.

"Ling Yuan's wounded. Take care of that while Frank and I go after Lannigan."

"It is nothing," Ling Yuan insisted, but Conrad and Frank were already running toward the parked buggy half a block away. Conrad called over his shoulder, "We'll meet you at your office later, Claudius."

It was a wild ride up and down the hilly streets and across town toward the bay. Conrad handled the reins, and Frank hung on for dear life.

Through the fog, Conrad saw the lights on the clock tower of the Ferry Building at the Embarcadero and steered toward them. The wharf used by the big ferryboats that plied the waters of San Francisco Bay was lit up, too. During the day, several ferries steamed back and forth almost constantly between San Francisco and Oakland, but at night there was only one boat in use.

"I don't see the carriage," Conrad said as he wheeled the buggy onto the wharf.

"Maybe they didn't come here after all," Frank suggested.

"Where else could they go? Lannigan's on the run. He's not going to stay here in San Francisco."

Conrad brought the buggy to a lurching halt in front of a small building on the wharf where a light was burning. He jumped down and ran to the door. Frank was right behind him.

The building housed the small office of the

wharfmaster. The main offices of the ferry company were in the big building behind them. The man on duty was middle-aged and had a drooping mustache. He looked up from the paperwork spread out on his desk as Conrad and Frank burst into the little office.

"When's the next ferry?" Conrad demanded.

"Forty-five minutes from now."

Conrad couldn't suppress a groan of despair. "One just left, didn't it?"

"Ten minutes ago," the man confirmed. "You and your friend want tickets on the next one?"

"Was there a fancy carriage on board the one that just left?"

The man frowned. "Say, how'd you know that? Friends of yours? Sorry you missed 'em, if they were."

"No, not friends," Conrad choked out. "Family. Some of them, anyway." He slumped into an empty chair just inside the door, trying not to give in to the feelings that gripped him. If the ferry wouldn't be back for its next run for forty-five minutes, that meant it would be well over an hour before he and Frank could reach Oakland to pick up the trail, giving Lannigan plenty of time to make his getaway.

A glimmer of hope came to Conrad. He stood up and said to Frank, "Let's go."

"You don't want them tickets?" the mustachioed man asked.

Conrad stalked out without answering.

"Where are we headed?" Frank asked once they were outside.

"Back to Claudius's office. We have preparations to make."

A grin stretched across Frank's rugged face. "That fella Diamond Jack knows where Lannigan's lodge is, I'll bet. I reckon we're going hunting, aren't we?"

Conrad nodded as he took up the reins. "Yes. We're about to do some hunting."

Chapter 29

The Diablo Mountains, one of the Coastal Ranges, rose on the eastern side of San Francisco Bay, behind the settlements of Oakland and Berkeley. As mountains go, they weren't particularly tall or rugged, but their wooded slopes provided a haven for some of San Francisco's wealthiest citizens who wanted a place to get away from the city.

It was certainly appropriate they were named after the Devil, Conrad thought the next morning as he watched the far side of the bay come closer from the railing of the boat Claudius Turnbuckle had chartered. Dex Lannigan might not be the Devil himself, but he had made a diabolical deal with Pamela Tarleton.

Since they were leaving the city, Conrad was dressed for more rugged surroundings. He wore boots, jeans, and a buckskin shirt without any fancy fringe on it. A broad-brimmed brown Stetson was on his head. He had the Colt on his right hip, and the Smith & Wesson .38 tucked away in a holster at the small of his back. He had a Bowie knife sheathed on his left hip, and cradled a Winchester in his left arm.

Frank came up to the railing beside him. "Lannigan's liable to have the local law up there on his side. Remember, he has the San Francisco police convinced you're loco . . . and dangerous."

Conrad nodded. "I know." Claudius Turnbuckle had warned them about that earlier.

"Don't tell me where you're going," the lawyer had said. "I don't want to have to lie to the police if they question me again . . . and it's likely they will. The captain of the boat doesn't need to know, either. It's bad enough he can tell the authorities that he dropped you on the other side of the bay."

"Don't worry, Claudius," Conrad had assured him. "As far as you're concerned, you don't know a thing about what we're going to do."

"I'm not worried about myself. I just don't want to have to tell the police anything that will hurt your chances of getting those children away from Lannigan. For what it's worth, I'll be filing suit this morning seeking to have the adoption set aside as being illegal because of fraud, and asking that custody of the twins be awarded to you."

"How long will that take?" Conrad had asked.

Turnbuckle's silent shrug had been answer enough.

Frank said quietly, "If you get your hands on those kids, you aren't going back, are you?"

"To put them through a long, drawn-out court case where they might be considered wards of the state and forced to live in an orphanage until things were decided?" Conrad shook his head. "No. Claudius can fight it out in the courts. Little Frank and Vivian and I will be somewhere nobody can find us."

"You'll be making a fugitive out of yourself, and them, too," Frank pointed out.

"Do you think I should do things differently?" Conrad asked sharply.

"Don't go by me. I've been a fugitive plenty of times in my life. Just because the law is the law doesn't mean it's always right. But it *is* still the law, and it's not a good thing to have it after you."

"I'll risk it," Conrad said. "For the sake of those two youngsters, I'll risk anything."

Frank nodded. "Reckon I know how you feel." He had risked his own life for Conrad on numerous occasions.

The boat belonged to a fisherman Turnbuckle had represented in a court case. The man wasn't wealthy like most of Turnbuckle's clients, but the lawyer took cases like that from time to time. He had prevailed in court, and the fisherman owed him a favor. He had agreed to ferry Conrad and Frank across the bay and drop them off in a secluded cove south of Oakland. A pair of horses would be waiting there, also arranged by Turnbuckle.

There had been no sign of Ling Yuan or any of Diamond Jack's other men. Conrad figured the tong leader was sitting back and waiting to see what was going to happen.

The fishing boat chugged into the cove, close enough for the captain to run a board to the shore. He shook hands with Conrad and Frank. "I don't know what you fellas are up to, but I've got a hunch it's somethin' pretty important. Best of luck to you."

Conrad nodded. "Thanks, Captain."

Trees grew almost to the edge of the water. The pair of horses were tied up about twenty yards into the woods, as Turnbuckle had promised. Frank took the big bay, Conrad the thick-chested dun.

Ling Yuan had drawn them a map to Lannigan's hunting lodge. "You've been there before, spying on him, haven't you?" Conrad had asked.

"Wong Duck says one of the keys to defeating an enemy is first observing him."

Conrad wondered why Diamond Jack hadn't had Lannigan killed before now. He supposed it was because such an assassination might trigger an all-out war between the tongs and the white underworld of the Barbary Coast.

If, on the other hand, Lannigan were to be killed by a couple white men, because of something that had nothing to do with the saloon owner's rivalry with the tongs, then Diamond Jack could claim he'd had nothing to do with it. That might be enough to avoid an orgy of bloodshed that could seriously cripple both factions.

They came to a narrow trail that Ling Yuan had marked on the map. "Lannigan's place is about five miles up in the mountains," Conrad said. "This trail is supposed to lead us around behind it. According to Ling Yuan, Lannigan doesn't know it exists."

"I wouldn't count on that," Frank cautioned. "Lannigan struck me as being pretty sharp. I'm not sure he'd have a back door into his place that wasn't protected."

"We'll just have to be careful. This won't be the first time I've snuck into somewhere that was guarded, and I'll bet it won't be for you, either."

Frank smiled in the shadows underneath the trees. "You'd win that bet."

They rode on, following the trail that was so faint, sometimes it was hard to see, even for a veteran frontiersman like Frank. They didn't lose it, though, and their route gradually took them upward, higher into the mountains. The trees thinned out some but were still thick enough to provide cover. Because the route twisted back and forth to avoid natural obstacles, they wound up traveling much farther than five miles. Hours passed as they climbed toward their destination.

Eventually Conrad came out on a shoulder that curved around the mountainside. He reached a spot where he could dismount and crawl forward to look over the edge of a bluff. The roof of a sprawling, two-story log building nestled in the trees was visible below. That would be Lannigan's lodge, according to Ling Yuan's map. The place matched the hatchet man's description, right down to the small barn and corral off to one side. Several horses were in that corral, including the six matched blacks that made up the team for Lannigan's carriage. Conrad had no trouble recognizing the horses. They had almost trampled him the night before.

Two men armed with shotguns stood near the lodge's rear door. Conrad spotted two more roaming through the trees. He figured there would be more guards in front of the lodge, and maybe on the sides of the sprawling building. There were bound to be gunmen inside the lodge, too, along with Lannigan, Winifred, and the twins.

Conrad heard a footstep behind him. A harsh voice said, "I don't know who you are, mister, but if you move I'll blow your brains out. You work for that Browning bastard?"

"No, I *am* that Browning bastard."

The man behind him let out a startled curse. Over the sound of it, Conrad heard a sudden rush of footsteps, then the solid thud of gun butt striking skull. He rolled over and saw Frank lowering the limp body of an unconscious man to the ground. The man's rifle lay where it had fallen.

"Figured there would be somebody keeping an eye on this spot," Frank said. "You drew him out just like we thought you would. That was quite a risk you ran, though. He could've just shot you in the back."

Conrad stood up and shook his head. "No, I figured he'd be curious about who I was and try to take me prisoner. Are you sure there was just one guard?"

"Pretty sure. After we split up, I circled higher and got above this shoulder. Had a pretty good view of the hombre sneaking up on you. He appeared to be alone."

"All right." Conrad glanced at the sky. It had taken them most of the day to climb to the lodge, and night would be falling soon. "Once it's dark, we can climb down that bluff and try to make it into the house."

"Those shotgun-toters will probably have something to say about that."

Conrad grunted. "So will we."

Frank grinned and slapped Conrad on the shoulder. "It's good working with you again, son."

"Likewise." Conrad paused. "Just don't expect me to start calling you Pa."

Conrad and Frank kept a close watch all around them as they waited for night to fall. It was possible another guard might come to change places with the man Frank had knocked out and tied up. No one else showed up, though, so Conrad suspected the shift change had taken place not long before he and Frank had sprung their trap on the luckless gunman.

They were up high enough on the western slope of the mountain that the sea was visible in the distance. Finally the sun sank into the Pacific, turning everything green and gold for a brief moment of beauty and tranquility.

That couldn't last. It would be a night of blood and death, Conrad sensed. But as long as his children wound up safe, that was all that really mattered.

He checked his Colt and slid the revolver back in its holster, then did likewise with the .38. Frank did the same thing. They left their Winchesters with the horses. Whatever happened in the lodge would be close work.

"I didn't see any badges or uniforms on those men standing guard," Conrad said. "I think we can assume they're all hired guns working for Lannigan."

Frank nodded in agreement. "There's bound to be a trail leading a long way around. That'll be how the guards get up here. Once things have settled down, one of us can come back up and get the horses. Then we'll ride out on that road we spotted leading through the trees to the lodge."

Conrad nodded. His father was assuming both of them would live through what was about to happen, and he hoped that turned out to be the case. But if it didn't . . .

"Frank, if I don't make it out of here—"

Frank held up a hand to stop him. "I'll see that

those youngsters are taken care of. You don't even have to ask."

"I know."

"Same goes for me." Frank chuckled. "Just don't tell them too many wild stories about their gunslinging granddad."

"I'll keep 'em away from those dime novels," Conrad said with a laugh of his own.

Frank's tone was a lot more serious as he went on. "We may have to kill Lannigan and the rest of those varmints. I reckon you can live with that, though, the way you went after the men responsible for Rebel's death."

"Yeah. This is the last hand, Frank. Pamela's down to her last card."

"You realize you're talking about gambling with a dead woman."

"That's the way it's been all along. Pamela's twisted game. I just didn't realize it soon enough."

"If we get those kids back safe and sound, it's soon enough."

Conrad couldn't argue with that. He went to the edge of the bluff, which was steep but rugged enough a man could climb down it if he was careful, even in the dark. Brush grew here and there, which helped provide handholds.

The bluff was about fifty feet high. Conrad and Frank took their time descending it. They didn't want to dislodge any rocks and send them clattering down the slope to warn the guards. Stealth was more important than speed. They had all night to make their approach to the lodge.

When they reached the bottom at last, Conrad put his mouth next to Frank's ear and whispered, "We'll take the guards who are patrolling first. You go left, I'll go right."

"Got it," Frank whispered back. He had been good about letting the younger, less experienced man call the shots, Conrad thought. At the same time, he knew if he was about to do anything really stupid, Frank would stop him.

Maybe it was just a matter of great minds thinking alike, Conrad told himself with a faint smile as he catfooted through the darkness.

As he made his way through the trees toward the lodge, he paused every few feet to listen. After several minutes he heard the soft rustle of feet on pine needles. Standing stock-still, he waited until he was sure which direction the roaming guard was moving, then he slipped to the side so his path would intercept that of the gunman.

Drawing his Bowie knife from its sheath, Conrad stopped and pressed his back against the trunk of a tree. A moment later the guard walked past him, unaware that he was there.

That was bad luck for the guard. Conrad struck without warning, looping his left arm around the man's neck and jerking him backward. At the same time he drove the big knife into the guard's back. The deadly keen blade slid easily through flesh, slipped between the ribs, and into the guard's heart. Conrad's arm was clamped across the man's throat like a bar of iron. No sound could escape from the dying man's mouth. He crossed the divide in silence except for the thud of his shotgun hitting the ground when he dropped it, and that was muffled by the carpet of pine needles.

Once again he had killed a man in cold blood, Conrad thought as he lowered the limp corpse to the ground. A part of him regretted it, but the steel at his core knew it was necessary. Lannigan's hired gun would have killed him without blinking, blasting him to bits with that shotgun.

He damned Pamela Tarleton for setting the tragic events in motion. He damned her for making him the man he was. Then he grimaced and wiped the blade on the dead man's shirt. Pamela might bear some of the responsibility, but not all of it. Not by a long shot.

He supposed there had always been a killer inside him. He just hadn't known it, and it had taken a great tragedy to bring that killer out. Once it was over . . . once his children were with him . . . he had to put that part of himself away. He had to bury Kid Morgan once and for all.

Conrad shook off his reverie and moved toward the house. Frank should have taken care of the other roaming sentry, and they had to deal with the men guarding the door.

Trees around the back of the house had been cleared away for a distance of thirty or forty feet, and a couple lanterns hanging on each side of the door cast a yellow half circle of light over that area. Conrad couldn't get close enough to strike with the Bowie without being spotted, and he doubted his ability to throw the knife with enough power and accuracy to kill one of the guards. Even if he did, that would leave another guard to sound the alarm.

Suddenly, from the woods a man called, "Hey, Toby! Lunsford! Get out here! I caught somebody tryin' to sneak up on the place!"

That was the other patrolling guard, Conrad realized as a shock went through him.

From the sound of it, he had taken Frank prisoner.

Chapter 30

The guards by the door reacted instantly, running toward the trees, shotguns at the ready. Conrad moved fast, too, circling swiftly through the pines toward them. He had to help Frank, and it was a chance to deal with those two guards without having to approach them across the open ground.

The hired guns ran into the trees. Conrad heard one of them exclaim, "What the hell!" Then a heavy thump sounded just ahead of him. He darted around a tree and saw one of the guards trying to swing his scattergun around to aim it at a shadowy figure. Knowing the guard was an enemy, Conrad lifted his knife and brought the brass ball on the end of the handle down hard against the back of the guard's head.

The man grunted in pain and stumbled forward as the shotgun's twin barrels drooped toward the ground. The shadowy figure leaped forward, grabbed the barrels, and forced the muzzles into the dirt. His other fist smashed into the guard's face and knocked him loose from the weapon. The guard toppled to the ground, out cold.

"Good teamwork," Frank said.

Conrad frowned in surprise at his father. "I thought you'd been captured!"

"Yeah, well, that's what I wanted those fellas by the house to think. The idea came to me when I jumped the one who was patrolling out here. Instead of killing him, I put my Bowie to his throat and made him call out to those two and lure them out here. I walloped one with my gun. I thought maybe you'd show up to give me a hand, and sure enough—"

"Where's the other guard, the one you used as bait?"

Frank gestured toward a shape on the ground nearby. "Knocked out, tied up, and gagged. He won't give us any trouble. We'd better do the same with these two."

Working quickly, they cut strips from the guards' shirts and used them to bind the men securely, as well as for gags to keep them quiet. That left the back door of Lannigan's lodge unguarded.

Conrad and Frank took the pistols worn by the unconscious guards. Having extra shots without needing to reload might come in handy. They trotted through the lantern light to the door and pressed their backs to the wall as they listened for any sounds of alarm. Everything was quiet. Evidently their approach hadn't been noticed.

Conrad reached over and tried the latch. He swallowed a frustrated curse as it refused to budge. Looking over at Frank, he mouthed the word *Locked*. They would have to find another way in.

Frank leaned back and looked up. Conrad followed suit. The roof overhung the door and slanted up to darkened windows on the second floor. Frank pointed up with his thumb, then bent over and formed a stirrup with his hands. Conrad nodded. He weighed less, so it made sense for him to go first.

Putting a booted foot in Frank's hands, Conrad stepped up and reached for the overhang. Frank heaved him up. Conrad's hands closed over the edge, the rough shingles providing a good grip. He hauled himself up, and Frank pushed from below. Conrad cleared the edge and rolled onto the sloping roof.

Once he was there, he unbuckled his belt and slipped it out of the loops on his jeans. After wrapping the tongue end around his hand a couple times, he lowered the buckle end to Frank, who grasped it with both hands and started climbing up the wall. In a few seconds, Conrad was able to reach down with his other hand and catch hold of his father's arm. With grunts of effort, he pulled Frank onto the roof.

They sprawled on the shingles for a few moments to catch their breath, then Conrad sat up, put his belt back on, and moved on hands and knees up to the nearest window. The room on the other side of the glass was dark and he hoped unoccupied. He tried to raise the window, but it wouldn't move. It was fastened shut.

Frank went to one of the other second-floor windows and tried it, then looked over at Conrad and shook his head. Chances were, they were all that way. Conrad took off his hat and drew his gun. Using the hat to muffle the sound, he rapped the gun butt sharply against one of the panes, just hard enough to crack the glass without shattering it. He pouched the iron, put his hat back on, and took out his knife. He got the tip of the blade into the crack and started working it back and forth gently.

The work was tedious, but it was important to be as quiet as possible. After several minutes, he managed to loosen a big piece of glass enough that he could get his fingers into the crack around it. Being careful not to slice his flesh open on the sharp edges, he worked the piece of glass back and forth some more and finally pried it loose from the window.

Conrad set the glass aside and reached into the room through the opening he had created. He felt around at the bottom of the window until he found the catch that held it closed. Thankfully, the window hadn't been nailed shut. He slid the catch over, pulled his arm out, and eased the window up.

Conrad went through the window first, with Frank following him.

Once inside the house, it was a matter of finding

the children and making sure they were safe before dealing with Lannigan and the rest of the man's hired guns. The odds were still steep against them, but that was nothing new for Conrad Browning and Frank Morgan.

Walking softly in hopes the floor wouldn't creak under their weight, they went to the door, which they could see dimly in the faint lantern light filtering into the room from outside. It appeared to be a bedroom, but no one was sleeping there at the moment. Conrad tried the door. The knob turned easily in his hand. He and Frank stepped into a corridor.

A staircase landing was a few yards to their right. The stairs led down into a big room filled with heavy, rustic furniture dominated by a huge fireplace with a massive stone mantel. A fire crackled in that fireplace, casting a garish, flickering glow over the man who stood in front of it with a drink in his hand.

Dex Lannigan.

Conrad looked around the room. He didn't see Winifred or the children, or any of Lannigan's hired killers, for that matter. The man appeared to be alone in the room. The way Lannigan stared pensively into the flames in the fireplace seemed to confirm that hunch.

Conrad and Frank glanced at each other. Taking Lannigan prisoner would give them the upper hand. They could force him to turn over the children, then take him as a hostage until they were safely away from the lodge.

Moving in absolute silence the way living dangerous lives had taught them, Conrad and Frank started down the stairs.

They had just reached the bottom when Lannigan turned abruptly from the fireplace toward them. They lifted their guns, but Lannigan didn't seem to be surprised to see them. He didn't drop his drink and try to claw out a weapon of his own. He just smiled. "I was expecting you."

"Don't move," Conrad warned as he looked at Lannigan over the sights of his Colt. "And don't yell for your guards."

"Or what?" Lannigan replied mockingly. "You'll shoot me? What good will that do you? I have a dozen men who'll be here in a heartbeat if they hear a gun go off. The only reason they're not in here already is because I want to talk to you, Browning."

"We don't have anything to talk about," Conrad snapped, "except for you telling me where my children are so Frank can go get them while I keep you covered."

"Your children," Lannigan repeated. "*Your* children." He laughed. "You damned fool. You don't *have* any children."

An ugly feeling had begun to crawl around inside Conrad as soon as he realized Lannigan wasn't surprised to see them. It was like a snake in his belly, and it told him something was very, very wrong.

"Little Frank and Vivian," he said. "Or David and Rachel, as you call them. You know good and well who I'm talking about."

"Oh, I know." Lannigan sneered. "But that doesn't make them your children. They're not here, anyway. They're back in San Francisco with their mother. When I left there last night, I figured you'd follow me without ever checking to make sure I hadn't left Winifred and the children behind."

That was like a fist in Conrad's gut. Every instinct he possessed told him Lannigan was telling the truth, about that part of it, anyway. The saloon owner had set a clever trap for him and Frank, and they had fallen into it. It hadn't even occurred to him that Lannigan might have left the children behind.

But the rest of it had to be a lie. Conrad said, "Pamela Tarleton—"

"You're about to tell me Pamela Tarleton is the twins' mother, aren't you?" Lannigan broke in. "How can you be so sure of that?"

"I was at the sanitarium in Cambridge where they were born. I talked to Dr. Futrelle—"

"Are you saying Futrelle couldn't have been paid to lie to you? I knew Pamela Tarleton, I don't deny that. When she set out to either destroy you or make your life a living hell, however it worked out, she tried to think of every possible contingency. She's always been two steps ahead of you, Browning."

Conrad shook his head. "You're lying through your teeth. Pamela went to that sanitarium—"

"With her maid, who was about to have a baby but had no husband to go with it." Lannigan shrugged. "I probably shouldn't talk this way about the woman who's now my dear wife, but at one time in her life she was rather free with her favors. When she found herself in the family way, it played right into her employer's hands. Pamela hatched the idea of making you believe the child was yours. As it turned out, there were two babies . . . but that just doubled the misery for you, didn't it?"

Conrad's pulse began to hammer inside his skull. He didn't want to believe the things Lannigan was telling him, but deep down he knew it was possible. Pamela could have done it all: fixed things so it looked like she had the children at the sanitarium, rather than her maid; written the letter to be delivered to Conrad after her death; acted like *she* was the twins' mother during the cross-country journey, rather than Winifred; struck a bargain with Lannigan to marry Winifred and take in the children, knowing if Conrad made it through all the death traps to San Francisco, he would jump to the conclusion that the twins were his . . .

All along, for months, he had played right into the hands of her twisted scheme.

"How do I know this isn't just one more of Pamela's clever lies you're telling me?"

Lannigan chuckled and shook his head. "You don't. That's the beauty of it, Browning. You're going to die not knowing for sure."

He looked up at the top of the stairs behind Conrad and Frank and nodded.

The roar of guns suddenly filled the big room.

Chapter 31

Lannigan's nod was enough to warn Conrad and Frank. They were moving even as the guns began to blast, and their superb reflexes flung them apart, Conrad going left and Frank going right, as half a dozen slugs burned through the space where they had been a shaved fraction of an instant earlier.

Conrad landed on his shoulder, rolled, and came up on one knee with the Colt in his right hand and one of the revolvers he had taken from the guards filling his left hand. Flame spouted from the muzzles as he fired up the stairs at the hired killers who had been waiting for Lannigan's signal to bushwhack him and Frank.

Two of the men staggered, stumbled, and doubled over as Conrad's bullets tore into them. Another man went down with blood welling from the hole in the center of his forehead where one of Frank's shots had caught him. Frank lay on his belly on the other side of the staircase, firing upward.

The gunmen retreated, driven back by the deadly accuracy of their intended victims. As the shooting entered a momentary lull, Conrad glanced over his shoulder toward the fireplace. Lannigan was gone. He had ducked out and left his men to deal with Conrad and Frank.

The men upstairs weren't the only ones they had to worry about. The front door slammed open, and several guards from outside burst into the room, brandishing shotguns. Conrad surged up from the floor and threw himself in a diving leap behind one of the heavy chairs as a guard touched off both barrels of a Greener. The double load of buckshot smashed into the chair, blowing stuffing and splinters into the air. The impact of the charge toppled the chair backward onto Conrad, who was unhurt but pinned down for a second.

Frank took some of the heat off him by opening fire on the shotgunners from the other side of the room. He darted behind one of the thick posts holding up the ceiling and put a bullet through the brain of one of the guards. The man collapsed with his shotgun still unfired.

Conrad shoved the chair aside and tipped his Colt up. The man who had loosed the blast at him was reloading, but Conrad didn't give him time to snap the Greener closed. He fired and sent a bullet ripping through the man's throat. The hired killer went over backward with blood fountaining from his torn jugular.

That left two of the shotgunners still on their feet. Conrad rolled desperately to avoid a blast from one of them. A few of the pellets stung his hide but didn't do any real damage. The gunman was smart enough to fire just one barrel, leaving him with another load of buckshot. He tried to track Conrad with that barrel.

The hammers of Conrad's pistols clicked on empty chambers. He dropped one, holstered the other and powered to his feet, grabbing the buck-shot-shredded chair as he came up. He heaved it just as the man fired. The chair blocked the pellets, then crashed into the gunner, knocking him back a step.

By then Conrad had drawn the Smith & Wesson. While the hired killer was off-balance, Conrad put a .38 round through his head. The man fell back on the stairs, which were painted by the blood and brains that sprayed from his ventilated skull.

That left one more man with a shotgun, but as Conrad swung around in search of that final target, he saw Frank had already taken care of the threat. The fourth guard was down on the floor, kicking out his life as crimson leaked from the bullet holes in his chest and belly. Frank stood nearby, smoking Colt in hand.

Three gunmen were left upstairs, and they had been waiting for a chance. They opened fire on Frank. He grunted and twisted around as a slug creased his upper left arm. A second later, Conrad tackled him and knocked him out of the line of fire. They rolled up against the wall where the gunmen on the second floor couldn't see them. The shooting stopped.

"How bad . . . are you hit?" Conrad asked breathlessly.

"I've cut myself worse shaving," Frank replied. "Anyway, it's not my gun arm."

Feet pounded on both sides of them. Men rushed into the room from right and left. Conrad and Frank were facing each other, so they fired *past* each other, downing the gunmen coming at their backs.

The shooting stopped again. Conrad and Frank reloaded while low voices came from upstairs. Conrad figured the surviving gunmen were debating what they should do next. If they charged down the stairs, they would be easy targets. On the other hand, if he and Frank moved away from the wall, they would be back in the line of fire.

It was a standoff . . . and Lannigan was still out there somewhere.

Quietly, Conrad said, "Frank, do you think Lannigan was telling the truth? About the twins, I mean."

Frank shook his head. "I just don't know. Sounded like it could have been that way, all right. You knew Pamela Tarleton a lot better than I ever did. Was she smart enough and loco enough to come up with a plan like that?"

"She was," Conrad answered without hesitation, "and evil enough, too. But that would mean . . . everything that's happened over the past few months . . . all the danger I put you and Claudius and Arturo in . . . all of it was for nothing. I did just what Pamela wanted me to do, like I was her puppet."

"Blast it, that's not the way it was at all," Frank argued. "Whether those kids are yours or not, you believed they were, and you acted accordingly. You acted like their father, and what you felt was real."

"But if they're not mine, then it was all a lie."

"All those fellas who tried to kill you were sure enough real," Frank pointed out. "This trap Lannigan set for us was real, and so is the score we have to settle with him."

Conrad took a deep breath. "Yeah. I guess when the bullets are flying, it's best to save the philosophical debates until later."

"You could say that," Frank agreed with a grin. "Now, are you ready to have it out with those hombres?"

"More than ready," Conrad said.

"Then I'll draw 'em out . . . and you finish 'em off."

Before Conrad could ask his father what he meant by that, Frank darted away from the wall, twisted around, and started firing both guns toward the balcony along the second floor. More shots came from above as the gunmen returned the fire. Frank staggered but stayed on his feet and kept shooting.

"Noooo!" Conrad shouted as he dived into the open, turning his body in midair so he landed on his back. From where he lay he could see all three gunmen standing at the balcony railing and firing down at Frank. The guns in Conrad's hands thundered as he sent a storm of lead sweeping across the balcony. The hired killers jittered and jerked as slug after slug smashed into them. They dropped their guns. Two of the bloody figures collapsed. The other one pitched forward over the railing and fell to the floor with a crash. He didn't move again.

Conrad scrambled to his feet. He wanted to rush over to Frank, who had fallen near the fireplace. But he had emptied his guns, and one thing Frank had taught him was to reload as soon as possible after a gun battle. Conrad holstered the .38 and started plucking .45 rounds from the loops on his gunbelt. With fingers trembling just a little, he slid the cartridges into the Colt's cylinder.

Only when he had a loaded weapon in his hand again did he hurry over to Frank and drop to one knee. Frank was still breathing, Conrad saw to his great relief. He rolled Frank onto his back and saw blood on his right trouser leg, as well as on his shirt.

Frank opened his eyes and grimaced in pain. "You get 'em?"

"Yeah," Conrad said. "I got them."

"Figured you would . . . if I drew 'em out."

"How bad are you hurt, Frank?"

"Not bad. Just creased a few more times. I'll be fine." Frank lifted a hand and clutched Conrad's arm. "Help me into a chair, and then you go . . . go find Lannigan."

"You need me to patch up these wounds—"

"Not yet. I'll bet . . . Lannigan's still around here . . . somewhere. You find him . . . settle up with him."

Conrad nodded, feeling a tightness in his chest and in his throat. He had lived most of his life unaware of Frank Morgan's very existence. The thought that Frank might not be around made Conrad feel like he couldn't catch his breath.

He lifted Frank and settled him in one of the big armchairs. Conrad reloaded his father's gun and slipped it into Frank's hand. "Just in case I didn't kill all those varmints and one or two still have some fight in them."

Frank nodded. "Don't worry. I can handle 'em."

"I know that. I'll be back."

He checked through the lodge quickly but found no sign of Lannigan. That gave him a chance to check all the bodies, and confirm the hired killers were all dead.

There was also no indication Winifred and the children were there, or had ever been there, for that matter. Lannigan had been telling the truth about *that*, anyway.

When Conrad returned to the big main room, he told Frank, "Lannigan's gone. But you don't have to worry about any of those other men. They're done for."

Frank grunted and hefted the gun in his hand. "I

wasn't worried." His voice sounded stronger. "Lannigan may still be waiting around outside to see what happens, or he might've lit a shuck away from here. Maybe you can find him, or pick up his trail."

"You'll be all right?"

"Better than all right. Now that I know I'm not gonna have to duck bullets any second, I can tie up some of these creases myself."

Conrad nodded. He went out the front door carefully, with his gun up and ready for trouble. Lamps on the porch cast a wide circle of light in front of the house. His eyes scanned the landscape around the lodge carefully, but he didn't see Lannigan anywhere. The road leading up the mountain from the bay ended in a large area covered with gravel. Conrad looked it over to see if he could find any fresh hoofprints, but he didn't spot any.

Gun in hand, he turned toward the dark barn. Lannigan might be hiding in there, waiting for some of his gunmen to come to him and report that the intruders were dead.

Conrad was about twenty feet from the open double doors of the barn when a mounted figure suddenly exploded out of them, spurring straight toward him. He caught a glimpse of Dex Lannigan's rage-twisted face as the man shouted incoherently. Lannigan had a gun in his hand. It roared as he jerked the trigger as fast as he could.

Conrad threw himself aside to keep from being

trampled or shot full of holes. As the galloping horse pounded toward him he dropped his gun and lunged, reaching for Lannigan as horse and rider flashed by. Conrad caught hold of Lannigan's leg and dragged him off the horse. Lannigan toppled out of the saddle with a startled yell and crashed to the ground, his gun flying through the air.

Conrad stood over the man. "Get up! Get up, Lannigan. We'll have this out, you and me."

Lannigan started to climb to his feet, then drove forward in a diving tackle that caught Conrad around the knees. Conrad expected a trick like that, but Lannigan's move was too fast to avoid. Conrad went down hard and Lannigan swarmed after him, hammering fists into his body.

Conrad brought a knee up and drove it into Lannigan's belly. At the same time, he caught hold of the man's shirt front and heaved him to the side. Lannigan rolled a couple times but snapped a kick behind him catching Conrad in the chest, knocking the wind out of him. He fought through the pain and launched himself at Lannigan again.

Gradually, both men struggled to their feet, pounding each other, and stood toe to toe, slugging it out. Blood dripped in Conrad's eyes from a cut on his forehead. Lannigan's eyes were swollen. They wheezed and fought for breath. No one could stand up for long to the sort of punishment they were each dealing out and absorbing.

Lannigan caught Conrad on the jaw with a looping right, then bored in and started to grapple with him. Conrad felt it when Lannigan plucked the Bowie knife from the sheath on his left hip. Twisting, Conrad got a hand on Lannigan's wrist just in time to stop the man from plunging the blade into his side. Conrad hooked a punch with his other hand into Lannigan's belly. Lannigan stumbled, off balance. Conrad gave Lannigan's wrist a hard twist, caught hold of his shoulder, and rammed his own body forward against the gambler.

Lannigan screamed as the collision sent twelve inches of cold steel slicing into his gut. Conrad had managed to turn the knife so it was pointing at Lannigan before they crashed together.

Conrad let go and stepped back. Lannigan swayed, his fingers still wrapped around the Bowie's handle. He pawed at it but couldn't pull it free. It wouldn't have mattered if he did. The damage was already done. Blood leaked out around the knife, and the crimson stain spread rapidly.

"Lannigan," Conrad said in an urgent voice. "Lannigan, is it true? What you told me about the children . . . is it true? You've got nothing to lose now by telling me."

Lannigan was looking down at the knife handle protruding from his belly. Slowly, he raised his eyes to meet Conrad's gaze, then started to laugh.

The laughter was so hard it shook him and made the blood flow even faster.

Then he gasped, made a grotesque gurgling sound, and blood spilled from his mouth. His eyes opened wide but no longer saw anything. He pitched forward and lay on the ground motionless, curled around the blade that had ended his life.

Conrad stood looking at the dead gambler when he caught a glimpse of motion from the corner of his eye. He turned his head and saw Ling Yuan standing there.

"It is done," the big hatchet man said.

"Yes, it's done. Diamond Jack's dirty work is done for him, so he won't have to go to war against the rest of the Barbary Coast. That's what he wanted all along, isn't it?"

Ling Yuan didn't answer.

"You've been lurking around here, haven't you?" Conrad went on. "You've probably got a dozen more hatchet men hidden in the trees. If Frank and I had failed, you'd have killed Lannigan and made it look like one of us did it. But now you won't even have to go to that much trouble. We took care of it for you."

"Is Mr. Morgan all right?" Ling Yuan asked.

Conrad jerked a thumb toward the lodge. "He's in there shot up a little, but he'll be fine."

Ling Yuan nodded and appeared to be satisfied. "His wounds will be cared for. We will bring your horses and help you get back to San Francisco."

Conrad started to respond angrily and tell the man they didn't need his help, but he changed his mind. Might as well get something out of this whole mess, he thought.

"Fine. I've still got business to take care of in San Francisco."

Chapter 32

Conrad took Claudius Turnbuckle with him when he went to Lannigan's house the next morning. Frank was back at the hotel, being looked after by Arturo, who seemed glad to have something to do again.

As they stepped down from Turnbuckle's buggy, the lawyer said, "Are you sure you don't want me to get Patrick Dugan and some of the other detectives who work for me? Lannigan may have left guards with orders to keep you from getting to his wife."

"If he did, I'll handle them," Conrad said. "I'm not sure they'll want to risk it when they find out Lannigan's dead."

"Mrs. Lannigan may call the police."

"If she does, I'll be gone before they get here." Conrad took a deep breath. "I have to *know*, Claudius."

Turnbuckle gripped Conrad's shoulder for a second. "Of course you do, lad. Of course you do."

"Wait here."

Conrad went up the walk, through the lush grounds, to the house. When he reached the porch, he was surprised to see the door stood open a few inches. He hadn't changed clothes since the battle at Lannigan's hunting lodge the night before, and his Colt was still in its holster. His hand went to his gun as a bad feeling came to life inside him.

He pushed on the door. It made a little noise as it opened all the way. The inside of the house appeared to be dark and quiet. He stepped into a richly-appointed foyer.

A voice came from the dim, shadowy parlor to his left. "Is that you, Mr. Browning?"

Winifred Lannigan, he thought. At least she was still alive.

Conrad drew his Colt as he moved into the sumptuously furnished room. Heavy drapes were drawn over all the windows, making it almost as dark as night. His eyes adjusted quickly, and he made out the figure sitting in a chair next to a fireplace. A large portrait hung over the mantel. Conrad's gaze flicked to it and saw four people, two adults and two children. A family portrait, he thought bitterly.

"Mrs. Lannigan . . ."

"You won't need that gun," Winifred said. "Dex left men here, but I sent them all away. They didn't want to go, but I insisted. I knew either he or you would come, and I have nothing to fear from either of you."

"Your husband's dead." He knew it was brutal to say it like that, so hard and cold, but one way or another, the woman had been a part of Pamela's scheme.

"I know. I knew as soon as you came in. I . . . had a feeling that's the way things would turn out. When I saw you at the Kimball mansion, I could tell you were the sort of man who wouldn't allow himself to be turned aside from what he wants." She laughed hollowly. "I'm sorry to say you can't have what you want, Mr. Browning. It doesn't exist."

Conrad tried to ignore the pulse hammering in his head and the sick feeling in his gut. "Then it's true. What your husband told me about the children."

"David and Rachel. My children. Yes, it's true. I knew Dex would tell you if he could. He planned to gloat about it before he killed you." She sighed. "He was an evil man. That's why he was so . . . well matched with Miss Tarleton. They should have been together. They were meant for each other."

"You sound like you didn't love him."

"You don't have to love someone to be married to them, Mr. Browning. Sometimes it's enough just to be . . . taken care of."

Conrad kept a tight rein on his emotions. "You could be lying to me right now," he snapped. "Just like your husband lied to me."

"I could be, but . . . you've never seen them, have you?" Winifred raised her voice. "David, Rachel, come down here, please!"

Conrad's breath caught in his throat as he heard the sudden clatter of small footsteps on the broad staircase leading down from the second floor into the foyer. He turned. He had left the front door open, so there was enough light for him to see the boy and the girl who came down the stairs and stopped in the entrance to the parlor.

They were beautiful. Thick, dark, curly hair. Clean, innocent features. Strong, sturdy bodies. Keen, inquisitive, intelligent eyes. The sort of children any man would be proud to call his own.

But they weren't his. That knowledge burned into his soul like a brand. No matter how hard he searched their faces, he couldn't find a trace of resemblance to either him or Pamela. When he looked back at Winifred Lannigan, he saw her in them. There was no doubt about that.

"Yes, Mama?" the little boy said.

The little girl looked up at Conrad. "Who're you?"

"Children, this is Mr. Browning," Winifred said. "He's come a long way to see you."

"To see us?" the little boy said. "Why?"

Conrad swallowed hard and struggled to find his voice. Finally, he said, "I came to tell you . . . what fine children you and your sister are . . . David. I've heard . . . so much about you . . . and now I see that it's true."

Both children looked at him like he had lost his mind. Maybe he had.

He managed to go on. "Why don't you go back upstairs and play . . . while I talk to your mother some more?"

They looked at each other and shrugged in the way children have of saying all grown-ups are crazy anyway, then turned and ran back up the stairs. Conrad swung around to face Winifred Lannigan across the parlor again.

"Thank you," she whispered. "It's going to be hard enough for them over the coming weeks and months." She lifted something from a small table beside her chair and held it out. "Here. This is for you."

It was a thick envelope. Conrad crossed the room and took it from her. "What's this?"

"Give it to Claudius Turnbuckle," Winifred said. "I've written down everything, going all the way back to Boston before any of this started. I've explained everything Miss Tarleton did, as well as Dex's part in it . . . and mine. It should be enough to clear your name with the authorities."

Conrad frowned. "Why would you do such a thing? Feeling guilty?"

"Of course," she answered without hesitation. "Wouldn't you if you'd helped torture someone the way Miss Tarleton and Dex and I tortured you? But I won't lie to you . . . If Dex had come through that door this morning instead of you, I wouldn't have said anything about this. I'd have burned what I wrote as soon as I got the chance, and I wouldn't look back. It would've been too late for that. I would have already been damned. Maybe this way . . ."

Her voice trailed off. Conrad could understand clinging to a hope of redemption. Sometimes that was all people had left.

Slowly, he nodded. "All right. Thank you."

"You don't have to thank me. Not after what I helped them do to you. This is a start, just a start."

A strained silence fell between them. There was nothing left to say. After a moment, Conrad cleared his throat. "I'll be going now."

She nodded but didn't reply.

He turned and went to the door, but paused there and looked back at her. "You have a fine pair of children."

A smile touched Winifred's lips. "I know. Sometimes we're blessed in ways we don't really deserve."

Conrad nodded. That was true.

And sometimes we're damned in ways we don't deserve, either, he thought as he left the house and walked toward Claudius Turnbuckle's buggy with the confession in his hand.

"Where are you going to go?" Frank Morgan asked.

"Don't know," said the man in the buckskin shirt. He smiled. "Thought maybe I'd just drift."

"But, sir—" Arturo began.

The man slapped him on the shoulder. "Not sir. Pard, maybe. That'll do."

Claudius Turnbuckle said, "Really, Conrad—"

"Don't know the man. My name's Kid Morgan."

"My God!" Turnbuckle exploded, and the outburst made the dun horse move around skittishly in the center aisle of the livery stable in Oakland where they had caught up to the man in the buckskin shirt. "You can't just turn your back again on who you really are. All the charges against you have been dropped. There's no reason you can't return to your old life."

The Kid took hold of the reins, put his foot in the stirrup, and swung up on the dun's back. His Winchester was snugged in the saddle boot, and he had a fully-loaded pack horse with him carrying plenty of supplies and ammunition. He looked down from the saddle. "You'll see to it the woman and her kids are taken care of?"

"Of course," Turnbuckle said, "just like you wanted. But I don't understand—"

"Life punishes some folks enough by itself," The Kid said. "You know what I mean, Frank."

"I do." Frank nodded. He had lived through plenty of tragedies of his own.

The Kid reached down and shook hands with Arturo. "I'll be seeing you again one of these days."

"I sincerely hope so, sir." Arturo summoned up a smile. "I mean, pard."

Turnbuckle sighed in exasperation and shook his head. "There's nothing I can do to talk you out of this, is there?"

The Kid just smiled. He lifted a hand to the brim of his hat as he turned the horse. He heeled the dun into motion and rode away. The three men watched until he vanished down the busy street.

"I just don't understand it," Turnbuckle said. "Where's he going?"

"Some place where nobody's ever heard of Conrad Browning," Frank said quietly. "Some place where the bullets are flying and there's powder smoke in the air, more than likely. Some place where he can forget what he lost . . . and what he never really had." Frank shook his head and spoke from experience. "Too bad he'll never find it. But sometimes . . . sometimes the only salvation people can grasp is in the looking."

TURN THE PAGE
FOR AN EXCITING PREVIEW OF
MASSACRE MOUNTAIN:
A Cotton Pickens Western
FROM WILLIAM W. JOHNSTONE
AND J. A. JOHNSTONE

Cotton Pickens doesn't go looking for trouble—
it's usually there when he wakes up in the
morning.

This time around, Cotton is made the town marshal in a Rocky Mountain silver mining settlement. Nobody else wants the job—reason enough
for him to keep moving on—but the always confident Mr. Pickens thinks he can handle it without
getting his head blown off the minute he sticks his
snoot out the door. But fate has other plans—and
Cotton is soon fighting it out with a greedy, dis-
honest mine owner, his bloodthirsty gunmen, and
townfolk who don't give an owl-hoot if he lives
or dies.

MASSACRE MOUNTAIN, On Sale Now
Wherever Pinnacle Books Are Sold!

Chapter One

They were fixing to fire me. That's what this was all about. There was no escaping it, neither. I'd messed up, and pretty quick now the job of sheriff in the county seat of Doubtful, in Puma County, Wyoming, would go to someone else.

All them politicos in their starchy shirts had collected at the log courthouse to have at me. Even my old friend George Waller, mayor of Doubtful, was in there sharpening his hunting knife.

Well, I'd get it over with, saddle up Critter, and go somewhere else and do something else. I ain't one to cry in my beer.

I walked into that courtroom, which was thick with the blue smoke of cheroots. A man could hardly be a politico in Wyoming without puffing away on five-cent cigars the color of a dog turd.

"Ah, there you are, Pickens," said Reggie Thimble, who was the big honcho in these parts. "Have a seat and we'll land on you directly."

He and Waller and Ziggy Camp were all parked in oak swivel chairs behind a big table. They'd brought in Lawyer Stokes, who was whetting his blades before he started carving on me. They were gonna make me stand. That's how it worked. They would sit and I would stand until my feet howled.

"All right, Sheriff, you just tell it in your own words," Lawyer Stokes said, a cheerful if slightly wolfish grin on his pasty face. I guessed he was going to be the prosecutor in this here inquisition.

"I got held up," I said.

"You, Sheriff Pickens, got held up?" asked Stokes, sounding like a funeral oration. "How could this be?"

"Yep. I was doing my rounds, like usual, and the night was plenty dark, no moon anywhere in sight. I peered into store windows looking for crooks, and I rattled doors making sure the places were locked up good and tight, and I checked out the saloons, them two that were still lamplit that late, and checked out the drunks. It was just what I always do. And then it happened."

Lawyer Stokes squinted ominously. "Would you care to elaborate?"

"Feller jumped out from between Barney's Beanery and Maxwell's Funeral Parlor, and waved a six-gun at me. He was wearing a black bandana and yelled at me to stop right there. I glanced around, looking for an accomplice, but this here bandit was alone, and he had a big old iron aimed at my heart.

"So I stopped. 'Your money or your life,' he says. And that sure got me to thinking some.

"I couldn't quite make up my mind. My money or my life? So I thought to humor the skunk for a little, and I said, 'You know, my pa always told me, Cotton, you ain't worth two cents. So I figure that's what I'm worth. You figure it'd be fine with you if I gave you two cents?'

"That bandit got plumb mad at me. 'Your money right now, toss it down right there in the dirt in front of me, or your life.'

"Well, I figured it was a fifty-fifty proposition. My life's worth about what I had in my purse, which was about a dollar and six bits. So I said to him, I said, 'Your choice.'

"That only made him madder. He said he'd blow my brains out. I said I didn't have any, least that's what my ma was always telling me."

"And then what happened, Sheriff?" Lawyer Stokes asked me, kind of oily.

"I told that feller, come and get it, or shoot me, whichever came first."

"And what did he do?"

"He shot my hat off. So I decided right smartly I'd give him the dollar and six bits, even though it meant going without breakfast for a while at two bits for pancakes, so I dug into my britches, found my bull-balls purse, and tossed it at him, real hard. It just bounced off his chest.

"Then he made me pull my pockets out, so I done it, and he got my Barlow knife.

"He says, 'Take off your boots,' so I done that too.

"'Your feet stink,' he said, and I nodded. Wasn't no arguing with him there.

"He said for me to turn around and start walking away, which I did, and after a bit I looked behind me and he was gone. I'd been robbed."

There was a real quiet in that room. They were all blotting up what I'd said. It came down to this: Doubtful, Wyoming, had itself a sheriff who'd allowed himself to be robbed right on the main street of town.

"And do you know who he was?"

"Nobody I ever seen before. Sort of blocky-looking."

"You're the sheriff and you don't know every lowlife in Doubtful?"

"Not this one."

"And he got away?"

"I sure didn't lasso him."

"And now word is out that the sheriff of Doubtful is, will we say, a pushover for the criminal element? That there's no good man keeping Doubtful safe? That the good citizens of Doubtful are in peril? That there's no one defending the worthy housewife in her kitchen, or the blacksmith at his forge, or the lawyer in his chambers?"

"Well, if you were to give me a raise, I'd be worth more," I said. "Make her forty-five a month and you'd fool my pa and my ma."

Lawyer Stokes peered at me sadly. Then he

turned to the others. "See how the man answers my questions. See where his deprived brain has led him. We are naked here in Doubtful."

Then it was Reggie Thimble's turn. "How come you didn't just draw iron and blast him? You chicken or something?"

"Well, I don't guess it'd get much done, not with a bullet through my gizzard while I'm clearing leather."

"We hired you for your speed with a shooting iron, Cotton Pickens, and we expect you to make use of your speed."

"Well, you got a point there, Mr. Supervisor, but I just didn't see that as anything that'd do anything but get me dead."

"You could have been a hero, Pickens. You could've sent a varmint straight to hell, even as you croaked. We'd have put up a statue of you in front of the courthouse."

"Well, you got a point there," I said.

Then it was Ziggy Camp's turn. "How come you didn't know this yahoo?" he asked.

"It was pretty dark," I said.

"You're supposed to know every lowlife in Doubtful."

"Well, I do, but this feller, he come out of the night."

"You's supposed to know them all by their voice. You mean to tell me you didn't even recognize his voice?"

"Can't say as I ever heard it before."

"What kind of voice was it? High and squeaky? Low and mean? What if it was a woman robbing you?"

"I don't rightly remember, Supervisor."

"Well, what kind of sheriff are you, anyway? How tall was this crook?"

"Neither high nor low, sir."

"What kind of answer's that, Pickens?"

"There wasn't much unusual about him, that's all I can say. Just an ordinary bandit."

Camp glanced at Thimble and sighed.

Then my friend the mayor, George Waller, came up to bat. He sort of smiled, to let me know that we'd still be friends after they fired me. "So what have you done about it, Cotton?"

He was using my first name, deliberately, too. He knew how I feel about that name that got hung on me by my ma and pa.

"I told every bartender in town to let me know if someone was on a drinking spree, spending like hell don't have it. I told my friend Studs, over at the poker palace, to snitch on anyone spending big-time."

"One dollar and six bits is big-time?"

"Is for me," I said. "That's why I want a raise."

"You want a raise? Now?"

"It's not every sheriff gets robbed and lives to tell about it."

They stared at me like I was a leper. I don't know what a leper is but I heard it's real bad and fingers and toes melt off. I still have all of mine, last I counted, but I sometimes have trouble getting past eight or seven, but they were all there last I took my boots off.

Lawyer Stokes intervened, flashing his fish-oil smile. "Well, gentlemen, you've heard the case in the sheriff's own colorful words. Right 'out of the mouth of babes,' as the saying goes. So we know where we stand. Doubtful, Wyoming, lies naked to the world. Our young maidens live in peril of being ravished. Our sturdy storekeeps shake with terror that they will be robbed. Our yeomen fear to be assailed in the night. Our wives and children are helpless against the malign forces of evil. Unless the town is swiftly protected by a competent man who knows how to ferret out crime and bring the world's meanest dregs to justice, then we are all at grave risk. I, for one, shall not sleep soundly in my humble bed as long as I know that there is nothing betwixt and between me and the thugs who prowl our streets as soon as the sun has set. Where will it stop? Who will stop the crime wave? Is our bank next? Will our citizens lie dead in the streets?"

He paused suddenly, turned toward me, and jabbed an ancient, arthritic finger into my chest. "Fire him," he said.

Then he quietly returned to his swivel chair, and swiveled clear around until he, too, was facing me, like the rest.

"You can take Doubtful and stuff it," I said, fixing to walk out.

"Whoa up, Cotton," Waller said. "We ain't fired you yet."

"Well, I'm quitting!" I yelled.

"We got no replacement yet," Waller said. "So we can't accept your resignation."

"What do you mean by that?"

"You can't quit because we don't accept it."

Now that was mighty strange logic in my book, but who am I to say? My ma always said I was a little slow.

"You got a couple of deputies over there, Burtell and De Graff, but they ain't sheriff material. They're better at taking orders than giving them. If anything, they're even less smart than you. They don't have your native cunning. You were smart enough not to argue with that stickup man, except a little, but if it was De Graff, he'd be plumb dead."

"Oh, George, you give Cotton Pickens too much credit," Reggie Thimble said. "I think we should just let Pickens here saddle up and find someone else."

"Like who?"

"Like Belle," Thimble said.

"Boardinghouse Belle?" Waller was aghast.

"Purse snatchers would be too busy looking at Belle's unforgettable chest to see her level her little revolver," Thimble continued. "She's got two aces and four kings."

There wasn't much anyone was saying about then. Me, I thought Belle might be a good sheriff, but there would be the little matter of persuading her to take the job. She had all she could manage running the boardinghouse for a dozen or so of us unattached males. She made good money, a lot more than she would hanging six-guns on her lush hips and patrolling Doubtful.

"Well, we could ask her," Ziggy Camp said.

Again, Lawyer Stokes intervened. "We're not going to hire that pneumatic female for our sheriff," he said.

"Then all we got is Pickens here, at least for now."

"We've been through this before," Supervisor Thimble said. "We had sheriffs by the cartload and they all croaked. Doubtful was on the ropes until we got Pickens here. He may not be the smartest man in town, but he's kept the lid on for some while. Fire him, and next thing you know, the Democrats will be taking over again."

I got to remembering that all them county people were anything but Democrats.

"I think I know where to go on this," said Lawyer Stokes. "It's time for us to have a little talk with Cyrus Ralston."

"Ah, there's a thought."

"Cyrus Ralston is a man of some sophistication. He'll know where to go to find a new sheriff."

"Why yes, my impression is that he's well connected throughout the West, with ties reaching into the great cities of the East as well."

"Ralston will give us the skinny," Waller said.

Lawyer Stokes smiled. "We're agreed then?" He turned to me. "We're going to have Ralston find us a new man, Pickens. Until then, you're still sheriff. "After that, you won't be."

"Well, I quit."

"Sorry, Pickens, that's quite impossible. We don't accept it."

I sure couldn't figure that one out. If I quit, I quit, but they was saying I didn't and can't.

Cyrus Ralston, the man in black pinstriped suits and Homburg hats who was finishing up the new three-hundred-seat Opera House on the main drag of Doubtful, would decide my fate. Durned if I could figure that out.

"Ralston will know how to deal with this crime wave," Lawyer Stokes said.

Chapter Two

So there I was, still sheriff until they could get another. That sure was a mess. I'd just as soon have pinned my badge on Lawyer Stokes and let him do the rounds every night, making sure Doubtful was locked up tight.

I didn't quite know how to spend my last days as sheriff, but I'd think of something. That whole business gave me a good excuse to visit the new opera house. That's what they were calling the place, but it looked like a theater to me. It had been going up pretty fast, three or four months, with a swarm of carpenters banging it together.

The front of the place was pretty fancy, with fieldstone facing the street, but the rest was just another frame structure. The stage was pretty small, but it'd do in a little town like Doubtful. They'd gotten a wine-red velvet curtain hung up, and the carpenters were bolting down a mess of seats that came in on the freight wagons. I'd never been inside a theater before, so I was taking a real gander at the whole outfit. Now, take the way the floor rose so that people sitting in the back were higher than people in front, and everyone could see real fine. That sure was a marvel.

Sure enough, there was Cyrus Ralston overseeing the whole deal, wandering around in a black pinstripe suit. I'd never seen one before, and it sort of reminded me of a barber pole.

"Ah, it's you, Sheriff," Ralston said.

"Just poking around," I said. "This place is as foreign to me as California."

"Well, glad to have you. We're close now. I've booked the first show for next week."

"Going to be an opera, is it?"

"Opera? An opera? Oh, no, not at all. It's a variety show. This is an opera house but that's a figure of speech."

"I've never seen a show, opera or other," I said. "What's the deal?"

"Lots of different shows around. Some come with music. Singers like Jenny Lind. Or Lotta Crabtree. Or dancers like Lola Montez."

"I never heard of any of them."

"Actresses, dancers, some of them quite, ah, bold."

"I'd sure come and look," I said.

"We'll have some fine entertainers coming, Sheriff. They're on the circuit."

"What's that?"

"Troupes go from one town to another, more

or less prearranged by booking companies. That way they've got work ahead, and know where they're going."

"They'll start rolling in, will they?"

"I'm working on it. Nothing's easy, Sheriff. You've got to persuade the booking companies that they can make some money coming here."

"Mess of fellers roll in and put on a show, is that it?"

"Gals, too, Sheriff."

"Where do they stay?"

"Well, that's a question. Some companies got their own little travel wagons with bunks. Most just book rooms in the town."

"We hardly got any rooms here in Doubtful."

"Yes, I'm working on that. It's hard to book a show here because of it. I've told Belle to put a wing on her boardinghouse."

I talked some with this Ralston, who seemed a lot smarter than anyone else in Doubtful, maybe because he was out of some big city somewheres. And I ended up with a pretty good idea of how this deal worked. Every couple of weeks a new troupe would arrive, and the old one would pack up and go to the next town.

"It sure took some figuring out," I said.

He smiled and nodded. He actually had a kind of cold gaze that missed nothing, and I think he was sort of humoring me when he wanted to be doing something else. But I was still wearing a badge, and people usually will palaver with me when I'm looking to know something. So I got around to the question that was on my mind.

"Mr. Ralston, the county supervisors are saying you know a lot about crime waves."

That sure got his attention. "They say that?"

"I mean, they're going to get in touch with you about finding a new sheriff. They're replacing me."

"Why should I know anything about that? Ralston's whole demeanor had changed, and he was suddenly wary. "And why are they replacing you?"

"I got robbed couple of nights ago, and they can't stand it. Sheriff of Doubtful getting stole from."

"And they're going to consult me? About your replacement?"

"That's what they were saying when they took the axe to me."

Ralston laughed suddenly. "Sheriff, there's some in the world, especially out here in the sticks, who think that show people are crooks and thieves and jailbirds. And that it takes someone like me, with some experience, to keep them toeing the line. That's hardly true. There's a lot of good troupes that cause no trouble; once in a while an outfit rolls in that's looking for ways to fatten their purses and aren't very careful how they do it. I can spot 'em, and I can usually keep the lid on. Time or two, I've cancelled the show and sent them out of town."

"Where was that?"

"Oh, Cheyenne, Deadwood, Miles City, Golden, Laramie. . . ."

"Yeah, but why did you come to Doubtful? We ain't half as big."

"Doubtful's future drew me. Some of the richest ranches in the state. Some mining in the Medicine Bow range. And the town's a stageline hub, coaches going off in three directions. And I'm not forgetting the hot springs, either. Pretty soon now you'll have the resort trade. So, naturally, all these good folks have some coin in their pockets and no place to spend it—at least not until I open up in a few days."

Ralston seemed almost amused, and I didn't much care for him. He seemed always to be talking down his nose, like I was a dummy. Well, maybe he was right. I'm slow. They all say it, starting with my ma.

"Well, the politicians are going to come talk to you about a new sheriff," I said. "Why is that?"

"You're all the sheriff I need, Pickens. I think you and I'll get along fine. Anyone running a show house needs an accommodating sheriff around."

"What's that word mean?"

"Means, you just stay relaxed, and I'll keep Doubtful happy. You look to be just the man I want, and if they come asking, I'll tell 'em so."

He was sort of smiling, but with cold eyes, and I figured I'd have to think about all this.

"You're going to tell them to stick with me?"

"I'll insist on it. You may not be aware of it, but I looked you over pretty closely even before I started business here. Having the right man wearing the star's important to a business like mine. I sell good times, Sheriff. There's lawmen that just don't like anyone having a good time in their towns, and then there's trouble. I wouldn't want to lay out a small fortune to build an opera house in some town where the sheriff hasn't got a happy bone in his body and doesn't want anyone else to be happy either."

"Yeah, well what's that got to do with enforcing the law?"

"Everything, Sheriff."

"I think I get it. If some actress wants to show a little leg you don't want me pinching her."

"Ah, you're mastering it just fine, Pickens."

"There's something you said about some of these outfits causing trouble. What kind of trouble?"

"You're a good man, Pickens. Asking the right questions. Every once in a while, there's a confidence man, or woman, traveling in a troupe. They usually work in saloons, getting suckers to bite on some fake deal or other. Once a pickpocket blew into town with a troupe, working the standup bars. You can do me a favor, and the town a favor, keeping an eye on the saloons when a troupe's playing."

"You put up with it?"

Ralston shrugged. "I don't control the acts. I book companies. If one's coming this way, I'll probably book it. That's why I'm glad to have this little talk with you. Company comes in, and you'll know what to look for, and you can collar the troublemakers. At the same time, you'll see that all the good citizens of Doubtful will be enjoying life at these shows, getting some belly laughs, and that's what I want. I want to sell tickets. Lots of tickets. I want to fill up the place every night. Sell out. SRO—that's standing room only. SRO every single night. You keep the lid on, but let the show go on too. You treat the performers and artists right, and I'll, say, make it worth your while."

Well, he was talking that subtle stuff I never did figure out, but it sounded a little like a bribe to me. 'Worth my while.' What did he mean? And 'treating the artists right?' What did he mean? And telling the county supervisors I'm the right man for the job, what would he do that for? I couldn't see he was doing anything wrong or causing trouble, but it sure got me to wondering some. I decided I'd keep an eye on the place, and the man. At least until the county supervisors pitched me to the dogs.

He got busy with the workmen, and I watched a while and headed into the sunlight, where it was a lot warmer than in that cold place. Doubtful was busy. There were carriages and wagons on the road. It hadn't rained, so the road kicked up dust, which was better than mud. It was still a raw town, but it was growing, and it seemed like I was seeing new faces every day. The ranches were some of the finest in Wyoming, and all a rancher had to do was push some skinny cows out, and pretty soon they fattened up and grew, and without much help from anyone, either.

Maybe it was a good time for an entertainment palace to come in. There were even a few ladies in Doubtful, but not many. Women were scarce around this place. Maybe a show with a few sweethearts in it would be good business. All them cowboys, living in bunkhouses with lots of other cowboys, most of them with smelly feet, would take to the opera house. That would be fine with me, long as they didn't shoot holes in the roof or scare the performers—Ralston was calling them artists—off that little stage.

I sure had learned a lot this day. I'd never heard of variety shows, and I still didn't know what went on, but I'd find out soon enough. It amazed me that there were regular companies wheeling around in coaches and wagons, setting up their acts in town after town, and then pulling up stakes and heading for the next one. It'd be strange folks, traveling like that, not ever putting down roots, never settling in any place. They'd be a lonely bunch, traveling like that. It all made me wonder how anyone would become a player in a variety show. That would be a hard life, too, moving in all kinds of weather, getting bogged down in mud, or stuck without shelter somewhere. But I guess some people liked it, or they wouldn't be doing it. Maybe a few even got rich, but I sort of doubted it.

So Doubtful was about to get a theater. I'd never met an actress in my life, and I decided I'd meet a few when they rolled in. What did they do for a living? I'd knowed a few female gamblers, slick with cards, and I'd met a few ladies of the night. I had a good idea of how them women got through life. But an actress, now that was a new side of beef for me. If they sang, if they danced, if they did little scenes, they must have gotten the practice of it somewheres.

All in all, I thought, Doubtful was about to get much better.

Chapter Three

Things were pretty quiet in Doubtful for a few days. I talked with a few barkeeps to see if anyone was spending that dollar and six bits, but no one was. I kept an eye out for thick, medium-high bandits with black bandanas, but there weren't any walking around town.

My deputies, De Graff and Burtell, they must have got wind of what was about to befall me, because they quit being my pals and stared away from me whenever we gabbed in the office. Maybe the supervisors had been asking if I done good work.

The one thing that did change was the color of Doubtful. All of a sudden there was these big red and blue and green sheets plastered to the side of buildings. I didn't know what to call them: playbills, or broadsides, or whatever, but Ralston was promoting his opera house and the opening show any way he could, and that meant posting these advertisements from one end of the county to the other.

He'd hung a sign on his new building, calling it "The Ralston." I guess that was better than calling it the Doubtful Opera House. And he'd had some kind of get-together in there, with all the town's bigwigs having a mint julep on stage. I wasn't invited, not being a bigwig.

I don't read so good, but I made out what was on them broadsheets. There was a lot of gorgeous women in that show, all dressed up in feathers. At least that's what the pictures looked like. That would sure draw a crowd in woman-starved Puma County, where there were about ten men for every gal, and the gals were all married. This outfit on its way to Doubtful was called the Gildersleeve Variety Company, run by Madame Magenta Gildersleeve, of the Slovakian Royal Ballet. There would be twenty beauties, along with the well-known comedian and tap dancer Horace Van Der Platz, the maestro of the top hat, cane, and white spats. And there would be a breathtaking tableau, featuring the famed women in the paintings of Rubens, displayed exactly as they appeared in his art.

I didn't know what a tableau was, but anything that displayed famous women would be worth a gander. I wondered if my badge would let me in free. Down there in the fine print it said the company traveled in thirty-six coaches, and had been the sensation of Prague, London, Cheyenne, Deadwood, and Denver.

Well, I had to hand it to that Ralston. He was going to fill his opera house, and maybe I'd even see this bevy of beauties a second time. Puma County was shy of beauties, although if Belle, who ran the boardinghouse, would lose a little flesh, she might qualify on a night when the light wasn't too bright.

Then one fine day I spotted Ike Berg meandering along our main drag. He was the sheriff over in Medicine Bow County, and I didn't need any help figuring out what he was doing in Doubtful. The supervisors were looking him over for my job. But there he was, dressed in his usual black suit and starched white shirt and string tie. He was the skinniest man I'd ever seen, almost skeletal, and his face was nothing but parchment over skull. He didn't have no flesh on him, just that parchment covering bone. But he was reputed to be as good as they ever got with his Peacemaker Colt. And there he was, grinning at me as we approached each other in front of the smithy.

"I guess I know what you're here for, Ice," I said. No one called him Ike. He was Ice Berg to the world.

"I hear you got a crime wave," Ice Berg said.

"Stickup man cleaned my purse," I said.

"Town fathers aren't happy with it. They're embarrassed. The sheriff got himself robbed."

Berg smiled, baring even, white teeth. I wonder whether teeth like that came with skinny.

"That was careless of you."

"You applying for my job?"

"The town's foremost citizens sent for me, Pickens. I'm here to oblige them."

He smiled again, like he knew things I didn't know.

"They offering you the job?"

"We're dickering about pay. I'm asking eighty a month and they won't budge from seventy-five."

"Seventy-five! I earn forty."

"We're usually worth what we're paid, Pickens."

His bony hand was actually hovering just over his piece, which sure made me wonder. Did he think I'd shoot him? Or was he just precautionary by nature? Shooting wouldn't be a bad idea, but my ma always said, don't shoot anyone unless it's a good idea.

He was standing there in the sunlight, chewing a toothpick, looking kind of smirky, and I thought that shooting him might improve the peace on Main Street. But I didn't, even though I knew I was faster than he'd ever be.

"When'll you hear?" I asked, since it bore on my future.

"They said there's a mess of petty crooks heading for town, theater riffraff, and they're going to see which of us keeps the lid on."

"You mean you're a lawman around here for a while?"

"Unofficially."

"I think I got the badge, Berg. No one's took it from me yet."

Berg, he just smiled and chewed on that toothpick.

I had to admit Berg would be a good man to have around if things got tough again. He'd come to Medicine City when it was a lawless mining camp, infested with every sort of crook and con man and bitch that ever set out to skin miners out of their metal. They all underestimated Ice Berg because he was so skinny, almost frail-looking. But he was quick and ruthless, and he slowly and almost secretly began locking up the worst, banging heads together, and causing a few funerals.

I'd done nothing like that, so maybe that's why I didn't get any more than some ranch cowboy was getting, but I got to live in town. But here he was, and I knew that Reggie Thimble and Ziggie Camp were studying on him. I don't think he weighed ninety pounds, but a lot of lawman came in that skinny package.

And here he was, my rival. I felt kind of low about that. I'd always thought Ice Berg was as good as they get, and he had always been sort of an idol of mine. Time or two, I'd found myself wishing I could be good as him. But here he was, walking the streets of my town like he already owned it. I sure had mixed feelings about that.

"You know anything about this variety show, Cotton?" he asked.

"I'll make a deal with you. You don't call me Cotton and I won't call you Ice."

"But I like my name. You don't like yours?"

"It got hung on my by my ma and pa, and I've always been a little tetched since they named me that. I've thought maybe I should get my name changed to Fat. Like Fat Pickens."

"Just call me Iceberg," he said. "It makes barflies shiver."

"I never seed a variety show in my life, but Ralston, he owns the joint, says there's gonna be pretty girls in it. To my mind, any girl's pretty. And there's so few women around that I can't tell pretty from plain."

"I don't like women, Iceberg said. "I can live without 'em."

"Can't get born without 'em," I said.

"Pickens, ain't that real bright," he said. He was smirking at me.

"Guess I'll see you around," I said.

"Maybe not," he replied.

He drifted off, studying our metropolis like it was dead meat.

My ritual is to patrol Doubtful at odd hours, never on a set schedule, because that's a good way to keep the peace. So that's what I did next. I started down Main Street, but I only got as far as the Puma County Merchant Bank before Hubert Sanders waved at me from his front stoop. He was the banker. He'd started it up two years earlier because Doubtful needed a bank, and now he operated with one teller and one bookkeeper, and his bank was thriving along with Doubtful. Hubert was a doleful man and his wife was even more doleful. They both wore wire-rimmed spectacles and their lips looked like they had just eaten pickles. They had gotten in a preacher and started up a Methodist Church, the first house of worship in Doubtful, which I suppose

I should have appreciated because it meant Doubtful was getting more civilized and less wild, but somehow, whenever I looked at that whitewashed wooden church I had an itch to get onto Critter and ride until I was about five counties away.

But there was Sanders, wiggling his skinny finger at me, as if he owned the plantation. I walked up the two stone steps into the red brick bank, eyed Willis the teller and Wally the bookkeeper with the green eyeshade and sleeve garters, and headed through a gate to the corner where Sanders had his desk and where he watched the world go by from his big glass window.

"Have a seat, Sheriff. I've been meaning to talk to you for some while now, he said, waving me to a hard oak chair. That was how Sanders operated. The harder the chair, the faster his visitors would get through their business and retreat before their tailbone howled at them.

"Perdition is arriving in Doubtful," he said. "Ruin. Sodom and Gomorrah. We'll all be fleeced."

"Ralston?" I said.

"Of course, Ralston. Do you know how these traveling companies work? They come into a small town like ours, run a few shows, clean out every spare dime the town has, and then head to the next town that is foolish enough to let them in." He eyed me with those owlish eyes. "The Ralston is a poverty machine. It is going to ruin our good ranchers and merchants. It is going to cause wealth to flee. It will empty my bank. My depositors will withdraw their funds and squander their cash on those theater hussies and vixens and worse. I tell you, Sheriff, this is a catastrophe in the making. And it gets worse. There never was a moral person treading the boards of a theater stage. We will have a Gomorrah here. There'll be no one attending church, and no one putting money in the collection plate. The sulfurous smell of hades will waft through Doubtful, stinking up our fair, clean, lawful city."

I was getting the drift, so I just nodded.

"It all depends on you, Cotton Pickens. It'll be up to you to rescue Doubtful from sin and poverty and madness. It'll be up to you not only to enforce the law in all respects, but to enforce the moral law. If those hussies on that stage bare anything more than an ankle, arrest them for violating public decency. If they dance, pinch them. Good people don't dance. It's against everything that proper people stand for."

"I just enforce the law, such as the legislature gives us," I said. "I got a book of it that I study sometimes."

"You're going to do more than that, Pickens. I'll insist on it. If you don't do what's required, I'll see about finding a man who will. You are going to find the means to shut down Ralston. That fellow is the devil incarnate. I didn't realize at first what he was up to, building that sin palace right on the main street of Doubtful. He didn't borrow a cent from me, and I don't know where his cash came from, but find out. It's probably tainted money."

He stared straight at me through those wire-rimmed spectacles. "Shut him down. You'll find reasons enough. A dozen reasons a night. Shut down any company that comes in. Shut them down for any reason you can think of. Arrest them. Charge them. Tell them to get out of town or they'll face worse."

So that was where Sanders was heading.

Me, I was feeling some heat from all sides. Ralston as much as said he'd welcome an open town, so people could have some fun. The supervisors were convinced a crime wave was cranking up. And now Sanders wanted me to shut the place down before it even got feet under it and started running. And there were a few vultures out there, or at least one anyway, looking to snatch my badge from me.

It sure was getting interesting.

"As long as they're lawful, I don't have any way to shut 'em down," I said.

"You'll find a way. Or a new sheriff will."

"Here's what you do, sir," I said. "You tell the supervisors what laws you want, and if they enact them, then I'll enforce them. It's that simple. You want some new laws, you go get the elected officials to put them on the books. Meanwhile, I'll do my best to keep this town as peaceful as I know how."

Sanders arose abruptly. "You are dismissed," he said.

So I was dismissed. I headed out into the sunlight and took a good look at them green-clad mountains off to the west, poking up into a bright blue heaven.